The
Chocolate
Bear Burglary

The
Chocolate
Bear Burglary

A Chocoholic Mystery

JoAnna Carl

Thorndike Press • Chivers Press
Waterville, Maine USA   Bath, England

This Large Print edition is published by Thorndike Press, USA and by Chivers Press, England.

Published in 2003 in the U.S. by arrangement with NAL Signet, a member of Penguin Putnam Inc.

Published in 2003 in the U.K. by arrangement with Penguin Putnam Inc.

U.S. Hardcover 0-7862-5103-4 (Mystery Series)
U.K. Hardcover 0-7540-8958-4 (Chivers Large Print)
U.K. Softcover 0-7540-8959-2 (Camden Large Print)

The text of this Large Print edition is unabridged.
Other aspects of the book may vary from the original edition.

Set in 16 pt. Plantin by Al Chase.

Printed in the United States on permanent paper.

British Library Cataloguing-in-Publication Data available

Library of Congress Cataloging-in-Publication Data
Carl, JoAnna.
    The chocolate bear burglary : a chocoholic mystery / JoAnna Carl.
        p. cm.
    ISBN 0-7862-5103-4 (lg. print : hc : alk. paper)
    1. Women detectives — Michigan — Fiction.
    2. Chocolate industry — Fiction.   3. Michigan — Fiction.
    4. Large type books.   I. Title.
PS3569.A51977C46 2003
                                                            2002042953

For Claire, Clay, and Eric —
the best grandchildren who ever were

Acknowledgments

As ever, I relied on many friends and relatives to research this book. The great people at Morgen Chocolate, Dallas, were invaluable — particularly my daughter, Betsy Peters; her boss, Rex Morgan; and the supervisor of production, Andrea Pedraza. Michigan friends Tracy Paquin, Susan McDermott, and Judy and Phil Hallisy were always patient and full of information. I also wish to thank Jim Avance, for information on law enforcement; Bob Bigham, sports car enthusiast; Marv Lachman, authority on classic mysteries; and Earlene Fowler, a generous mystery writer.

Chapter 1

The bear wasn't cuddly or cute. His eyes were squinty and mean, and his face was grimy. A harness — or was it a muzzle? — was around his snout, and he looked as if he resented it. In fact, he looked like he might take a bite out of anybody who tried to take a bite out of him.

"I don't care how much milk chocolate you load into that mold," I said. "That bear's never going to be a teddy."

The other bear molds looked dirty, too. The metal clamps that held the backs and fronts together were all askew, and their silver-colored metal seemed to be tarnished. All of them looked as if they needed to be soaked in soapy water and scrubbed with a brush. I wasn't impressed with the cleanliness of the dozen antique chocolate molds Aunt Nettie was arranging on the shelves of TenHuis Chocolade.

"I'd be glad to wash all these," I said.

"Wash them!" Aunt Nettie teetered on the top step of her kitchen step stool. "You don't wash them!"

"But they're dirty-looking."

"Those are chocolate stains."

"Naturally, since they're chocolate molds. But you don't let the modern-day molds sit around dirty. Wouldn't the antiques look better if they were cleaned up?"

Aunt Nettie clasped the mean-looking bear to the bib of the apron that covered her solid bosom. She looked so horrified that I could tell my suggestion was making her wavy white hair stand on end, right up through the holes in the white food-service hairnet she wore.

But she spoke patiently. "Lee, the plastic molds we use today won't rust. These antique ones are tin-plated, and they can rust. So the normal way to maintain them — back when they were in general use — was to put them away without washing them. The coating of chocolate was like oiling them. It kept them from rusting. When the old-time chocolatiers started on their next batch of chocolates — maybe a year later — then they'd wash them."

"But since we don't plan to use these, but just to display them . . ."

"No, Lee. The chocolate traces show that the molds are authentic." She held out the mold of the mean-looking bear. "This one has been washed, and it wasn't dried properly. It's rusted already. I pointed that out to Gail Hess when she brought the molds by, so she'd know we didn't do it. Washing them would be like putting a coat of acrylic on a genuine Chippendale table."

I didn't argue.

My aunt, Jeanette TenHuis, is the expert on chocolate and is the boss of TenHuis Chocolade. I'd had to be told that lots of chocolate people use the European spelling — "mould" with a "u" — for the forms they use for shaping chocolates, and reserve the American "mold" to refer to that stuff along the hem of the shower curtain. No, I'm just the bookkeeper — business manager, if you want to sound fancy. I pay the bills for the butter, cream, chocolate, and flavorings Aunt Nettie uses to make the most delicious bonbons, truffles, and molded chocolates ever placed into a human mouth, but I don't take any part in how she assembles the ingredients.

"Anyway, I think the molds will get us into the teddy bear spirit," Aunt Nettie said.

"The chamber of commerce committee ought to approve," I said. "They're going to look nice, even if they are a bit dingy."

The little retail area of TenHuis Chocolade was looking quite festive. Warner Pier, already tourism central for western Michigan in the summer, was making a special push to draw winter visitors, and the chamber of commerce had decided on "A Teddy Bear Getaway" as the theme for a late-winter promotion. The amateur theater group was putting on a production of *Teddy and His Bear*, a comic look at the hunting exploits of Teddy Roosevelt. The Warner Pier Sewing Society had costumed the high school choir as toys, and the kids were going to present a concert with "The Teddy Bears' Picnic" as a theme. The twelve blocks of the Warner Pier business district and dozens of the town's authentic Victorian houses were festooned with bear banners, and cuddly bears shinned up the pseudo-gaslights on each corner. The Warner Pier restaurants — the ones that are open off-season — were serving honey cakes and Turkey à la Teddy. There's a bed-and-breakfast on nearly every corner in Warner Pier, and the ones that were taking part in the promotion were so full of teddy bears there was hardly room for the guests. Their special Getaway rates had been advertised as far away as St. Louis and New York. The weather seemed to be cooperating, providing picturesque snow that made us look as if we were decorated with stiffly starched antimacassars, but didn't block the roads. The snowmobile rental places were gearing up, and volunteers were checking the cross-

10

country ski trails. Even the Warner Pier bars were offering specials — bear beer and teddy tonics. The official Warner Pier greeting was a bear hug.

We were cuddly as all get out.

TenHuis Chocolade, one of the specialty shops catering to the town's wealthy visitors and part-time residents, was getting into the spirit by displaying antique chocolate molds, loaned to us by Gail Hess, who ran the antique shop across the street and who was chairman of the promotion.

"I want to have these up by the time Gail comes back," Aunt Nettie said.

I left Aunt Nettie to arrange the molds and got down on my knees to festoon swags of red velvet ribbon along the edge of the glass showcase. Since I'm close to six feet tall, I would have had to bend way over to do it standing up, but kneeling put the counter almost at eye level for me. Of course, it also meant that the glass front of the showcase reflected my face in a frightening close-up. I'm not used to seeing every strand of my Michigan Dutch blond hair — pulled back George Washington style — and every speckle in my Texas hazel eyes jump at me in such detail.

The showcase was already filled with an artfully arranged selection of TenHuis teddy bear specialties. We had a milk chocolate teddy who was much more jovial than that cranky-looking antique one, tiny teddy bears in milk or white chocolate, a twelve-inch-high teddy with a white chocolate grin and dark chocolate eyes. Interspersed among the large molded items were miniature gift boxes of gold and silver, each stuffed with yummy TenHuis truffles and bonbons and molded bears. Tins painted with teddy bears beating toy drums held larger amounts of truffles, bonbons, and bears. Best of all, I thought, were the gift certificates — beautiful parchment scrolls peeking out of backpacks worn by eight-inch chocolate teddy bears or held in the paws of cunning six-inch cubs.

There were no peppermints or hard candies here. TenHuis makes only fine, European-style chocolates — bonbons, truffles, and molded treats.

I had just put the final red velvet swag on the counter when the door opened and Gail blew in.

It wasn't really a pun. Gail Hess walked and talked so fast that a conversation with her was like standing out in a high wind. She was fiftyish, maybe twenty years older than I was, and she wore her frankly fake red hair cut short and tousled — as if it had been styled by a hurricane. She always left me feeling as if I were back in my hometown on the Texas plains, facing into one of our thirty-mile-an-hour breezes.

Gail began talking as rapidly as usual. "IsOliviahereyet?"

My Texas ears didn't understand a word she said. Aunt Nettie seemed to, though she looked surprised. "Olivia VanHorn?" she asked.

"Yes. I invited her to come by."

"I didn't even know she was back in town."

"She's clearing out her mother's house. I was afraid she would be here before me. Nettie, the molds look lovely!"

Aunt Nettie gave an antique teddy a final tweak, then climbed down from her step stool. She seemed puzzled. I wondered what was bothering her. It couldn't be the arrangement of the chocolate molds. Gail had just admired them, anyway. It must be the mention of this Olivia person.

"Who is Olivia VanHorn," I said, "and why does she want to see the display of molds?"

Gail looked at me. "Oh, Lee, I keep forgetting you're almost a stranger in Warner Pier. Being Nettie's niece and all. Though I will say you two don't look as if you're related."

"We're not blood relations," Aunt Nettie said. "Phil was Lee's mother's brother. Lee has the TenHuis head for business. I bless the day she agreed to help me out."

"And I bless the day she agreed to help me get out of Dallas," I said.

We both laughed. The secret, of course, is that Aunt Nettie and I just love each other. And we respect our differences. So we're able to work together all day and share a house at night without getting on each other's nerves too often.

"Phil always handled the business side, so I was lost after he died," Aunt Nettie said. "Lee's got me back on my feet."

I gritted my teeth at that one. Aunt Nettie's business was still teetering, and we had an obnoxious banker leaning over our shoulders to prove it. But I didn't want to tell the other Warner Pier merchants that, so I changed the subject. "Now, back to my question. Who is Olivia VanHorn?"

"Oh! Olivia's a Hart," Gail said.

"I thought you said her name was VanHorn?"

"It is. Her maiden name was Hart."

"The Harts have always summered here," Aunt Nettie said. "Olivia's great-grandfather was one of the original group of Chicago people who built cottages in the 1890s."

Warner Pier society has three castes — I'd found that out a dozen years earlier, when I was sixteen and worked for Aunt Nettie during summer vacation. First, there are the "locals," divided into subcastes such as natives, newcomers, retirees, commuters, and so forth. Then there are the "tourists," who make brief visits to Warner Pier and who count only as contributors to the community's economic kitty. And then there are the "summer people," who spend the warm-weather months in cottages or houses they own in Warner Pier or along the shore of Lake Michigan. A lot of the summer people are wealthy — some are socially prominent or others even famous — and a lot of the families have been coming to the area for seventy-five or a hundred years. They are taxpayers, but rarely vote in Warner Pier. They get special treatment even though they aren't considered "locals." It's a complicated system, but knowing that the Harts had "always" summered in Warner Pier assigned Olivia Hart VanHorn to her proper station in life.

"I thought she'd never be back," Aunt Nettie said.

"She hasn't been since her husband died — more than fifteen years. And I guess she won't be back again. She and her brother

15

are putting the cottages on the market." Gail leaned close to Aunt Nettie and lowered her voice. "The gossip is that she wants the money for Hart's campaign."

It took me a second to place "Hart." Then I remembered that Hart VanHorn was a state legislator who was being talked up as a candidate for Congress. This Olivia VanHorn must be his mother.

Aunt Nettie raised her eyebrows. "Then he's definitely running?"

"That's the way Olivia talks."

"Are they going to sell the whole compound as one piece of property?"

"I think they'd like to." Gail used both hands to muss her hair up even more. "Three year-round houses, plus the bungalow. I'm hoping to handle the estate sale."

"Good for you," Aunt Nettie said. "The contents of all the houses?"

"Yes. Of course, it's the usual story. The family's taking the good stuff. But Timothy gave me the chocolate molds on consignment."

I spoke up. "Then the antique molds belong to this Olivia VanHorn and her brother?"

"Yes. Her grandfather started out in the chocolate business — some of the molds were actually used in his original shop in Chicago. Then he invented some special machine used in making chocolate. He sold out to Hershey in 1910."

"I'm surprised that no one in the family wants to keep the molds," I said.

Before Gail could answer, the door opened again, and I knew that the woman who entered had to be Olivia Hart VanHorn. She simply had the look of a woman whose family had a "compound" on the shore of Lake Michigan, whose grandfather had sold out to Hershey in 1910, and whose son was running for Congress. Think American duchess, and you've got it.

She wasn't beautiful. But when I'm sixty, I'll settle for flawless skin, a slender figure, erect carriage, dark brown eyes, and white hair arching back from a patrician forehead. If I can have all that, I won't complain about the big hooked nose and the thin neck. They might prevent conventional beauty, but they definitely added character.

Olivia VanHorn smiled with complete graciousness and an air of command. "I hope I'm not late."

If this gal was ever late, the clock would back up and wait for her. I almost curtsied.

Instead, Gail introduced us, and Mrs. VanHorn and I shook hands. Aunt Nettie greeted her as "Olivia," and she spoke back to "Nettie." They exchanged How-are-yous and You-haven't-changed-a-bits. Olivia VanHorn was friendly, but not effusive.

Gail gestured toward the shelves behind the cash register. "What do you think of the display?" She and Aunt Nettie turned toward the molds.

Olivia VanHorn looked at the molds, too, and slowly, very slowly, the life drained out of her face.

She stood as still as death, not even breathing. Her stillness was frightening. And she was beginning to sway. I realized she was going to faint.

I grabbed a chair, one of two we keep in the shop for people who have to wait for their orders, and I scooted the chair behind Olivia VanHorn. "Here," I said. "Sit."

I don't know if Mrs. VanHorn sat or if her knees simply buckled. But she wound up in the chair.

"Head between the knees," I said.

Instead, she leaned back in the chair. "It's all right," she said. She took a deep, sobbing breath.

All this had happened in about two seconds, and Gail and Aunt Nettie had spent those seconds staring at the chocolate molds. Now they turned around, and both of them gaped at me and Olivia VanHorn.

Mrs. VanHorn was getting her color back. "I'm fine," she said.

Gail Hess began to fuss around. "Goodness, Olivia, what happened?"

"Oh, it's nothing! I have these turns. I'm sorry if I frightened everyone. They go away quickly."

She was looking much better. "My doctor assures me it's nothing serious."

"I hope not! Shall we call a doctor?"

"Oh, no! Hart drove me in. He went down to the bank to speak to George Palmer. George chairs the party for Warner County, you know, so Hart needs to keep in contact with him. But I'm fine now."

She might be fine, but the mention of George Palmer had nearly made *me* faint. George was the local bank manager and Aunt Nettie's loan officer, and I found him annoying. Plus I'd had a real friendship with his predecessor, Barbara, so every time I had to deal with George, I missed her.

Mrs. VanHorn looked at me and smiled graciously. "Your niece reacted quickly, Nettie."

The smile froze me. It was gracious as all get out, true. But the dark eyes stabbed

19

right through me. I had punctured the dignity of a great lady by noticing that she was about to fall down in a dead faint. Embarrassed, I moved back behind the counter.

But Olivia VanHorn wasn't through. "Thank you very much for the first aid, Lee."

I had to respond. "We have lots of practice," I said. "Everybody swans over Aunt Nettie's chocolates."

I'd done it again. Gotten my tongue tangled and used the wrong word. Gail and Olivia VanHorn stared at me and even Aunt Nettie looked puzzled.

"I'll try that one again," I said. "All our customers swoon over Aunt Nettie's chocolates."

Everybody smiled, and I went on. "Sparklin' re-party ain't my fort-tay," I said. "I git my tang tongueled."

Aunt Nettie laughed, so Gail decided I'd done it on purpose that time, and she smiled. Olivia VanHorn gave a perfunctory chuckle. I gestured at the shelves. "If you're feeling better, I hope you are pleased with the display of chocolate molds."

Olivia VanHorn looked at the display and nodded. "They look wonderful, Nettie."

"I'm going to put one or two in the showcase," Aunt Nettie said. "I'd like for people to be able to see the detail, but I know they are quite valuable. I don't want anybody picking one up to look it over."

"It's a beautiful collection, Olivia," Gail said. "I was really surprised when Timothy said you wanted to sell them. I remember the lovely display your mother had in that wonderful oak china cabinet in the bungalow. And they're highly collectible."

I'd been around enough antique dealers to know how to translate "highly collectible." It meant "nice commission for me."

Olivia VanHorn nodded. "Timothy gave them to you?"

"They were with some other things he brought in on consignment. Didn't he tell you?"

"No, my idiot brother didn't tell me. I'm delighted that you're using them for your display, Nettie. But Gail, I really don't want them sold."

"Then we'll take them down immediately," Aunt Nettie said.

"No, no! They're perfect for the Teddy Bear Getaway theme. I'll pick them up after the promotion is over." Now Olivia VanHorn gave a rather stilted laugh. "After Timothy has a piece of my mind."

Gail began to apologize profusely, but Olivia brushed her words aside. "Gail, it's not your fault in any way. In fact, it's not Timothy's fault. I remember he said he was going to take a box of old kitchen things from the basement of the bungalow to an antique dealer, and I assured him it was all right. I didn't realize the molds were in the box."

Olivia VanHorn was looking much better. She stood up, and she and Aunt Nettie began to look at the individual molds. "I always remember this one, the acrobat bear wearing a fez," Mrs. VanHorn said, tapping the shelf in front of that one. "When I was a little girl, I had a book about a circus and a bear who did tricks. I always thought this was a mold of him. Actually, of course, it's a German mold."

"Oh, yes," Gail said. "An Anton Reiche. It dates from around 1929. But it's not the most valuable in the collection. I have a friend in Chicago, Celia Carmichael, who's a real expert on chocolate molds. I believe she evaluated them for your mother, Olivia. Celia is coming up this way in the next few days, and she wants to stop by and see them."

This comment made Olivia blink, and Gail hastily spoke again. "I'll be sure and tell her they're not for sale. But she'll enjoy seeing them."

The three of them continued talking about the molds, each from her own angle. Aunt Nettie looked at their historical connection to the chocolate business, Gail at their value to collectors, and Olivia VanHorn at her childhood memories.

I stood by and listened. We weren't exactly swamped with customers that day — in fact, winters are really slow for nearly all Warner Pier retail businesses. The "hairnet ladies," the women who actually make the chocolates, stay busy with mail orders and commercial accounts, but Aunt Nettie and I don't bother to keep anybody on duty at the counter in the winter. If customers walk in, one of us runs up to wait on them.

I was considering going back to the paperwork piled up on my desk when the phone rang. I answered the extension behind the counter. "TenHuis Chocolade."

"Lee? I'm glad it's you."

It was Joe Woodyard. Calling me at the office. That was strange. Joe and I were circling around a love affair, but for a lot of complicated reasons we — or maybe just Joe — didn't want to become an item for Warner Pier gossip. So Joe phoned me several times a week, but we'd agreed that he would always call me at home.

"Hi," I said.

"Lee, I just caught a kid trying to break into your house."

"What?"

"I'd have called the cops, but —" Joe stopped talking.

"But what? Joe, if someone tried to break in . . . Who is it?"

"He claims he's your son."

Chapter 2

My son?

I was so astonished I think I hung up without saying another word. I headed for my office. I stepped into my boots, pulled on my ski jacket, and walked past Aunt Nettie, Gail Hess, and Olivia VanHorn without speaking. I went out the street door, leaving them gaping after me. Or Aunt Nettie and Gail gaped; Olivia merely raised a well-bred eyebrow.

I drove off in my van, which had been Michiganized with the proper license plates and three fifty-pound bags of kitty litter, carried as ballast and for emergency traction.

The day was sunny and the streets fairly clear, either covered with hard-packed snow and ice or melted through to the pavement. Snow several feet deep covered the lawns and fields I passed on the way to Aunt Nettie's house on the outskirts of Warner Pier. I drove cautiously, like a Texan in snowy weather, but I didn't really pay a lot of attention to the road. I was too upset at the thought of my "son." My son the burglar.

I'd figured out who it must be.

I was glad I'd stopped for my boots as soon as I pulled into the driveway, a sand lane about a hundred yards long that connects Aunt Nettie's two-story white farmhouse — built in 1904 — with Lake Shore Drive. Every town on Lake Michigan has a Lake Shore Drive, of course. Aunt Nettie and I lived on the inland side, but this time of the year we could glimpse the lake through the bare limbs of the hundreds of trees between us and the water.

I saw that the drive was blocked by Joe's truck — a blue pickup with "Vintage Boats – Stored and Restored" on the side — and by a sporty gold SUV. Even from the road I could see that it was a Lexus RX300. That figured, if I was right about who the burglar was. The Lexus was half off the road and obviously stuck. That figured, too. The kid who drove it probably thought an SUV could go anywhere; it couldn't.

Aunt Nettie hires a man who plows the drive when it needs it. (He also scrapes the snow off the porch roof, because that roof slopes so gently it can collect enough of Warner Pier's "lake effect" snow that it might collapse. I'm not in Texas anymore.) So the drive was fairly clear, but since the snow melts and refreezes on a regular basis, its surface was icy and rough. If the Lexus had stayed on the road, though, it shouldn't have gotten stuck. I parked my van behind Joe's truck, got out and began slipping and slogging toward the house. As I passed the Lexus, I noted its Texas tag. Again, just what I expected.

Joe — six feet plus, with dark hair, blue eyes, lots of brains, and skillful hands — was standing on the front porch of Aunt Nettie's house. Sitting on the porch steps, with his head down nearly to his knees, was a skinny kid in a down jacket, jeans, and tennis shoes. He wore thick glasses, and he had a gold ring in his left eyebrow. His ears were pierced, too — no, they were more than pierced. They had big eyelets in the lobes, as if he expected to tie shoelaces through them.

The kid didn't seem to have gloves or a hat. Joe wasn't wearing gloves or a hat either, but somehow he looked macho, as if the winter didn't faze him. The kid just looked cold.

Joe and I exchanged nods, but I didn't stop to talk. I went right around him, to the kid. I could have whacked him, but I tried to stay calm.

"Hi, Jeff," I said.

The kid lifted his head to glare at me, and

I saw that he also had a stud in his lower lip. Then he ducked his head and studied the walk some more. He didn't speak.

"He claims he's your son," Joe said.

"He used to be," I said. "He's Jeff Godfrey. For five years he was my stepson."

Joe looked relieved, then tried to hide it. I fought an impulse to laugh. I guess finding out I had a teenaged son would have come as a shock to him.

"Y'all might as well come on in," I said.

I knocked the snow off my boots, unlocked the front door, and went inside. Joe held the storm door open, but he had to gesture before Jeff got up and preceded him into the living room.

There was a mat by the door, and Jeff and Joe had already knocked most of the snow off their feet out on the porch. I kicked my boots off and walked around in my heavy socks. Then I looked Jeff over. I hadn't seen him in two years — it had been at Christmas two years and two months earlier. His dad, Rich Godfrey, had insisted that Jeff join us on Christmas Eve, and Jeff had sulked and sneered the whole evening. Rich had finally blown up at him. It hadn't been a happy holiday.

Jeff had grown taller, of course. He was still scrawny, but he had reached his dad's height, maybe an inch shorter than I am, and he had Rich's light brown hair. But his face was thin like his mom's, and the gray eyes behind his glasses weren't like either of them. He wasn't as spotty as he had been two Christmases earlier. Between the glasses and the jewelry installed on his head, he seemed to glitter.

"Well, Jeff, have you had lunch?" I said.

Jeff finally spoke. "No, but I'm not hungry." I was having a hard time not staring at the huge holes in his earlobes, and the stud in his lip seemed to bounce around.

"I'll fix you a sandwich anyway. Joe? Ham sandwich?"

"Thanks."

Joe took his jacket off and hung it on the hall tree by the front door. He seemed watchful, and I realized he was keeping an eye on Jeff. Did he think the kid was going to go berserk?

Would Jeff be likely to go berserk? I hadn't the slightest idea. He'd been eleven when I married his dad and sixteen when I divorced him. I'd tried to be a nice stepmom, but Jeff had always avoided me like poison.

I didn't know him at all.

I turned up the furnace heat, then showed Jeff where the bathroom was; in

Aunt Nettie's old house you get there by way of the kitchen and the back hall, so it's kind of tricky. Then I started making five ham sandwiches, three on white and two on rye.

Joe came into the kitchen while I assembled bread, cheese, and ham. "How did you happen to catch Jeff?" I said.

"I was headed down to Benton Harbor to look at a boat. I thought I'd take the lake road and check on how the ice is treating the beach. I saw the Lexus stuck in your drive, so I stopped. The kid was up on the porch roof, trying to get in that window."

"The one over the stairwell?" I was horrified.

"Right. He's lucky he didn't succeed and break his neck." Joe lowered his voice. "How well do you know this kid?"

I kept my voice low, too. "Not well, I'm afraid."

"I could still call the cops."

"Let me talk to him first."

But that didn't prove easy. Even after Jeff sat down at the dining room table and decided he would eat a ham sandwich and have some milk, he was determined not to give out any information.

"How'd you wind up in Michigan?" I asked.

"Got in the car and drove."

"Why?"

Jeff took a big bite, chewed and swallowed before he answered. "I wanted to see a new place."

"You turned eighteen in July." Jeff looked up sharply at that, maybe surprised that I remembered his birthday. "Did you start college this year?"

"Yeah. SMU."

Southern Methodist. In Dallas, his hometown, but a good college, not easy to get into. Jeff had been doing something right.

"Are you still working for your mom?" Jeff's mom, Dina, has an antique shop.

"I was. Saturdays. I made some deliveries, polished stuff."

"Does your mom know where you are?"

That got a quick and angry reply. "No, and I don't know where she is!" Bite, chew, swallow. Then, "I don't live at home anymore."

"You living in the dorm?"

"I was."

"Did your dad send you up here?"

That brought a gape that made the lip stud bob around. "No! He wouldn't send me anyplace!"

Jeff's reaction was genuine enough to settle that particular suspicion. Rich hadn't sent his son as a go-between of some sort. Good. Maybe Rich had quit trying to salvage his hurt pride.

"Then why did you come?"

"Not because I wanted to see *you*."

"Jeff, please don't ask me to believe that you wandered a thousand miles from home and college and just happened to get stuck in the driveway of your former stepmother."

Bite, chew, swallow. Glare. No answer.

I was getting impatient. "Come on, Jeff! Joe still thinks we should call the cops. Explain yourself."

Now Jeff pouted.

"If you did come all this way to see me, Jeff, for heaven's sake why didn't you come by the store? Why didn't you phone? Why did you try to break into the house?"

He scowled and rubbed at one of his earlobes. I fantasized about sticking my little finger through the huge hole in it.

"I thought maybe you'd loan me some money," Jeff said. "Then when I found your house, I got stuck. I was trying to get in to use the phone."

He raised his head and shot Joe an angry glance. "This guy . . ." He stopped talking, ducked his head and stared at his sandwich. "At least he had a cell phone."

Joe raised his eyebrows. "When I drove

up he was halfway in that upstairs window," he said. "I could take a look at it. Has Nettie got a ladder?"

"In the garage. The key's hanging in the broom closet off the back hall."

Joe stood up. "I won't be far," he said.

Jeff sullenly ate two more bites of his sandwich, but after we heard Joe go out the back door and saw him pass the dining room windows, he glared at me. "Does that guy live here?"

I swallowed a sharp answer, then tried to speak calmly. "Obviously not, Jeff. If he lived here he'd have a key. Joe's just a friend. He's not even a frequent visitor."

"I saw him in the papers. He's the guy you were mixed up with over that murder."

"His ex-wife was murdered, true. Neither of us had anything to do with it."

"Dad said —"

"Quit trying to change the subject, Jeff. What are you doing here?"

"I'm broke. Like I said, I thought maybe you'd lend me some money."

"I haven't got any money to lend. Why don't you call your mom."

"I told you. I don't even know where she is."

"Then call your dad."

"He won't talk to me."

"What happened?"

Jeff squirmed and made a low, growling sound. Then he whacked his fist on the table and yelled, "They both threw me out!"

I could see Joe whirl around and start running back toward the house. But Jeff was back into his sullen mode, staring angrily at his plate. I got up and went to the back door to assure Joe the situation wasn't out of control.

As I walked back to the table, I thought about what Jeff had said. I wasn't sure I believed it.

If Jeff had had a specialty, it had been playing his parents against each other. When I pointed this out to Rich, he got mad at me instead of at Jeff. It was hard to believe that Rich and Dina would ever have stopped fighting over Jeff long enough to throw him out; Jeff would have figured some way to divide them and ruin the plan.

Jeff might well have deserved to be thrown out. He'd always been bratty, and his ear, eyebrow, and lip jewelry would have given his dad a stroke. But I found it hard to believe that his parents had actually tossed him. Jeff's mother had always doted on him, and so had Rich, in his own selfish way. Rich saw the other people in his life merely as reflections of his own success. Dina got a big settlement when they divorced, so he could brag to his friends about how she took him to the cleaners. For Jeff, Rich had always provided the best private schools — best, as in most expensive — and the best bicycle and the best summer camp and the fanciest tennis shoes. I had benefited from Rich's largesse, too; I'd always had jewelry, a snazzy car, a fancy house.

The only thing Rich hadn't given any of us was respect and love, but he didn't have much of that to spare.

When I walked out and left the jewelry, the car, the house, and the clothes behind, I was trying to convince Rich I loved him, not his money. His reaction had shown me the truth — Rich saw his money as an extension of himself. When I rejected the one, I had rejected the other. He hadn't forgiven me.

But if Rich loved anybody, it was Jeff. It would take a lot to make him throw the kid out. I needed more details.

"What do you mean, they threw you out? How could they throw you out if you were living in the dorm?"

"Just what I said. They finally agreed on something. They didn't like my grades. They didn't like my credit card bills. They ganged up on me and said I had to get a job flipping hamburgers and make it on my own. Earn my own spending money. Buy my own gasoline. Pay my own car insurance."

Yeah, I thought, "make it on your own" from a dorm with room and board paid. I guess I was jealous. My parents hadn't been able to help me with college.

Joe came in with the ladder and went to work on the window over the stairwell. He began by putting a footstool even with the bottom step, to make a level space large enough for both legs of the ladder. Joe then climbed up the teetery ladder to close the window Jeff had opened from outside. I held the ladder and prayed, as Aunt Nettie had a month earlier when I did the same stunt so I could change the lightbulb over the stairs.

I could see how Jeff had been entrapped. He had tried to get in a window in a row that was easy to reach from the porch roof. The one Jeff had tackled had a storm window that was warped in some way and hung a little crooked. Which, I'm sure, was why Jeff had climbed from the porch railing to the roof and up to that particular window.

Since he'd never been inside the house, Jeff had no way of knowing that the handy-dandy window was over the stairwell. He'd been darn lucky that he hadn't fallen in headfirst, tumbled fifteen feet down to the wooden stairs, and broken his neck.

I shuddered at the thought of having to tell Rich and Dina that I'd come home from work and found their son dead in my house. Jeff wasn't the only one who had had a narrow escape.

Jeff finished his sandwich and milk, then voluntarily got up to go outside and help Joe with the storm window. This time he held the ladder while Joe climbed onto the porch roof. Joe whacked the wooden frame of the storm window with a hammer and got it to fit a little better. I found a pair of Uncle Phil's old boots and lent them to Jeff. He and Joe collected a couple of shovels from the garage and went down to dig out Jeff's SUV.

As soon as they left the house I called Jeff's dad, the guy I've nicknamed Rich Gottrocks. He's a big-time real estate developer in Dallas. Or maybe he just thinks he's big-time. He had acquired a receptionist with a British accent.

Miss Brit told me Rich was unavailable. And his executive assistant was unavailable, too, she said. No, she had no idea when either of them would be back. She'd be only too happy to take a message.

I left one. "Jeff is here in Warner Poor. I

mean, Warner Pier. In Michigan! Please call." I gave my name, but didn't identify myself as an ex-wife. Then I called Jeff's mom at her antique shop. I got her answering machine. Her message said the antique shop would be closed for a week, but it didn't give me a hint about where she was or why she'd closed. I left a message there, too. Next I called information and asked for a home number for each of them. Both were unlisted. Rats!

Two long-distance calls wasted. I was still standing beside the telephone trying to figure out what to do when the thing rang.

Could it be Rich? Or Dina? I snatched the phone up, hoping I could shift the responsibility for Jeff onto one of his parents.

But the phone call was from Aunt Nettie. "Are you all right?" she asked. "You ran out like something was after you."

"Just a dirty secret from my past," I said. "You may have forgotten I used to be a wicked stepmother."

"Oh, my! Rich's son called?"

I could always count on Aunt Nettie. She knew all my secrets and loved me anyway. I poured out the whole story — Jeff's unexpected arrival, his attempt to break in, the lip stud, the eyebrow ring, the earlobe eyelets, the sullen attitude, and all the danger

38

flags he was running up in my mind.

"So I don't know what to do about him," I said. "If he's broke, I don't really want to turn him away. I tried to call both his parents, but neither of them is available. He's apparently walked out on college. But I certainly can't see giving him money, even if I had any to give."

Aunt Nettie didn't hesitate. "What he needs is a job," she said. "He can stay there at the house, and we'll put him to work packing chocolates for TenHuis Chocolade."

Chapter 3

TenHuis Chocolade couldn't afford another employee. Aunt Nettie knew this as well as I did. She and I had even cut our own salaries to help make ends meet. This was one reason I wasn't enrolled in the review course for the CPA exam.

But we could use some packing help. And I didn't see any other way to keep Jeff corralled, to try to have a little control over him. So I offered him a job.

Jeff was not enthusiastic about becoming a chocolate packer. But I made it clear that neither Aunt Nettie nor I — and certainly not Joe — was likely to come up with a loan, so he grudgingly said he'd try it. Somehow I didn't expect him to be a long-term employee.

Jeff was also unenthusiastic about staying at the Lake Shore Drive house, but he accepted Aunt Nettie's invitation. When I quizzed him, he said he was down to less than five bucks. So he didn't have much choice.

Joe left, headed for Benton Harbor, and Jeff and I unloaded the Lexus and put his things in the bedroom across the upstairs hall from mine. He had apparently left his dorm room in a hurry, because he had nothing but a change of clothes and a laptop computer. Then I drove the two of us into town; Aunt Nettie's house is inside the city limits, but in an area that's not fully developed, so we always talk about "going to town" when we mean to the Warner Pier business district. There are plenty of parking spaces in the winter. I parked on Peach Street.

"How come all the streets in this town are named for fruits?" Jeff said.

"Because it's a big fruit-growing region," I said. "But there are a couple of non-fruity streets. Dock Street. West Street. Lake Shore Drive."

"Yeah. And Orchard and Arbor."

I made a mental note of that comment. Evidently Jeff had driven around Warner Pier before he went out to the house. At least he'd read the names of the streets in the downtown business district and identified Warner Pier's main drags. In fact, he had seemed to know which street led to TenHuis Chocolade. But if he'd driven by there earlier, why hadn't he come in? His story was full of holes.

Jeff's entrance into TenHuis Chocolade was interesting. He walked straight across the shop, went behind the counter, and looked at the dirty bear mold that had distressed me earlier.

"Your aunt collects antique chocolate molds," he said. "That's a dandy."

"It's borrowed," I said.

Jeff had moved on to the mold of the acrobat teddy bear wearing a fez. "That's a really old one."

"I was told it's a Reiche, if that means anything to you."

"I don't know a lot about them, but Reiche was one of the big guys."

"Does your mother's shop handle chocolate molds?"

"Not many. But she's got a customer — a guy who runs a Dallas chocolate company — and she keeps her eye out for anything he might like."

Aunt Nettie came in, and I introduced Jeff. She greeted him with her usual beaming smile. "Jeff, we're glad to get a little help down here. Have you ever done packing or shipping?"

"Furniture. I've packed furniture. Sometimes dishes. But not chocolates, Miz TinHouse."

Jeff's Texas pronunciation of the family name made Aunt Nettie smile, though a kid born and raised in Dallas sounds much less like a hick than a person like me. I lived in a small town out on the prairie until I was sixteen, and even two years with a speech coach hasn't removed all the twang from my voice.

"It rhymes with 'ice,' Jeff," I said. "Tenhice."

Aunt Nettie still looked amused. "Lee said it just the same way, the first summer she worked here. But don't worry about it. You can call me Nettie, or Aunt Nettie. And the first thing you need is a sample chocolate. Every TenHuis employee gets two each day."

Jeff didn't look sullen about that. He picked an Italian cherry bonbon ("Amareena cherry in syrup and white chocolate cream"), and while he didn't gush about how good it was, he looked pleased enough to suit Aunt Nettie.

"Now, come on back and I'll show you where to put your coat," she said. "We need you, because this is still our busy season. Do you know how to use a tape gun?"

Aunt Nettie took him away, and I got back to work. She wasn't kidding about this being our busy season. The summer tourist rush is busy enough. It keeps the front shop going hard, as our summer student helpers sell bonbons, truffles, and molded chocolate to the thousands of tourists and summer residents who pour into Warner Pier every year. That rush ends at Labor Day, or whenever the Chicago schools go into session.

Then things really pick up. Halloween, Christmas, Valentine's Day, Easter, and Mother's Day are big holidays for our mail-order side, with Thanksgiving, Hanukkah, New Year's, and Father's Day also bringing in business. In addition to the sixteen types of truffles and bonbons we always keep in stock, TenHuis makes fancy molded pieces and specially packaged boxes of chocolates — like the teddy bears on display in the showcase. We ship them all over the United States. Aunt Nettie has twenty women making chocolate all winter.

Our winter hours are different, however. In the summer Aunt Nettie comes in about seven thirty and leaves at midafternoon, and I come at one and stay until the shop is closed and cleaned up, around nine thirty. Between Labor Day and Memorial Day we all work nine to five, unless we're behind on orders and need to put in overtime.

And in our current financial position, I was trying to keep Aunt Nettie from supporting overtime.

I went into my office, which has big windows overlooking both the workroom and the retail shop, and called our supplier in Grand Rapids for an extra order of heavy cream. Then I checked the figures I needed when I faced our loan officer that week. I was fighting the despair that exercise always caused when the bell on the front door chimed and a customer came into the retail shop.

I jumped up and went out to the counter. "Can I help you?"

The customer looked familiar, but I didn't think I knew him. He was a distinguished-looking older gent with a beautiful head of white hair, a perky gray mustache, and a red face. Who did he remind me of?

"I've come in to apologize," he said. "I've been told that I've pulled a major boner." He leaned forward in a sort of bow, and he gave a smile that must have wowed the sorority girls forty years earlier. "I've come to sheek your forgiveness."

The "sheek" gave me a clue about his condition. Then his head bounced around like a toy clown's. Whoever he was, he'd drunk his lunch.

"I'm sure, whatever it is, it will be all right," I said. "Your apology is accepted."

"M'sister scolded me severely," he said. "According to her, I'm selling the family

45

treasures for filthy lucre, and I embarrashed her in front of your aunt and the antique woman."

I was beginning to figure out who this must be. "Are you Mrs. VanHorn's brother?"

"Timothy Hart, m'dear. An embarrassing limb of the Hart family tree."

"I'm Lee McKinney, Nettie TenHuis's niece." We shook hands.

He looked at the display of chocolate molds behind me. "Mama's collection looks very nice."

"My aunt arranged it. It's a lovely collection. I understand why Mrs. VanHorn wants to keep it in the family."

"I don't understand it! Olivia's spent years trying to live down that particular side of the family. They're my favorite anchestors, but she finds them a bit too earthy. She always wants to remember that Great-grampa Amos invented the Hart centrif — centrifi — centrifugal molding machine and forget that he worked as a candy butcher. He walked up and down the cars of the Illinois Central, selling candy, apples, and bananas from a basket."

I warmed to Timothy. "But that's inspiring! A real American success story. I can see y'all have a wonderful family connection with the chocolate business."

"But if Olivia values the collection so highly, why did she toss it in a box in the basement?"

"Sometimes things get put away in the wrong place."

"True. I mustn't be too hard on her. She hasn't been around for the past fifteen years. Couldn't face the Warner Pier house after Vic died there."

"Vic? Was that Mr. VanHorn?"

"Congressman VanHorn. She's spent fifteen years grooming her son to take his place. Though that ambition may elude her."

"A political career could be very rewarding, but it's always uncertain."

"That's so." Timothy Hart shook his finger at me. "That sweet Southern accent has me pouring my heart out, Miss McKinney. I'd better leave."

"Not without a sample of TenHuis chocolate."

Mr. Hart selected a Jamaican rum truffle ("The ultimate dark chocolate truffle"). "A small additional taste of the good stuff won't hurt," he said. "I'm not driving. Lost m'license years ago." Then he shook his finger at me again. "Now, don't tell m'sister I came in here. She told me an apology would make things worse."

"You haven't made things worse at all, and I've enjoyed meeting you, Mr. Hart." I waved as he went out the door. Yes, Timothy Hart was quite pleasant — for a drunk. But if he pulled this stunt very often, I could see that his relatives would get tired of it.

I sighed, looked at the clock and went back to the office. Closing time was almost here, and I hadn't gotten started on the accounts payable or reached Jeff's parents. I called Rich's office and Dina's shop again. Both still unavailable. I left new messages. I wanted them to know about Jeff as quickly as possible.

I heard the UPS man come in the back, and Jeff appeared. I saw that Aunt Nettie had found him a baseball-style cap; at least he wouldn't have to wear a hairnet.

"They sent me for the UPS paperwork," he said.

I handed him the forms. "How's it going?"

"There's a lot more to it than I thought there would be." He took the papers and rushed back.

I smiled as I went back to my computer. Maybe a few days as a peon would do Jeff some good. Every overprivileged kid needs a lesson or two before he develops respect for the skills ordinary working people have — such as packing fragile chocolate rabbits so carefully that they can be shipped clear across the country without arriving in pieces and ruining Easter bunny sales for Neiman Marcus.

I had the bank figures done by quitting time. It was going to be close, but we weren't going to have to increase our loan. Not that my report would suit our new loan officer. He wanted us to have to refinance; then he could increase our interest.

I could hear Aunt Nettie's hairnet ladies calling out as they left through the back door. Soon Jeff came up, saying Aunt Nettie had asked him to drive home with me. She would stop at the store and get something for dinner. I told Jeff to pick out his second chocolate for the day, and he picked a Bailey's Irish Cream ("Classic cream liqueur interior"), but he said he'd take it along to eat afterward, so I gave him a small box to put it in. I sorted my paperwork into piles, and Jeff and I drove back to the house on Lake Shore Drive. It was dark when we got there, but we could still see that the yard was covered by snowmobile tracks. The crazy people who drive those things are always riding around on the lawn and cutting through all the little paths that link us with our neighbors. It annoys Aunt Nettie.

Aunt Nettie came in a half hour later with chicken breasts and tomato sauce. Jeff was subdued — or maybe just sullen — during dinner, but he asked Aunt Nettie lots of questions about making and shipping chocolates. I was glad that he gave some impression of being interested in his job. I still couldn't take my eyes off the quarter-inch holes in his earlobes. They were more eye-catching than the lip stud.

I expected Jeff would want to check his e-mail after dinner, and I steeled myself for an argument when he was told he'd have to pay for any long-distance calls, including those made to his e-mail server. But Jeff didn't suggest that. He put stuff away in his room, then I showed him how to operate the washing machine, and he washed some underwear and a sweatshirt. As I said, he hadn't brought much, though he did have a few warm clothes, including the ski jacket he'd had on that afternoon.

While his clothes were in the dryer, I sat him down at the dining room table and tried again to quiz him about why he'd left college. He muttered something about his grades.

"I can't believe you can't do college work, Jeff," I said. "You were always a good student."

"There's a lot more to life than college."

"True. Like packing chocolate."

He scowled. "Look, my dad wants me to learn to handle money, stuff like that, but he wants to make all the decisions — my major, where I live, the kind of car I drive, how I dress. I just need to try it on my own."

I might have believed him if he hadn't cut his eyes at me. I knew he was checking out how I was taking his story. Jeff had cut his eyes the same way when he was thirteen and was trying to convince me his mother rented X-rated movies for him to watch.

At ten thirty the dryer buzzed, and Jeff folded his underwear, then said he'd take a shower. He was still pouty, but he didn't make any comments about our strange bathroom.

Aunt Nettie's house was built by my great-grandfather and originally was the TenHuis family's summer cottage. My grandparents decided to live there full-time, so they winterized the house in the late 1940s, but the bathroom hasn't changed much since the family got indoor plumbing in 1915. For one thing, there's only one bathroom in the three-bedroom house. For another, we still have an old-fashioned claw-foot bathtub. Uncle Phil had changed the plumbing to allow for a shower. He hung a circular rod over the tub, and Aunt Nettie put up a shower curtain on each side. That was the shower. It wasn't exactly like the facility I knew Jeff had in his mother's house — his own bathroom with a tiled, walk-in shower. So I was surprised that Jeff didn't complain. He'd grown up in a house full of antiques; he wasn't likely to think the claw-foot tub was quaint.

As soon as I heard the shower, I knew the noise would keep Jeff from hearing anything else. I looked at the phone and again wished I could talk to Rich or Dina, but I still had no home numbers for either of them. So I called Joe Woodyard.

Several nights a week Joe called me. But Aunt Nettie's house not only has only one bathroom, it also has only one phone. And that phone is in the kitchen. So when I talk to Joe I sit on a stool by the kitchen sink. Aunt Nettie tactfully stays in the other room. I didn't want to carry on a conversation with Joe while Jeff was digging in the refrigerator for a bedtime snack or otherwise standing around with his ears hanging out. I told Joe as much.

"So you and Nettie took the kid in," he said.

"Aunt Nettie's too kindhearted not to. But there wasn't really anything else to do."

"You could send him to a motel."

"I suppose my credit card would stand it, but Jeff claims he left college because he wants to be on his own. Lending him money doesn't seem like a good thing to do, and neither does paying his rent. And I could hardly send him to the homeless shelter."

"You could send him to jail."

"No, I couldn't, Joe. That's not a realistic opinion. I mean option."

"Maybe not. But — listen, how about if he comes over here?"

"No! You don't have any room for him." Joe was living in one room at the boatyard. He had a rollaway bed, a hot plate, and a microwave.

"I've got an air mattress and a sleeping bag. I don't like him alone in the house with you and Nettie."

"Don't be silly."

"I'm not. The kid definitely tried to break into the house this morning. That's a criminal act. You admit you don't know him too well. How long has it been since you saw him?"

"A couple of years."

"Have you heard anything about him in the meantime? Like, was he president of his Sunday-school class?"

"No, I haven't heard much about him

since Rich and I divorced, and I doubt he's president of his Sunday-school class, since I never heard of either of his parents taking him to church. But I'm not afraid to have him in the house."

"Well, put a chair under your doorknob."

The water stopped then, and Joe and I hung up on that slightly antagonistic note. It seemed that a lot of our conversations had been ending that way lately.

I guess I was getting tired of sitting home by the telephone. Joe kept telling me he wanted us to start dating, but we didn't seem to be getting close to that goal.

Joe was a Warner Pier native; his mother ran an insurance agency across the street from TenHuis Chocolade. I'd first known him — or known of him — twelve years earlier, when Joe was chief lifeguard at Warner Pier's Crescent Beach, and I was one of the gang of teenaged girls who stood around and admired his shoulders. Joe had been a high school hotshot — all-state wrestler, state debate champion, straight-A student, senior class president. He got a scholarship to the University of Michigan and did well there and in law school. Aunt Nettie says his mother glowed every time his name was mentioned.

But after law school Joe surprised his

mother by going to work for a Legal Aid-type operation instead of the big firm she'd pictured. His mom wasn't as excited about that.

Then Joe met Clementine Ripley. *The* Clementine Ripley. One of the nation's top defense attorneys, the one the movie stars and big financiers called before they called the cops.

Ms. Ripley went to Detroit to defend one of Joe's clients pro bono. Before the trial was over, he'd fallen for her in a major way, and she had found him a pleasant diversion. Joe convinced her that they should get married, even though she was more than fifteen years older than he was.

Warner Pier says that it was doomed from the start, and Joe says he was naïve — only he uses the word "stupid." He also might not have expected the attention the marriage drew from the tabloid press: TOP WOMAN DEFENSE ATTORNEY WEDS TOYBOY LOVER IN MAY-DECEMBER ROMANCE.

That was followed by TOP WOMAN DEFENSE ATTORNEY BUILDS SHOWPLACE HOME IN TOYBOY HUSBAND'S HOMETOWN. Next, TOYBOY HUSBAND OF TOP WOMAN DEFENSE ATTORNEY QUITS LAW CAREER, DENIES PLAN TO BECOME HOUSE

HUSBAND. Finally, TOP WOMAN DEFENSE ATTORNEY SPLITS WITH TOYBOY HUSBAND. AGE NOT FACTOR, BOTH CLAIM, with a subhead, "Ex now repairing boats."

Joe's version is that Clementine Ripley's approach to the practice of law crystallized his disappointment in the morality of a legal career and made becoming an honest craftsman seem a more honorable way to make a living. So he bought a boat repair shop in his hometown. Specializing in antique wooden boats, he did beautiful work, work to be proud of. But his mother had quit glowing whenever his name came up.

Then, just when Joe had thought he'd escaped from the glare of the media, Clementine Ripley was murdered in her "showplace home in toyboy ex's hometown." The tabloids came back.

The crime was solved — that's how Joe and I met each other again. Then Ms. Ripley's lawyers dropped another bombshell. They revealed that she hadn't changed her will after her divorce from Joe. Joe inherited her entire estate, plus he was named executor. The tabloids stuck around.

To complicate matters further, Clementine Ripley left an extremely involved estate.

Joe was having to spend several days a week with accountants, attorneys, court appearances, even finding a new home for her champion Birman cat, who now lived in Chicago with a former housekeeper. Joe swore he wasn't going to keep any of the money — and he said there wasn't going to be much left, anyway — but it was forcing him to spend a lot of time concentrating on his ex-wife's affairs.

Not on his own affairs. Not on my affairs. On Clementine Ripley's affairs. The woman was haunting him.

The tabloid press was haunting him, too. They seemed to have some conduit into Warner Pier. Any little thing Joe did popped up in the tabloids. The previous week he had talked to the mayor, to see if the city was interested in owning the fifteen-acre Warner Pier estate Clementine Ripley had left behind. Two days later the headlines read, TOYBOY HEIR OF FAMED ATTORNEY SEEKS BUYER FOR MANSION.

Our mayor, Mike Herrera, swore he hadn't told anybody but the park commissioners. How had the tabloid found out?

Neither Joe nor I wanted to see ourselves splashed across the *National Enquirer* — TOYBOY HEIR OF FAMED LAWYER ROMANCES TEXAS EX-BEAUTY QUEEN

WHO WAS WITNESS TO EX-WIFE'S DEATH. So I understood why Joe and I were having a telephone romance. But I was getting tired of it.

Jeff went up to bed, and I said good night to Aunt Nettie and went up, too. I didn't get undressed, but I wrapped up in a comforter and read by my bedside lamp, which is rather dim. I got interested in my book, forgot Joe, and barely heard Aunt Nettie moving around as she got ready for bed.

Then, across the hall, I heard Jeff's bed creak. His door opened, he came out, and he stopped outside my door.

Instantly, I remembered what Joe had said about putting a chair under my doorknob.

My heart jumped up to my throat. I told myself I was being crazy, but that didn't do any good. Joe's warning had created suspicions, and it was no good denying they existed. I was scared.

I lay still, not breathing, just listening. It was ludicrous. Jeff was on one side of the door, listening to me, and I was on the other, listening to him.

I didn't breathe again until I heard Jeff move on and start down the stairs.

Stupid, I told myself. Even kids have to get up to go to the bathroom now and then.

I wondered if Jeff *was* going to the bathroom. Or if he was going to Aunt Nettie's room. That gave me another stab of fear.

So I listened carefully to his progress through the house. I'd spent a lot of time in that house. I could tell who was walking where without moving anything but my ear.

Jeff crept down the steps to the living room, then turned toward the dining room. He went into the kitchen.

Good. He was going to the bathroom.

But when he got to the kitchen, he stopped. He fumbled with something that thumped. Was it the hall tree where all the winter jackets had been hung?

I heard a click. I was sure the sound was the lock of the back door.

The door opened, then shut. I heard Jeff's footsteps cross the back porch, then scrunch through the snow in the side yard, moving toward the driveway and off into the night.

CHOCOLATE CHAT

GOLDEN AGE CHOCOLATE

One of the most famous books of the Golden Age of Mysteries is *The Poisoned Chocolates Case*, by Anthony Berkeley, published in 1929. It's based on a short story Berkeley wrote, "The Avenging Chance," published a year earlier.

In both the short story and the novel a box of chocolates is mailed to a member of a London men's club, and the man is asked to sample it as part of a marketing survey. Since the recipient dislikes chocolates, he gives them to an acquaintance, who takes them home to his wife. The wife eats one and dies — poisoned. The detectives, of course, try to figure out who had it in for the man who received the chocolates and passed them on to his fellow club member. The solution, however, is that the second man knew his fellow club member did not like chocolate and arranged to be beside him when the box arrived. The wife was the intended victim all along.

All very logical — except that part about the first man disliking chocolate. That's completely unbelievable.

Chapter 4

What the heck was Jeff up to?

I quickly turned off my bedside lamp, slid out of my cocoon of comforter, and went to the window. I pulled the curtain aside and peeked out.

Could Jeff be creeping outside to smoke? Aunt Nettie didn't have ashtrays out, true, but he hadn't asked about it. The kid would have to be a confirmed nicotine addict to go outside for a cigarette in fifteen-degree weather.

Did he want to get something from his SUV? Unless he'd hidden something under the seat, I didn't think there was anything left in it to get. I'd even given him a plastic grocery bag for his trash, and he had filled it with soft-drink cups and fast-food debris that afternoon. The SUV had looked empty.

Was he going someplace? That didn't seem likely. For one thing, I'd noticed that his gas tank was close to empty. I'd planned to buy him a tank of gas the next day, but I hadn't told him that yet. Besides, if he wanted to leave, Aunt Nettie and I had made it clear we weren't going to try to stop him. There was no reason for him to sneak off in the middle of the night.

And it was the middle of the night. My watch read 1:00 a.m.

But middle of the night or no, the interior lights flashed inside Jeff's SUV; then I heard the motor start. But only his running lights came on when the Lexus began to move. He backed down the driveway slowly. This was definitely as surreptitious a trip as he could manage.

Where was he going? I had to know. Or at least try to find out. Maybe if I followed him, I'd get a clue as to why he had left Texas.

I was still dressed, so I grabbed my purse and rushed down the stairs in my stocking feet, hoping that I wasn't waking Aunt Nettie. At the back door I stepped into my boots and pulled on my jacket and cap. By the time I got outside, Jeff's taillights had turned onto Lake Shore Drive, and his headlights popped on. I ran to my van, thudding along the cleared walk and then scrambling through the snow along the drive. I pulled the no-lights stunt until I was past the house. I was still trying not to wake up Aunt Nettie, but I half expected to see her standing at her bedroom window as I went by; Aunt Nettie doesn't miss much.

Even without lights, it was easy to see where I was going. Our part of Michigan is heavily wooded, but there are only a few evergreens; nearly all the trees are bare in winter. The snow on the ground reflected what light there was, giving the night a luminous quality. I drove about a quarter of a mile before I turned on my headlights.

By then I was asking myself if I was wasting my time. Jeff had about a three-minute head start, and even one minute would give him enough time to get away from me completely. But a few factors were working in my favor. If Jeff had gone anyplace but Warner Pier, I might as well forget the chase and go home. But if he had gone into Warner Pier, it was just a small place; I could drive up and down every street in the town in fifteen minutes. Plus, his gold Lexus RX300 was really noticeable. There probably wasn't another car like it in Warner Pier in the winter. So if I spotted one, I'd know it was likely to be him even before I saw the Texas tag.

Besides, if Jeff had sneaked out because he wanted to buy something, there was only one place in Warner Pier that was open all night, the Stop and Shop out on the state highway, at West Street and North Lake Shore Drive. I didn't consider that a strong possibility. Jeff had claimed he had less than five dollars in his pocket.

So I crossed the Warner River on the Orchard Street bridge and drove up and down the streets of Warner Pier. I was all by myself; the town shuts down completely on a winter night. Streetlights made the snow glitter at every corner, and the Victorian houses looked like wedding cakes.

The Dockster, a beer joint that rocks until dawn in the summer, was shuttered for the winter. The Warner Pier Inn had closed its dining room at nine. Dock Street Pizza, where the locals hang out, had closed at ten. The Holiday Haven, one of the two motels that stay open all winter, was dark, though a dim light in the office hinted that an on-site manager would have appeared if I had banged on its doors. I saw no reason to do such a thing. There was no Lexus SUV in its parking lot.

Even the Warner Pier Police Department, which occupies a corner of City Hall, had only one light inside and a security light outside. The Warner Pier Volunteer Fire Department was locked up tight as well. The police and fire station share a dispatcher with the county, and in case of emergency, I guess the dispatcher knows who has the keys.

The only human being I saw was the guy spraying water to form a new layer of ice on the tennis courts. Warner Pier's tennis courts are flooded and turned into a skating rink every winter, and some poor schnook has to maintain them after the skaters have packed it in.

By the time I reached the intersection of West Street and North Lake Shore Drive — where the state highway enters Warner Pier — I had just about decided that Jeff had headed back to Texas on an empty gas tank. I glanced at Warner Pier's other open motel, the Lake Michigan Inn. It looked busier than the Holiday Haven had looked; one guest room had a light in the window and there were a few cars parked outside, though none of them had Texas tags.

I drove around the corner and pulled into the Stop and Shop to turn around, and there, under the lights next to the building, was Jeff's gold Lexus.

Luckily for my surveillance project, there was no sign of Jeff himself. I flipped a U-turn through the parking lot and wheeled my old van across the street. I pulled into the circular drive of Katie's Kraft Shoppe and parked close behind the shop's van. I cut my lights and watched the Stop and Shop.

So Jeff had stopped for gas. Did he have more money than he'd told me he had? Or did he have a credit card he hadn't mentioned? Or had he bought gas? He wasn't parked at a pump.

I didn't see Jeff. It crossed my mind that he might be robbing the joint. My heart jumped to my throat. His car was in plain sight, however, nosed in near the entrance door. If he'd planned to commit a crime, surely he wouldn't have been stupid enough to park that noticeable car in so obvious a spot. Maybe he had just dropped by the Stop and Shop to buy a bag of potato chips. I tried to calm down.

The inside of the store was visible through big plate-glass windows, and I scanned the shelves and aisles. It wasn't a big place, just a half dozen aisles. There was no sign of Jeff. I turned the van's motor off. I would sit there until I got cold, I decided. If he didn't show by then, I'd go home to bed.

But I had waited only about five minutes when Jeff appeared. He came into the store from the back room, waved at the clerk, and walked out the front door.

What the heck had he been doing in the back room of the Stop and Shop?

Oh, God! Were they dealing drugs there? My heart leaped back into my throat, then dropped to my toes, and began to pound like crazy. But I had no reason to think Jeff was into the drug scene, I told myself. He hadn't acted high, and his eyes looked normal, even if his earlobes didn't. Maybe he wanted to use the Stop and Shop's restroom.

Jeff started his car, backed out, and drove toward the Warner Pier business district. I waited until he was several blocks down the street, then cautiously followed him.

He didn't seem to have any idea I was there, and he seemed to know where he was going — if he was heading back to Aunt Nettie's. At least, he turned where I would have. If I were going home myself, I'd cut over to Dock Street by way of Fifth, a route that would take me past TenHuis Chocolade, near the corner of Fifth and Peach. I was once again made aware that Jeff was more familiar with the layout of Warner Pier than he should have been.

I hung back a couple of blocks as we drove. I was beginning to wonder what I was going to tell Jeff after we both parked in Aunt Nettie's driveway.

So he caught me completely by surprise when he suddenly turned off his headlights, pulled over, and parked beside the curb, right in front of TenHuis Chocolade. I stopped a block away, as far away from a streetlamp as I could, and turned off my headlights.

But Jeff wasn't paying any attention to me. He remained motionless inside his SUV for about a minute; then he jumped out and ran across the sidewalk. I could see him silhouetted against the dim security light we leave on behind the counter.

Now what?

I decided I'd better intervene. I drove on down the street. By this time Jeff was running back and forth in front of the store, looking up and down the street. As I pulled in beside his car, he shaded his eyes from my headlights. His glasses glittered. He seemed to be peering at me, trying to see who I was.

I opened the van's window and leaned out. "Jeff! What are you up to?"

"Lee?" His voice was a harsh whisper. "Oh, God, you're here!"

"Yes. And so are you. Why?"

He waved frantically and whispered again. "Be quiet! Call the cops! Somebody's broken into the store!"

I got out of the van. "That's silly. This is Warner Pier."

"I don't care if it's the moon! The glass is broken out of the front door! And I saw somebody moving around. Now they're in the back room. They've got a flashlight!"

The whole thing was ridiculous. Burglaries don't happen in Warner Pier, at least not in winter. I moved toward Jeff, into my headlights.

"Warner Pier has practically no crime in the wintertime," I said. "The tourists take it home with them."

I could see myself reflected in the shop window as I crossed the sidewalk. But when I moved in front of the entrance door, my reflection disappeared.

For a moment I was reminded of a funhouse mirror — now you see it, now you don't. But when I stretched out my hand toward the door, my glove went right through the glass part of the door.

"The glass is gone," I said stupidly.

Jeff whispered again. "That's what I've been trying to tell you! The glass in the door is smashed, and there was somebody moving around inside."

Right then we heard a motor start, followed by squealing tires.

"They're getting away!" Jeff ran toward the corner.

I had an awful vision of Jeff tackling burglars, ruthless and desperate burglars armed with guns and knives.

"Jeff! Stop!" I ran after him.

It was half a block to Fourth Street, and we pounded along until we got there. But when Jeff reached the streetlight at the corner he stopped abruptly. I careened into him, and we both slipped on a patch of ice. I grabbed Jeff, he grabbed me, we both grabbed the base of the streetlight. We wound up sitting on the sidewalk, but neither of us hit the ground very hard.

Jeff was still facing up Fourth Street. "There they go! And I didn't get a good look at the car."

I twisted around in time to see taillights disappearing around a corner. "He turned on Blueberry," I said. "Or I think he did. And his taillights look funny."

"The left one is out," Jeff said, "but that's not going to be a lot of help. I think it was some kind of sports car. Maybe."

We walked back to the store. "You don't have a cell phone, do you?" Jeff asked. He made it sound like a major personality flaw.

"Sorry," I said. "But I have a key to the shop."

"We shouldn't go in the front. We might destroy evidence."

"Well, I'm not going around to the alley," I said. "It's too dark and snaky back there. Besides, the burglar must have gone out the back door, it's easy to open from inside."

"How far is the police station?"

"Just a couple of blocks, but there's nobody there. We have to call the county dispatcher."

There was little glass on the sidewalk, of course, because the burglar had knocked the glass inside. We gingerly walked in.

"If the burglars came in this way," Jeff said, "they're gonna have glass in the soles of their shoes."

I turned on the lights and looked at the display shelves.

"Thank God!" I said.

"Yeah," Jeff said. "The molds are still there."

Since the moment the word "burglar" had sprung into my mind, I'd been dreading finding the Hart collection of chocolate molds gone. They were the only thing in the shop that was valuable.

I called the dispatcher, and in about ten minutes a patrol car pulled up. I was relieved to see a tall, lanky figure get out — Abraham Lincoln in a stocking cap.

"It's Chief Jones," I said.

The chief waved at me. "Just what have you been up to now, Lee?"

"I'm a victim, Chief. Or at least TenHuis Chocolade is."

The chief stepped in through the broken

glass, and I introduced him to Jeff. "You two better go in the office and close the door," the chief said. "We'll hurry up out here."

"Yeah. Chocolate gets funny-looking if it freezes. I'll call Handy Hans and see if he can do something about that door."

"Have you called Nettie?"

"No. I'll do that, too."

Telling Aunt Nettie that someone had broken into her beloved shop wasn't easy, but she took it calmly.

"Nobody's hurt?"

"Not Jeff or me. I hope whoever broke in slashed their wrists on broken glass."

"Any sign of that?"

"Nope. Apparently they — he — parked around behind, but he must not have been able to open the back door from the outside. So he came around to the front, smashed the window in the door, and got in that way. But Jeff must have disturbed him right away, and the guy ran back to the break room, opened the door to the alley and got out the back."

"I'll be right down."

Aunt Nettie's big Buick showed up within fifteen minutes. By then a second patrol car had arrived and Patrolman Jerry Cherry was taking pictures. The chief had allowed Jeff and me to start cleaning up the glass, so Aunt Nettie was able to enter the shop in a more traditional manner.

Soon afterward Handy Hans — his last name is VanRiin — arrived with a sheet of plywood, which he used as a stopgap measure against the cold, and Aunt Nettie joined Jeff and me in the office.

She looked puzzled. "What I don't understand is why you two were down here in the middle of the night. And why did you come in separate cars?"

Jeff glowered and stared at the floor.

I was going to have to tell them that I had followed Jeff. "I heard Jeff leaving," I said, "and my curlicue got the best of me. I mean my curiosity! I admit it, Jeff. I wanted to know where you were going, so I followed you."

Glower and mutter. He shot a glare at me.

I felt embarrassed and angry. "If it's any consolation, you lost me, and I found you again just a few blocks before you pulled up in front of the shop." I thought Jeff looked relieved, but he didn't speak. I went on. "I feel responsible for you, Jeff. You won't tell us why you showed up here. I can't get hold of your parents. I need to know what you're up to!"

"Good question." The comment came

from the door to the office, and I looked up to see Chief Jones come in. He unwrapped a mile of wool scarf from around his neck, pulled off his stocking cap, and took a chair.

"Okay. Jeff, you did good work, scaring the burglar off like that. But what the heck were you doing down here anyway?"

Jeff's lips pursed, and his brows knitted. He looked as if he were trying to decide whether he should yell or burst into tears.

But before he could do either, Aunt Nettie took over. "Chief, does Warner Pier have a curfew?"

"No, Nettie. You know it doesn't."

"Then is there any legal reason that Jeff shouldn't have been driving around in Warner Pier, even if he did it after midnight?"

"No, there isn't, Nettie. He wasn't breaking any law by merely driving around the business district. It's just a little unusual."

She turned to me. "Lee, Jeff isn't a little boy anymore, and you're not married to his father anymore. So, if he wants to drive around all night every night, he's welcome to do so."

Then she addressed the chief. "It's getting to be time for breakfast. Let's form a caravan out to the house — you and Jerry are invited. I've got a couple of pounds of sausage in the freezer, and I've got a dozen eggs. Let's go eat."

She zipped her heavy blue jacket and pulled on her own woolly cap and gloves. She shook a bulky finger at us. "And not one of you is going to ask Jeff a single question. He saved the Hart molds, and I'll be eternally grateful to him."

She sailed out the door — solid as a tugboat, but regal as an ocean liner.

When I looked at Jeff, he had tears in his eyes.

Chapter 5

Of course, Aunt Nettie was right.

Or I had convinced myself that she was by the time I had driven out to the house. My Texas grandmother would have said Jeff was simply "bowing his neck," acting like a mule fighting the harness. He wasn't going to be badgered into telling us anything. The only way we were likely to find out why he'd come to Michigan was by killing him with kindness. It was the same technique Aunt Nettie had used twelve years earlier, when she was saddled with an angry sixteen-year-old niece for the summer.

We had to let Jeff learn that he could trust us. Which made me a little ashamed that I had followed him. But not too ashamed. When I finally got hold of his mom or his dad, they were likely to have a fit because he had left college in the middle of the semester and driven to Michigan. I didn't want to quarrel with them, and they wouldn't like it if I had let him wander around western Michigan in the snow and hadn't even tried to figure out what he was up to.

And I did wonder about those tears in Jeff's eyes.

Jeff offset the tears, however, by pouting and sulking all through breakfast. By the time Aunt Nettie had fed Chief Jones, Jeff, me, and herself — Jerry Cherry hadn't joined us — it was close to six a.m. The chief insisted on helping Aunt Nettie with the dishes, and Jeff delighted us all by going to bed. I was exhausted, but too keyed up to sleep. So I put on my jacket and boots, took my flashlight and walked down the drive to get the Grand Rapids paper out of the delivery box across the road.

Getting out and walking around in the snow is another part of my campaign not to act like a Texan who'd never seen cold weather before. Actually, it can get darn cold in Texas, but it doesn't last months and months, the way it does in Michigan.

I'd just taken the newspaper out and turned to go back across the road when headlights came around the curve. I stopped to let them go by. But the headlights didn't go by. A pickup screeched to a halt, and Joe Woodyard got out.

"Are you okay?" He sounded all excited.

"Yes. Are you?"

"No, I'm pretty upset." He came around the front of the pickup.

77

"What are you upset about?"

"You," he said. And then he threw his arms around me.

I tipped my head back and looked at him, astonished.

So he kissed me. Thoroughly.

I enjoyed it thoroughly, too. In fact, it felt so good I had to fight an impulse to throw him in the back of the pickup and tear his clothes off, beginning with his puffy nylon jacket and working down to the long underwear I could see peeking out at his cuff. But a little voice kept nagging in the back of my head. *What brought this on?* it asked. And, *Is this a good idea?*

It was about five minutes before I could ask my questions out loud. "Wow!" I said. "I'll have to upset you more often. What's the occasion?"

"Chasing burglars! What would have happened if you caught 'em? Don't you know I couldn't make it if anything happened to you?" Then he kissed me again. For just four and a half minutes this time.

When he worked around to nibbling my neck, I was able to talk. "Nothing did happen to me," I said. "I'm enjoying this, but I don't quite understand it."

Joe moved his head back, but he didn't let me go. We were standing sternum-to-sternum and talking nose-to-nose. "You and that kid! What were you two doing waltzing around with burglars?"

"I haven't the slightest idea, when you get down to it. How'd you find out about our adventure?"

"I had coffee with Tony out at the truck stop." Tony Herrera was married to one of my friends, Lindy. Tony, who happened to be the son of Warner Pier's mayor, drove into Holland every day for his job as a machinist. He and Joe had been friends since elementary school.

Joe went on. "We ran into Jerry Cherry."

"I see that the Warner Pier grapevine is in good shape. How come Jerry realized you'd want to know about our excitement?"

"He didn't. There was a whole table of us. I tried not to seem too interested."

He had tried not to seem too interested? Suddenly I was hopping mad. I pushed myself away from Joe.

How could he act as if I mattered to him when we were alone or when we were talking on the telephone, but pretend he hardly knew me in public?

"Oh, I think you could justify some interest in a local burglary," I said. "After all, you're a Warner Pier property owner. All the Warner Pier citizens are shocked and

79

appalled by local crime, right?"

"Sure. Everybody was interested. But —" He cocked his head. "Are you mad?"

"No. I'm furious."

"About the burglary?"

"Not exactly." I stopped talking then. It was awfully hard to tell a guy that your relationship stunk when you didn't have a relationship. I decided I'd better not try. "I suppose I'm just tired."

"Well, yeah. You've been up all night."

"That's not what I meant, but I guess it's close enough."

"Hop in, and I'll drive you up to the house."

"Better not! Chief Jones is up there. He might see you."

I guess my sarcasm finally sank in. Joe's lips tightened, but he didn't say anything.

"I'll talk to you later," I said. Then I pushed on past him, but he caught my arm.

"If you think I like this situation, you're wrong."

"If you think I like it, you're wrong, too."

We stood there, glaring at each other. Then I pulled my arm away. "I'm completely out of patience with adolescent piccalillis — I mean peccadilloes."

"Thanks! I'm really thrilled at being lumped in with that kid."

"Actually, you and Jeff are acting quite differently. He won't talk at all, and you won't do anything else."

"What do you want me to do?"

"I don't know! But it's not real complimentary if you don't even want people to know —" I broke off. "Oh, forget it! It's a dead end anyway."

I stalked across the road. Joe followed me. "I didn't come to quarrel," he said.

"Then why did you come?"

"To see you. To make sure you were all right."

"You've seen me. I'm all right."

"And I wanted to find out just what that kid —"

"That kid's name is Jeff."

"Okay! To find out just what kind of a story Jeff told about the burglary."

"Jeff had nothing to do with the burglary. I was following him. I saw him pull up in front of the shop. I saw him get out of the SUV. He did not break the window."

"Maybe not, but Jerry said he doesn't think the chief is satisfied with his story."

"I'm not satisfied with his story either. I want to know why he went into town in the first place. But I don't think he broke the window. I do think he scared the burglar off."

"Maybe so, but . . . Jerry said that the burglar apparently went off in a car with a broken taillight."

"We think so."

"Well, Brad Michaels said —"

"Who is Brad Michaels?"

"He has the gas station south of town, down at Haven Road. Right on the interstate. And he says a kid driving a gold Lexus SUV with a Texas plate stopped there around seven a.m. yesterday. He didn't buy gas, just candy bars and chips."

"Sounds like Jeff. So?"

"So Brad says there were two Texas vehicles. The other driver didn't get out, but Brad thinks they were together."

Maybe I would have reacted differently if I hadn't already been mad. But I *was* mad. Plus tired and plain old out of sorts. I didn't want any more bad news. So I tried to kill the messenger.

"I suppose that your pal Brad says the other Texas car had a taillight out," I said.

"No, he —"

"I suppose you asked him that."

"Yes, I —"

"And I suppose you made sure he told Jerry about it."

"No! He didn't mention it until Jerry had gone."

"But I suppose you urged him to tell Jerry. Or Chief Jones."

"They're gonna find out. Warner Pier is a small town."

"Well, let them! But I'm not getting involved in any more efforts to quiz Jeff. He knows I want to find out just what he's up to. He'll tell me something when he's ready. Or he'll tell Aunt Nettie. Or the chief will question him. But right now I'm cold and I'm tired and I'm going back to the house."

I walked away without looking back. This time Joe didn't follow me.

When I got back to the house I took off all my outdoor paraphernalia, then sat in the living room pretending to read the paper. I felt pretty miserable. Joe was suspicious of Jeff even without knowing the most damning part of the situation. Nobody, including Chief Jones, knew that Jeff had been aware that the molds were valuable, but I did. Should I tell Chief Jones? Like Joe said, the chief was bound to find out. I just didn't want to be the person who caused Jeff more problems, even though he was causing me a lot.

Darn Joe Woodyard anyway! Why had he reminded me of Jeff's odd behavior? And why did I care what Joe thought? I shook the newspaper angrily. How had I wound up in this dead-end relationship?

For six months I'd been patient about Joe's hang-ups over his ex-wife and about his fear of the tabloids, but right at that moment I was sick of the situation.

Oh, maybe I'd brought part of it on myself, making it clear I wouldn't sneak around to go out with him. He had to take me out in public, or I wasn't going to go at all. And I certainly wasn't going to get too cozy with a guy I wasn't officially dating. So there'd been no weekends when we both just happened to be in Chicago and staying in the same hotel, no surreptitious meetings at the boat shop, no nights in a B&B a hundred miles up the lakeshore.

Joe wasn't the only one who had survived a bad marriage; I wasn't interested in having my self-respect further flogged by a clandestine affair, an affair that would have made me feel cheap and used.

Maybe I wasn't sure what I wanted out of a new man in my life anyway. So I had only myself to blame over the crazy relationship Joe and I had fallen into, I told myself. I half resolved to end it. Or maybe I already had. After the things I'd said, maybe I'd never get another of those eleven o'clock calls from Joe. Maybe we'd never hold each other again, never kiss like that again. Maybe I'd felt that melting sensation behind my navel for the last time.

I didn't like that idea either.

When Chief Jones left, I still hadn't decided what to tell him about Jeff. I put any decision off and simply called out a goodbye.

Aunt Nettie said she was going to bed. "We'd all better sleep as long as we can," she said. "I'll call the shop and leave a message. Telling them we'll be late."

I thought I couldn't possibly sleep, but I forced myself to undress and lie down, and the next thing I knew, it was eleven a.m. I could hear Aunt Nettie in the shower downstairs, and Jeff was snoring gently across the hall. I groaned and got up. Aunt Nettie had left the house by the time I got out of the shower.

I managed to get to work by one p.m., to find Aunt Nettie going crazy. "Thank goodness you're here," she said. "I can't get any work done for answering the phone and gossiping with the neighbors."

"I guess the news about our burglar got around."

"Naturally. The Warner Pier grapevine is up and running; we don't need radio or television or newspapers in this town. But everybody wants a personal account."

"I'll try to keep them away from you."

"I've simply got to make the bakjes for the crème de menthe bonbons today. Hazel's working on them, but she needs to get busy on the Neiman Marcus bunnies." Aunt Nettie froze and looked out the front window. "Oh, no! It's Mike Herrera. I can't be rude to him."

"Go on back to the shop and get up to your elbows in chocolate. I'll deal with him."

I shooed her toward her bakjes. Bakjes, pronounced "bah-keys," are the shells of bonbons, the part that holds the filling. First you cast the bakjes, then cool them, then fill them, then run the whole thing through an enrober, a special machine that gives the bonbons a shower-bath of chocolate. After that the tops are decorated, and you've finally got a goodie ready for the customers to drool over.

Aunt Nettie had washed her hands and moved to a stainless-steel worktable by the time the door opened. I greeted the newcomer. "Mayor Mike! Did you come to check our damage?"

Mike Herrera looked puzzled. "It's just so strange," he said. He closed the smashed front door behind him, then examined the plywood that blocked it temporarily. "We just don't have burglaries in

86

Warner Pier this time of year."

Mike Herrera is an attractive middle-aged man who owns several successful restaurants and a catering service. He was the first Hispanic to own a business in Warner Pier and the first to be elected to public office. He's the father of Joe's friend Tony and the father-in-law of my friend Lindy Herrera; in a town of twenty-five hundred, people tend to be related.

But I'm careful not to bring him up around Tony because Lindy told me her husband isn't real happy with his father since he changed his name from Miguel to Mike. Tony's reaction to the name change was to grow a thin Latin mustache and start teaching their children Spanish. The Herreras are typical of the American experience, I guess. One generation tries to assimilate; the next clings to its roots.

Mike kept looking at the damage.

"Handy Hans called the glass installers," I said, "but they can't get here until tomorrow."

We heard a crack like a pistol shot, and Mike craned his head to look into the shop. "What was that?"

"Aunt Nettie's making bakjes. She whams them on the worktable to get the edges right."

"Can I talk to her?"

"As long as we don't stop her work."

It was hard to refuse Mike. He knew that Aunt Nettie could make chocolates with her eyes closed. Mike followed me into the shop and greeted Aunt Nettie, commiserating with her over the break-in. Aunt Nettie kept pouring melted dark chocolate into a mold about the size of an ice-cube tray — an ice-cube tray with forty little compartments.

"I just wondered if anybody suspicious came in yesterday," Mike said.

Aunt Nettie had apparently filed Jeff in a nonsuspicious category. "I can't think of anybody," she said. "The antique molds were the only thing valuable in the shop." She turned her filled mold upside down over her work pan, and went tappity tappity tap on its edge with the flat side of her spatula while the excess chocolate drained out. She scraped the top of the mold, wielding her spatula like a conductor wields his baton. Then she flipped the mold over and slammed it onto the sheet of parchment paper that covered the work-table. Wham!

Mike jumped about a foot. Apparently he hadn't realized that making bonbons is that noisy. The bakje molds are polycarbonate, a tough resin, and they're hard. Whacking them onto a stainless-steel table makes a sharp crack.

"Who knew that the molds were here?" Mike said.

"Everybody who works here knew." Aunt Nettie flipped the mold upright again, then placed it behind her, on the conveyor belt that led to the cooling tunnel. "All the Hart and VanHorn family knew. How about the retail customers, Lee?"

"We had only a few retail customers yesterday afternoon," I said, "and none of them acted very interested in the molds. Except Timothy Hart."

Aunt Nettie had filled another mold with more dark chocolate. She flipped it and began the same routine.

"Maybe it was just a coincidence," Mike said. "Maybe the burglar was looking for money. Not for the molds."

Aunt Nettie frowned, sliding her spatula over the top of the mold. Then she flipped it, and before Mike could get set, she whammed it onto the table.

Mike jumped again. "Why are you doing that, Nettie?" He's a foodie, after all. Curious about cooking.

"I'm sorry to be so noisy, Mike, but whacking it that way keeps the bonbon shell thin and gives it an even edge. Plus, it gets rid of air bubbles." She moved the mold over to the cooling tunnel. A dozen other bakje molds were already making their five-minute trip through the tunnel's sixty-five-degree air.

Aunt Nettie took several bakje molds from the opposite end of the cooling tunnel. She moved to a second table, flipped the molds over and popped the little square chocolate shells out onto more parchment paper. She was already refilling one of those molds with dark chocolate, and while she worked — tappity tappity tap; swish-swish with spatula; flip mold — she talked. "You know, Mike, I don't care what the burglar was after, but I want those molds out of here. Lee is going to call Gail and ask her to come and get them. And I'm not going to ask Olivia VanHorn's permission to take them down."

Wham! She whacked the bakje mold onto the table, as if emphasizing her determination.

That time Mike didn't jump. "Mrs. VanHorn is just another Warner Pier absentee property owner. I don't care what she thinks. But you're still going to take part in the Teddy Bear Getaway, aren't you?" Mike Herrera is not only Warner Pier's political chief, he's our biggest tourism promoter.

He'd pushed hard to make sure all the merchants took part in the special winter tourism campaign.

Aunt Nettie's magic hands kept working. "My ladies have made and hand-decorated hundreds of teddy bears. We certainly hope to sell them." She whacked another tray onto the parchment paper.

"They'll have to do double duty as decorations in the shop," I said.

I guess I sounded impatient, because Mike spoke soothingly. "Oh, chocolate teddy bears will be fine decorations! I'm sorry if I sound worried, but I am. It's just so odd — why break in here? If there's any place in town that's not likely to leave cash in the register, it's y'all." Mike is another transplanted Texan, raised near Dallas, and his accent is an interesting mix of Southern and Hispanic.

He looked at me. "And I know, Lee, that you can swear that this stepson of yours didn't break the glass. But he is driving a Texas car."

"That's hardly incriminating," I said.

"I know, I know — it's that I'm concerned about that car they found over at the Superette."

"What car?"

"Greg Glossop . . ."

I groaned. Greg Glossop operates the Superette's pharmacy and he's notorious as the biggest gossip in Warner Pier. Joe suspected Glossop was the pipeline to the tabloids.

Mike Herrera made a calming gesture. "I know, I know, Greg's not the most popular man in Warner Pier, but he doesn't miss much. He noticed a car with a Texas tag in the parking lot this morning. It had apparently been there overnight. Some kind of a small Ford, several years old. The chief says the gas tank was empty."

I immediately thought of the car seen by Joe's buddy who worked at the station out on the highway. It was likely the mayor had also heard the truck stop gossip and was thinking the same thing.

"Jeff wasn't doing anything illegal last night," Aunt Nettie said. "I'm not going to let anybody gossip about him. He kept the burglar from taking anything." She gave Mike a firm look, then whammed another mold onto the stainless-steel table for emphasis.

Mike left, still frowning, and I called Gail Hess to ask her to come and get the molds. I got her answering machine.

I left a message, then hung up, wondering where Gail was. I also wondered why she hadn't been over first thing in the morning, or even in the middle of the night. Everybody else in Warner Pier knew about our break-in.

Then I called Mercy Woodyard, Joe's mother, because she handled our insurance. I got her answering machine, too, and left another message.

And I called the two Dallas numbers for Jeff's parents. More answering machines. Was there a human being left near any telephone in the universe?

I got a packing box from the back room. I took all the antique molds down and heaped them on the counter. Then I wrapped each of them in tissue paper and packed them in the box. That made me feel better. If Gail didn't show up to take them away, I'd take them home with me that night. Or put them in the bank. Or something.

I actually got some work done in the next thirty minutes, despite a call from the obnoxious George Palmer, our banker, reminding me we had an appointment at four o'clock. I'd just assured him that I'd be there when the bell on the street door chimed. I hung up on George to go out to the counter to wait on a customer, a great-looking guy.

He seemed familiar, but how did I know him?

His face was young, but his beautiful head of dark hair was beginning to be shot with silver. It looked soft and silky. I found myself wanting to rub my cheek against the top of his head. He would have had to sit down for that, because he was at least my height. His eyes were a dark brown, with black lashes. Then I recognized him, and I knew we had never met.

"I'm Hart VanHorn," he said. "You must be Mrs. TenHuis's niece."

He was Olivia VanHorn's son. The state senator who was rumored to be running for the U.S. House. Of course he looked familiar. Not only did he have his mother's eyes, but I'd also seen him on the evening news and in the *Grand Rapids Press*. Neither medium had shown how sexy he was, however.

He smiled, giving me lots of eye contact. Aware that I was standing there gawking at him, I quickly extended my hand in shaking position. "I'm Lee McKinney."

"Oh. It's not TenHuis?" He took my hand.

"My mother was a TenHuis. My father is a Texan."

"I see. Uncle Tim said you had a charming Southern accent."

"I don't know how charming it is, but I

94

can legally y'all." I realized I was still holding his hand. Yikes! I was about to drool on his snow boots. I dropped his hand and stepped back behind the counter. "I enjoyed meeting your uncle yesterday. He's a charmer."

Hart VanHorn grinned. "Uncle Tim is one of my favorite people. He has his problems, but ordinary human meanness was simply left out of his character."

Also sobriety. Time to change the subject. "Did you come in to see the mules? I mean the molds." Curses! My tongue was tangled up again. "I already packed them up."

"Oh? You're not going to display them?"

"After the break-in, I didn't want to take the chance."

"Mother wouldn't mind, but I understand how you must feel. I wanted to make sure that you and your aunt weren't upset by the excitement last night."

"We were just grateful that the burglars didn't take anything. Particularly the molds."

"Down at the post office I heard that your stepson scared the burglars off."

"My former stepson. Yes. He saw someone moving around in the shop as he drove by, so he stopped. Then he saw that the glass in the door was broken."

"I'd like to give him a reward."

"That's not necessary, but it's very nice of you."

"May I meet the young man?"

"Not right now. We all slept late, and Jeff isn't here yet. I'll tell him you came in."

That seemed to bring the conversation to a halt, and I expected Hart VanHorn to smile his beautiful smile and say good-bye. But he lingered. "I also need some candy."

"That I can take care of!"

I didn't correct his terminology directly. In the chocolate business, the word "candy" means hard candy — lemon drops and jaw-breakers. Our product is "chocolate."

"We have lots of chocolate," I said, "and it's all for sale. What do you need?"

"Well, the board members from a Grand Rapids shelter for battered women helped push a bill I'm sponsoring in the legislature. They worked really hard, and I'd like to give them all something in recognition. It should be versions of the same gift — you know, not singling any one person out. So, my mother suggested a box of candy for each of the twelve board members."

"Of course. I think they'd all be delighted. We have four-ounce, eight-ounce, and one-pound boxes."

"Oh, I think at least a pound."

"That would make a very nice gift. The one-pound boxes are thirty dollars. If you want tins, it's a dollar more." I always work the prices in early in the conversation. Not everybody is pleased to pay thirty dollars for a pound of chocolates — even chocolates as delicious as TenHuis's. A purchase of twelve boxes could run him three hundred sixty dollars, plus tax. That would make some people decide on a thank-you note instead.

But Hart VanHorn didn't turn a hair of that beautiful head. "Fine," he said. "And the boxes are okay. But — well, could you put one of those chocolate teddy bears in each? They're collecting teddy bears for the children who come to the shelter. And could you wrap each box a little differently? I mean, different-colored ribbon or something?"

"I'm sure I can come up with something. And for an order that size I can give you a fifteen percent discount. When do you need them?"

"Today, I'm afraid. I have to run up to Grand Rapids, and I wanted to take them along." He smiled. "Their board meets tomorrow. Is that too soon?"

"Oh, no. I have enough ready. Unless you want them individually packed?" I pulled ready-to-go boxes from a shelf against the wall and showed him the assortments inside. I demonstrated how I could substitute a molded teddy bear for four of the chocolates, and Hart VanHorn approved the plan. Then we discussed the decorations. I found ribbons in different colors — gold, silver, red, green, blue, plaid, peppermint stripe. And the boxes came in white, gold, and silver, so making each one different from the others wasn't difficult.

I gave Hart VanHorn a dozen gift cards, and he stood at the counter writing them out while I fixed up the boxes of chocolate. He didn't refer to a list, which I found awe-inspiring. I couldn't remember the names of my twelve closest relatives without looking them up. He kept writing, but it seemed that whenever I looked at him, he was looking at me. I began to feel as if I should say something.

Finally I thought of a question. "How is your congressional campaign going?"

"It may not go at all."

"Oh? The newspaper says you're the front-runner."

"I suppose I have a good chance, since the incumbent isn't running and my mother's pulling in all her chits. But I'm not sure that's how I want to spend the rest of my life." He smiled. "That's one reason we're down here without any staff. I'm trying to make up my mind."

His mother had already made hers up, judging from her comments the day before. I didn't bring that up, just smiled and kept working. And Hart kept writing. And staring at me.

As I worked I reminded myself that Hart VanHorn was a politician, so eye contact would be his standard operating procedure. Though I did remember that the *Grand Rapids Press* had identified him as one of Michigan's most eligible bachelors.

I was impressed with him. His selection of gifts was tactful — equal, but easy to tell apart. And he didn't seem embarrassed to credit his mother with the inspiration for the twelve boxes of chocolates. That was interesting, too, though I wasn't sure of its significance. Was he a mama's boy? Or simply secure enough to admit her influence? Was she making the decisions on his campaign? Or was he? How long were her apron strings?

I tied up the final box and took out a large white shopping bag with "TenHuis Chocolade" printed near the bottom in the classy sans-serif type Aunt Nettie uses in her logo.

"Anything else?" I said. "Are there any children on your shopping list?"

Hart VanHorn grinned broadly. "Do I want fries with that?"

I laughed. "Retail sales are not my specialty. But I'm trying to learn all the tricks. How about a box for your mother?"

"Your aunt gave Mother a box yesterday."

"Then how about a free sample for yourself?"

"Sure!" Very few people refuse a sample of TenHuis chocolate. Hart VanHorn picked a double fudge bonbon ("Layers of milk and dark chocolate fudge with a dark chocolate coating") and ate it with eyerolling relish. Then he sighed and leaned his elbows on the counter next to the cash register.

"Ms. McKinney," he said, "I know I'm being what my mother would call forward. But honestly, I'd love to get out of dinner with her and Uncle Tim one night this week. They're not going to be good company. And you would be. Would you consider going out to the Dock Street and splitting a pizza with me tomorrow?"

Chapter 6

I almost clasped my hands to my bosom and said, "Sir! This is so sudden." In spite of the eye contact and chitchat, I had not been expecting Hart VanHorn to ask me out.

Not that I don't get asked out now and then. But I've never accepted too many invitations. When I was in high school, I was a drudge. I knew I'd have to put myself through college without much help from my parents, so I always had a job, plus I was still afraid of serious relationships because of my parents' divorce. I was too cautious for either commitment or casual sex. It made for a lot of boring Saturday nights.

But during my senior year my mom and dad decided I might be less gawky and lacking in poise if I did something public, so they pushed me into the beauty-pageant circuit. That didn't help my social life. A little success there, I discovered, meant the guys I met were either awed or thought I must be easy. I never liked either kind — a date who was too scared to say anything or a date I had to fight off before he bought me a Coke.

College didn't change much. I still lived

with my mom — couldn't afford a dorm or my own place — and the pageant circuit didn't add glamour, though it meant enough money to pay for a speech coach, once I learned where to buy used evening gowns.

I was still trying to get through college when I was twenty-two, and I met the guy I thought was my dream man — Jeff's father. He was old enough and successful enough not to be impressed by having a wife who had once been a loser in Miss Texas competitions. He was settled in life, I told myself. I could trust his love.

Wrong again. Rich didn't love me. He loved his idea of me — a blonde who could look good when we went out with his business associates and who was barely smart enough to punch in the phone numbers for the right caterer and the right decorator.

I was still trying to finish my accounting degree when we got married, and he encouraged me to enroll in a full class load the next semester. I overlooked the patronizing way he wrote my tuition check, but I caught on when I brought my grades home. I made the President's List, and Rich sulked for three days. Then I asked a few accountant-type questions about his business, and Rich was furious for three weeks. Because I get my tang tongueled all the time, he'd thought I was stupid. And that's what Rich had wanted me to be. When he found out there were a few brains under my natural blond hair, it ruined our marriage.

I'd wasted five years on Rich. Then I wasted nine months on Joe Woodyard. Now Hart VanHorn was standing there, smiling at me and offering to buy me a pizza at the Dock Street. A lot of emotional baggage might have flashed through my mind, but I answered him within fifteen seconds.

"That sounds wonderful," I said.

"Great! About seven?"

"Fine. But are you sure you want to make it the Dock Street?"

"Nearly everything in Warner Pier is closed this time of the year. Doesn't the Dock Street have the best food of any place that's open?"

"Oh, yes. But the Dock Street is gossip central for Warner Pier."

Hart laughed. "I don't mind. But I don't live here. If you'd rather go into Holland . . . ?"

"No, the Dock Street is fine."

"Good. Now you tell me just where to pick you up."

I described the landmarks that identified Aunt Nettie's drive. "This time of the year you can see the house easily," I said. "I'll leave the lights on in front and in back, and you may want to come around to the kitchen. That sidewalk's easier to get to, since the drive curves around to the side of the house."

"I know the house you mean," Hart said. "It's not far from our place. I'll be there."

I rang up his chocolates. While he was signing the MasterCard slip I stood there beaming because one of the most eligible bachelors in Michigan had asked me out to a highly public place. Then our boarded-up front door opened and admitted an attack of guilt.

Joe Woodyard's mother came in.

I almost ducked down behind the counter. I'm sure I did turn red and look guilty. For a mad moment I was sure she was going to accuse me of being untrue to her son.

"Hi, Lee," she said. "Sorry I wasn't in the office when you called. Of course your insurance covers your break-in — after your deductible."

"Oh!" I'd forgotten that I'd called her. "Handy Hun called the grass destroyers."

Joe's mom and Hart VanHorn both stared at me incredulously. I'd reached a new standard in scrambled language.

I spoke again, slowly and carefully. "I mean, Handy Hans called the glass installers. They'll be here tomorrow." I gestured toward Hart. "Mercy, have you met Hart VanHorn? Aunt Nettie and I were terribly relieved that the burglar didn't take Mrs. VanHorn's mold collection."

Mercy Woodyard's whole demeanor perked up. She beamed at Hart. "No, we haven't met, but I heard the speech you gave at the insurance convention last summer. On the state violence-against-women bill. It was excellent."

They shook hands. I left them chatting about women's shelters and insurance coverage for battered wives and went to tell Aunt Nettie that Mercy was there. By the time I got back, Hart was going out the door. He waved at me. "See you later," he said.

I hoped Mercy Woodyard hadn't seen the way he lifted his eyebrows. I interpreted the lift as indicating he intended to see me at a specific time. I was flooded with confusion again, and I was afraid I was blushing.

Mercy Woodyard, however, was smiling. "Now that's one politician I might be able to support," she said.

I tried to sound noncommittal. "Oh?"

Mercy laughed ruefully. "And to think

Joe could have been a member of his law firm."

"Oh?"

"Oh, yes. When he quit the Detroit job and moved over here he was contacted by one of the partners. They offered him a nice deal." She shook her head. "Joe can't do anything by halves. He stuck with the boats. But Barton and VanHorn — of course, there's a whole string of partners. It would have been a good opportunity."

Then she looked at me sharply. "Maybe you could convince Joe he should go back into law, Lee."

I almost gasped. I had assumed Joe had told his mother nothing about me. Did she know about our telephone courtship? I decided to change the subject.

"You know, Mercy, there's one thing I've been wondering, and I'm sure you know. What happened to Hart VanHorn's father?"

"Vic VanHorn? I'm afraid he wasn't much of a loss."

"He was a U.S. congressman, right?"

"Yes. At least he would have been until the next election. He had become more and more irresponsible in the way he talked. I believe the technical term is 'shooting his mouth off.' Even Olivia couldn't restrain him. The voters were getting fed up."

"People around here talk about his death as if the circumstances were common knowledge. But I'm a newcomer. Did he die there at the Hart-VanHorn compound?"

"Yes. It was a freak accident. He had come down with Olivia and Hart. And I believe Timothy Hart was there, too, but he was staying in his own house. It was in the summer, and one of those wild thunderstorms rolled in off the lake. Sometime in the night Vic VanHorn apparently walked down to the lakeshore to take a look at the lake or watch the lightning. Or something. Of course, no one will ever really know why he went down there. But he got too near the bank, and it gave way."

"How awful!"

"Nobody knew he had gone out. I guess Olivia woke up early and discovered he had never come to bed. She found his body, down on the beach."

"Then he was drowned?"

Mercy frowned. "Actually, I think the fall killed him. I seem to remember that he fell about twenty feet and hit his head on something when he landed. His body had been in the water though. Luckily, it got caught on a log and didn't drift off."

"So Olivia VanHorn didn't come back to Warner Pier for fifteen years because of the sad association?"

"Apparently so." Mercy leaned over the counter and lowered her voice. "I heard — from a really reliable source — that the governor offered to appoint her to finish out Vic's term. But she refused."

"That's surprising. She seems so interested in politics."

"I guess she'd rather work behind the scenes."

Aunt Nettie came up to the counter then, and I went back to my office. But I couldn't help looking out into the shop, to see if Mercy was acting unusual in any way.

Joe's mom is a perfectly nice woman, as far as I can see. She's trim and attractive, in her fifties. She's fairly tall, but not a giant like me. She's blond, though I suspect she originally had dark hair. We blondes who don't need "touching up" tend to feel a little smug about blondes who do.

If Mercy Woodyard has a distinction, it's that she's the best-dressed woman in Warner Pier. Or perhaps I should say she's the most professionally dressed woman in Warner Pier.

Warner Pier is, after all, a resort community. Our customers are likely to appear in bathing suits and shorts, so the clerks in the shops and the tellers at the bank and the receptionists in the offices would be ill-advised to dress as if they were working on Fifth Avenue. The clerks TenHuis Chocolade hires in the summertime wear khaki shorts or slacks and chocolate-brown polo shirts. The high school principal wears a blazer and khakis. The receptionist at City Hall wears jeans, and the mayor presides at council meetings in khakis and a sweater. I used to dress up when I worked in a Dallas office, but now I consider L.L. Bean my prime fashion consultant. That day I was wearing flannel-lined jeans and a turtle-neck.

So Mercy Woodyard's power suits stand out. She could walk into any Dallas bank or Chicago brokerage firm and look as if she belonged there. And while the rest of us wear ski jackets and woolly parkas in winter, she appears in well-tailored dressy coats. Her wardrobe, I suspected, was designed to set her apart as proprietor of a "professional" business.

I had no idea what Joe thought of her. Which is significant, I guess. During the past nine months, he and I had spent hours talking on the phone, discussing every subject under the sun except his mother. He'd mentioned her a few times — saying he had things stored at her house, for example, or describing a visit the two of them made to his one remaining grandparent at Thanksgiving — but he'd never mentioned anything his mother had done, repeated anything she had said, or expressed any opinion of her.

And he'd never indicated that she knew he and I had become anything more than casual acquaintances. I didn't know what to make of her earlier comment that I might influence Joe, urge him to go back into the practice of law.

I was getting out the checkbook to write up the payment on our loan when I heard Mercy Woodyard raise her voice. "I'm going to land in the middle of Gail, anyway."

"She was only trying to help the Teddy Bear Getaway promotion," Aunt Nettie said.

"She was only trying to help Hess Antiques," Mercy said. "She's wild to handle the sale of the VanHorn furnishings. That would be quite a coup for her."

"Gail runs a nice auction."

"Of course. But I'd expect the VanHorns to deal with someone a little more upscale. Allen Galleries, maybe. Or someone from Chicago or Grand Rapids. Gail shouldn't have brought those molds over here."

"I should have realized how valuable they are. A lot of chocolate people collect them, but Phil and I simply never had time for such things. I never thought about anything happening to them."

"Gail did know they were valuable, and she should have put a rider on them if she was going to display them somewhere outside her shop. I'm going to make sure this doesn't happen again." Mercy nodded firmly and left.

Aunt Nettie was frowning as she went back toward the shop. She stopped in the door of my office. "Mercy would make a powerful mother-in-law," she said.

I laughed. "Well, it looks like that's not going to be my problem."

"Oh, dear! Did you and Joe quarrel?"

"I guess so. And then — Hart VanHorn asked me to go out for a pizza. I said yes."

"Oh, my, Lee! And Jeff turns up, too. Your life is complicated."

"I'd forgotten Jeff! I'll break the date with Hart."

"Why?"

"I don't want to leave you stuck with Jeff."

"Oh, I can manage Jeff for a few hours." Aunt Nettie raised her eyebrows. "I assume a few hours is all you had in mind?"

"It certainly is. And as far as I know it's all Hart has in mind. He may be Michigan's most eligible bachelor, but he can't be that fast a worker."

"Times have changed so much that I can hardly keep up."

"Maybe so, but right at the present moment, your niece is living a celebrate — I mean celibate — life. And that situation doesn't seem likely to change. Certainly not over one date, even if it's with Hart VanHorn."

I stood up and reached for my red jacket. "And now, it's time for me to beard George the Jerk and extend our loan."

Aunt Nettie patted my hand. "I really appreciate having you to handle that, Lee. Take him a bonbon or two. He likes Mocha Pyramids."

I put two Mocha Pyramids ("Milky coffee interior in dark chocolate") and two Amaretto truffles ("Milk chocolate interior flavored with classic almond liqueur and coated with white chocolate") in a box and headed down the block to the bank. As I walked, I psyched myself up. You're the customer, I told myself. The bank needs you more than you need them. George Palmer is your servant, your flunky. Treat him like dirt.

Of course, that wasn't my actual intention. I really intended to kill him with kindness — à la chocolates — and snow him with figures. I'd already discovered that one reason George acted so snotty was that he didn't really understand numbers. His main qualification for being branch manager had apparently been marrying the daughter of one of the bank's more important board members. Despise him, I told myself. But I still felt intimidated.

When I got to the bank, however, I looked through the glass wall that kept George separated from the rest of the bank, and I discovered he had his own problems. He was having a meeting with Olivia VanHorn.

Olivia was seated in an armchair, her casual mink thrown onto George's small sofa. She looked to be completely at ease; not a hair of her thick white hair — Hart's was going to be just like it — was out of place.

George, on the other hand, looked nervous. He was smoothly handsome and sleek, with dark hair and eyes. Like Mercy Woodyard, he wore city suits — garb I felt sure was designed to make us yokels feel our yokelhood. But even his suit wasn't helping George right then; Olivia VanHorn was obviously making him feel like nobody.

113

In winter the Warner Pier branch bank has a very small staff that doesn't include a receptionist, so I nodded to the only other employee present, a young guy at the one open teller station, and sat down in a chair outside George's office.

I eyed George and Olivia's conversation — she talked and he listened — and I got curious about what they were talking about. So I did a wicked thing. I decided to use the ladies' room.

That may not seem wicked, but it was. Because I knew a secret about that ladies' room and why its exhaust fan was kept running all the time. The previous branch manager, my friend Barbara, had revealed it to me over lunch one day. Because of a quirk in the heating system, she whispered, every word spoken in the manager's office was broadcast through the ductwork and was plainly audible in the ladies' room. Naturally, whatever happens in the ladies' room is also audible in the manager's office.

For this reason, Barbara never used her office for confidential conversations. And she also installed a fan in the ladies' room that ran all the time, effectively covering the noise of flushing and hand washing, so these sounds wouldn't be heard in her office.

When Barbara was given a new assignment, apparently no one had told her replacement about this little quirk. George used the manager's office all the time, closing his door and assuming his conversations were private, whether the exhaust fan was on or not.

When I quizzed one of the women tellers about it, she giggled. "We *tried* to tell him," she said.

Anyway, the more I looked at George and Olivia talking, the more I was dying to know what they were saying. I left my jacket and the file folder that held my bank records in my chair and went to the ladies' room. When I entered the tiny room, the furnace was on, and its fan added to the background noise. I took the opportunity to reach up high and unplug Barbara's specially installed exhaust fan. In a minute the furnace fan went off, and the next sound I heard was the voice of Olivia Hart VanHorn.

"You can assure Bob that Hart is definitely going to run," she said.

She sounded as if she were right in the room with me. My heart pounded for a minute. It seemed impossible that she wouldn't know I was listening.

George spoke. "To be honest, Mrs.

VanHorn, that's not what Hart said to me yesterday."

Olivia spoke again. "I admit that my son has a serious handicap for a political candidate. Modesty. He sometimes doubts his own abilities. But I've helped him turn this into an advantage."

"In what way?"

"Hart is never unwilling to share credit. And since the legislative process requires cooperation and . . ."

"Back-scratching?"

"Dickering. Trading favors."

I stared at the vent. Maybe I should be feeling guilty, but I wasn't. I felt curious. After all, I had accepted a date with Hart for the next night. If he and I were going to be friends, I had a right to know what others thought of him.

Sure, I did. I threw any qualms in the trash with all the used paper towels and extended my ear toward the heating vent.

George was speaking. "Bob says you're the best politician in Michigan." I realized the Bob he and Olivia had been talking about was his father-in-law, a well-known political and business figure in Michigan.

Olivia laughed a ladylike laugh. "Oh, I'm not sure that's right. Michigan has a lot of expert politicians. But I have had experience in back-scratching, as you call it."

"Why have you never run for office your-self?"

There was a pause before Olivia an-swered. "Perhaps I might have, George, if I were thirty years younger. But back when I convinced Vic he should seek office, it was still somewhat rare for women to enter the political arena. I would have had to get in-volved in the Equal Rights Amendment, in support or opposition of pro-choice legisla-tion. I would have been smeared as a woman who neglected her son, her hus-band."

Huh, I thought. Other women ran for office then. They made their positions known on those issues. You just wanted to be a kingmaker, the power behind the throne.

"No, I've always thought I made the right decision," Olivia said. "I've been able to pursue my goals through my work with Vic, with the party. And now through Hart."

"If Hart runs."

"Oh, he's going to run. Hart has a com-plete, perfect background for national office, beginning with Boy's State and his success in high school debate. Then there was Harvard, study abroad, a law degree *and* a graduate degree stressing government theory. He handled the right kind of law cases, backed the right kind of legislation, supported the right social causes."

George didn't sound convinced. "Hart has the reputation — well, I've heard he's been seeing . . ." His voice faded away, as if he couldn't bear to finish the thought.

Olivia laughed. "You're worried because Hart has never married. Well, he's a perfectly normal man, and he sees lots of women. But Hart has had no serious entanglements. No scandals are going to surface. And he's only thirty-five. I feel certain that soon Hart will find the right woman."

Olivia sounded as if she already had the right woman picked out. And somehow I didn't think that Hart's wife would be a blond divorcée with a tangled tongue. Maybe I represented rebellion to Hart.

George stammered out a few unintelligible words, but Olivia kept talking. Her voice became more triumphant. "There are no skeletons in Hart's closet. Absolutely none. Hart has the VanHorn looks and charisma and the Hart family's drive, ambition, and brains. Hart is going to go far, George, and if you're smart, you'll go along with him."

I was mesmerized. Then the furnace fan started again. It broke the spell I was under. With its noise as cover, I plugged in the exhaust van again. Then I dashed out of the restroom before George noticed the difference in the sound of the fan and I got caught. I sank into the chair where I'd left my jacket, whipped out my loan folder, and pretended to study the papers inside.

Wow! That Olivia VanHorn was something. Her ambition for Hart took my breath away; she obviously thought the U.S. House was just a step on the ladder. But she made me sad, too. Why had she turned that ambition loose on her husband and her son? She had even refused to serve in Congress when she had the chance, if what Mercy had said was right.

Aunt Nettie had thought Mercy Woodyard might be a difficult mother-in-law. Mercy would be a piece of cake compared to Olivia VanHorn. Suddenly I wasn't so sure I wanted to go out with Hart after all. Maybe I'd be seen as a threat to his political career, and if I were, Olivia would trample me flat.

Though Hart did seem to have the gumption to stand up to her. At least he was hesitating to commit to a run for Congress, a run she'd plainly decided he was going to make, like it or not. It was going to be interesting to see who won.

But I think at that moment I knew —

though it gave me a twinge of regret — that I was never going to be seriously interested in Hart VanHorn. I had my own problems.

In a few minutes I saw George helping Olivia into her mink jacket. She nodded to me regally as she left the bank, and George motioned me into his office.

I thought he might make some comment about Olivia, but he didn't. He seemed troubled, and he barely spoke. I had no need to snow him with my figures; he didn't try to talk me into refinancing at all. He merely accepted my check, and we both signed the papers for the loan extension — at the same interest rate. Then I gave him his chocolates and left.

I was back in my own office, still thinking about what I'd overheard, when the next commotion started.

The outside door to TenHuis Chocolade was opened so suddenly and with such force that it nearly flew back into one of the show windows. A figure hooded in emerald green dashed inside and slammed the door.

I stared. When the newcomer pushed her hood back, I saw that it was Gail Hess. She was panting slightly.

"Lee!" she said. "I just heard about the burglary! Is it true you and Jeff saw the burglar's car? Tell me all about it!"

CHOCOLATE CHAT

THE CULINARY KILLERS

Mysteries, emphasizing the physical world as they do, have always paid attention to food. Even Sherlock Holmes and Dr. Watson checked out the clue of the curry in "Silver Blaze." But more recently a whole field of culinary mysteries has bloomed.

And plenty of these emphasize chocolate. Just a few . . .

- Diane Mott Davidson wrote *Dying for Chocolate*, starring caterer Goldie Bear.

- Joanne Fluke's detective, baker Hannah Swenson, solved the *Chocolate Chip Cookie Murder*.

- Heaven Lee, the caterer-detective created by Lou Jane Temple, appears in *Death Is Semisweet*.

- Magdalena Yoder, the operator of a bed-and-breakfast in Pennsylvania Dutch country, was created by Tamar Myers for a series of comic mysteries.

Although Magdalena has not so far starred in a book that features chocolate in the title, in *Too Many Crooks Spoil the Broth*, Magdalena's sister, Susannah, almost loses her miniature dog when the pet, who habitually rides about in Susannah's bra, falls into a pan of Chocolate Oatmeal Drops. The little dog is not injured.

Chapter 7

I stared at Gail. "Are you just hearing about our excitement?"

"I went over to Lansing last night, so I could go to a sale this morning. I just got back. Mercy Woodyard told me about it. What happened?"

"We had a break-in. The molds are safe."

"Thank God! What did they take?"

"Nothing. My former stepson —" Suddenly I realized Gail didn't know anything about Jeff. I sighed. "It's a long story. Let me start at the beginning."

I sketched out Jeff's arrival — leaving out his trying to break into our house — and ended with his interrupting the burglar.

"So the burglar might have been after the molds, Gail. That's why Aunt Nettie and I want them out of here."

Gail seemed to think deeply. "It could have been coincidence. I mean, why? Is it true you and your stepson got a look at the burglar's car?"

"It was turning onto Blueberry before I saw it."

Gail leaned over the counter, and — I swear — her eyes sparkled. "Mercy said that one of the taillights was out."

Her reaction mystified me. "Jeff said one of them was. I didn't get a good look."

"So you don't know what kind of car it was?"

"Jeff might. Guys that age are up on cars. He thought it was some kind of sports car."

Gail looked at me with those bright, excited eyes. "It's funny that the burglar came in through the front door. I'd have tried the alley, myself."

"The door back there is steel and has a dead bolt. It would be almost impossible to get through. And the window has steel mesh. The front door may be more public, but it was a lot easier to break in."

"It's just lucky your stepson saw the burglar."

"Yes. We owe Jeff a lot."

"I guess he didn't even know there was anything valuable in the shop."

I cleared my throat. "Well, uh, Jeff's mom owns an antique shop in Dallas. He did recognize the molds as collector's items. The chief . . . well, he'll have to know about that. But Jeff had no reason to break in."

Gail smiled gleefully. "Of course he didn't! It will probably be one of those unsolved crimes." The thought seemed to delight her.

Gail took the box of molds and went back to her shop, still excited. But she'd left me down in the dumps again.

Gail's questions had reminded me about Jeff. It was now after four o'clock, and we hadn't heard a word from him.

I called the house. The phone rang eight times, and I was about to hang up when Jeff answered with a sullen, "Yeah."

"Jeff? Were you still asleep?"

"No." There was a long pause before Jeff went on. "Sorry I didn't get down to work."

"I just wanted to make sure you were okay."

"Yeah, I'm okay. I'd have come down, but that policeman showed up."

"Policeman! What policeman?"

When Jeff answered, he didn't sound quite as sullen. "Cherry? Officer Cherry? He wants me to go down to the police station, Lee."

Was I imagining the slightly plaintive quality in Jeff's voice? "Oh! I can meet you there."

Then the tough Jeff was back on the phone. "Butt out!" he said. "It's no big deal. I can handle it."

He hung up.

He hung up on me? I made my mind up to quit feeling worried about Jeff and let him take care of himself. I angrily slammed a few things around on my desk. Then I tried to call both of Jeff's parents one more time. Both were still unreachable. I even asked Rich's British receptionist for Alicia Richardson, who had kept books for his company since it was founded. Alicia knew where all the bodies were buried. But she wasn't there either. I still didn't want to tell Miss Brit about Jeff's problems.

My stomach lurched. How would Rich react if he learned his son had run away, come to Michigan, and gotten arrested for burglary? It was like a pit opening under my feet.

It was no good. I checked the time. It had been a half hour since I talked to Jeff. I was still worried about him. I decided to walk down to the Warner Pier City Hall and find out what was going on — even if Jeff didn't want me to. I wanted to know what Police Chief Hogan Jones was up to.

Chief Jones is not your typical small-town lawman. He'd spent most of his career on a big-city force and had been headed up the final steps of the promotions ladder until Clementine Ripley, prominent defense attorney and Joe Woodyard's ex-wife, turned him inside out on the witness stand. I don't know all the details, but after that Hogan

Jones retired and moved to Warner Pier, where he and his wife had long spent their vacations. A year later his wife died, and Jones, maybe feeling the need for a new interest in life, had taken the job as chief of Warner Pier's police — in charge of all three patrolmen and a part-time secretary. He seemed to get along fine in Warner Pier, maybe because his retirement income wasn't dependent on city politics. He was quite willing to tell the Warner Pier merchants and city officials where to get off. Consequently, they didn't fool with him a lot.

I put on my ski jacket and hollered at Aunt Nettie to tell her where I was going, then I went out the front door.

Warner Pier's business district is incredibly picturesque. One of the town's attractions to tourists — besides great beaches, miles of marinas, and an art colony — is its Victorian ambiance. The town was founded in the 1830s, and by the 1860s and '70s was a prosperous center for growing and shipping peaches. The captains of the lake steamers and the wealthy fruit growers built classic Victorian houses along the Warner River and on the bluffs along the lake. When the artsy crowd moved in during the 1890s, they added Craftsman-style homes and cottages. Luckily, the same families owned many of these for years, and sentiment prevailed; only a few of them had been "modernized" — another word for "ruined" in the view of the historic-preservation crowd.

The Warner Pier downtown isn't all quite as authentically Victorian as Aunt Nettie's "Folk Victorian farmhouse." Some new construction did creep in during the 1950s. But today's merchants know what's good for business; genuine and faux Victorian features abound — including several blocks of fake Victorian condos that challenge the architectural imagination.

The shops along Dock Street face the river, with a strip of park separating the business district from the marinas. Dock Street is the busiest part of town in the summer, when the river is lined with yachts, near-yachts, sailboats, and fancy power boats. Now, at the end of February and with all the boats in storage or moved to southern climes, it still looked pretty.

There was even a little weak sunlight that day, and the sidewalks had been cleared. The temperature had climbed to nearly forty. I enjoyed the fresh air on my walk to City Hall, even if I wasn't happy about my errand.

City Hall is one of the authentic Victorian buildings, originally a private home. I went up the redbrick steps, across the white front porch — decorated with the approved Victorian lanterns and a few teddy bears — and in through a front door with a beveled-glass panel.

When I came in, Patricia VanTil, the tall and rawboned city clerk, jumped to her feet and almost ran to the counter. "Oh, good, you're here," she said. "I was debating with myself about calling you."

"Why?"

"Well, I wanted to be sure you knew about your stepson being down here."

I tried to act calm. "I'm sure it's just ravine. I mean routine. Jeff did stop the burglary last night. But I'll go on back to the police department and see what's going on."

I gave what I hoped was a gracious smile — it probably made me look like one of the chocolate skulls TenHuis makes for Halloween — and went past the counter and down the corridor that leads to the two or three rooms of the police department.

Jerry Cherry was out in the main room. "Hi," I said, determined to be friendly and casual. "Don't they ever let you go home?"

"Oh, I got a few hours' sleep." Jerry looked at me suspiciously. "What can I do for you?"

"I hear the chief has Jeff in for more questioning. I decided I needed to keep informed on the situation."

"He's not under arrest or anything, Lee."

"I'm glad to hear it." In fact, about half my stomach muscles relaxed at the news. "But just what is going on?"

Jerry sighed. "I'll tell the chief you're here."

He knocked on the door of the chief's office, looked inside, and spoke. I heard the rumbling voice of Hogan Jones. "Come on in here, Lee!"

I went into the office. Jeff was sitting in a chair across the desk from the chief. Only the two of them were present. I thought Jeff looked a little relieved when he saw me, but he didn't say anything. I tried not to stare at his earlobes.

"What's up?" I said.

"I needed to ask Jeff a couple of questions. Nothing serious."

"You mean I don't need to call him a lawyer?"

Chief Jones laughed. "Oh, we're a long way from that kind of thing. Jeff's a hero, right? Stopped the only burglary the Warner Pier business district has had since Labor Day."

"He certainly did."

"As a matter of fact, I didn't want to ask him about the burglary at all."

Jeff burst into speech then. "It's some car, Lee. They think I might know something about it."

"What car?"

"We found it in the parking lot at the Superette. Out of gas. The manager called and asked us to tow it."

"Why would Jeff know anything about it?"

"It has a Texas tag." Jeff sneered. "Like I know every car in Texas."

The chief chuckled. "Yeah, that's pretty silly, isn't it? But the guy who runs the station down at Haven Road — that's five miles south of Warner Pier, Jeff, on the interstate — he said a young man in a gold Lexus RX300 with a Texas tag pulled in there early yesterday and bought some chips and stuff."

"Okay," Jeff said. "That was me."

"The guy says you weren't alone, Jeff."

"He's wrong!"

"He says another car with a Texas tag pulled in at the same time. A small Ford."

"Maybe so. But I was alone."

The chief shrugged, but he didn't say anything. I couldn't think of anything to add, so I didn't say anything either.

The silence grew until Jeff finally spoke. "No shit. I was alone. I pulled in there and bought some chips and a Coke. I sat in the parking lot and counted my money. I didn't have enough for gas, so I decided that I'd have to call Lee, see if she could help me." He turned to me. "I knew where you were because of all the newspaper stories last summer."

The chief spoke again. "You didn't see the other Texas car?"

"It was still dark!"

"Had you driven all night?"

"I pulled over and slept some."

"Mighty cold for sleeping in a car."

"I left the motor running. Guess that's how I used up all my gas." His eyes had grown wide and innocent-looking, then cut at the chief, the way they did when he was lying.

The chief's voice took on a fatherly tone. "And just why did you come to Michigan, Jeff?"

Jeff's lips tightened, but his eyes stayed wide. "I'm old enough for a road trip, if I feel like one."

"Right in the middle of the semester?"

"I wasn't so excited about my classes anyway."

"And without telling your parents?"

Jeff didn't answer.

"Jeff," I said, "I've been trying to call both your parents. I know they're worried."

"No, they're not. They're not interested in me right now."

I ignored his comment. "I haven't been able to reach either of them. Do you know where they are?"

Jeff glared at me.

"How about your mom? She always acted pretty interested in you, Jeff."

"Mom?" He gave a snorting laugh. "She's got other interests."

"And how about your dad? I couldn't get along with him, true, but he's not a bad person. Does he know where you are?"

Jeff looked up, and he looked, well, curious. "Look, Lee — what the hell did you say to Dad last summer?"

I hadn't been expecting that question. "We only spoke one time since our divorce, Jeff. It wasn't a very friendly conversation."

"Did you tell him something about he was so dumb he didn't know one Great Lake from another?"

I tried to laugh it off. "It was just a wisecrack, Jeff. He called up here when I was in the middle of that mess after Clementine Ripley was killed, and he offered to help me. I guess I should have been grateful."

"Where did the Great Lakes come in?"

"He offered to fly up. I'm sure he meant well, but right at the moment I took his offer as meaning he thought I was too dumb to help myself. So when he said he'd fly into Detroit, I made some remark pointing out that Warner Pier is a lot closer to Chicago than Detroit. I told him that if I needed help I'd get it from somebody who knew Lake Michigan from Lake Erie."

Jeff laughed. "Yeah. He would have flunked fourth-grade geography."

"I wasn't being fair, Jeff, and neither are you. He simply thought of the biggest city in Michigan. Besides, Detroit isn't exactly on Lake Erie. It's just closer to Lake Erie than it is to Lake Michigan, and telling him he didn't know the difference between Lake Michigan and Lake St. Claire wouldn't have been funny. Anyway, your dad's a Texan! Admit it, all us Texans tend to think the other states in the union are tiny little places where all the cities are just a few miles apart."

Chief Jones had been enjoying this exchange thoroughly. "How about Alaska?"

"Alaska? Never heard of it," I said. "Real Texans ignore the existence of Alaska. Jeff, what does my smart-aleck exchange with your dad have to do with the current situation? Where is he? Where is your mom? I find it hard to believe that both of them left home at the same time, and neither of them told you where they were going."

Jeff sighed. "Well, they're in Mexico."

"Both of them?"

He looked up at me angrily. "Don't you get it? After you and Dad had that fight, it was like he finally admitted he could be wrong about something. I mean, if he didn't know Lake Erie from Lake Michigan?"

"Okay. But what does that have to do with his going to Mexico?"

"Everything! See, he went to see a counselor. Kind of caught on to what a jerk he'd been to you. And to Mom."

I was beginning to see the picture.

Jeff looked at me angrily. "Get it? Mom and Dad are thinking about getting married again. They're off on a trip to Mexico together!"

Chapter 8

I didn't know if I should laugh or cry. Was this the crisis that had made Jeff walk out on college and take to the road? But wasn't seeing his parents back together the dream of every child from a broken marriage? It had been mine.

On the other hand, Jeff was a real expert at playing his parents against each other. If they started speaking to each other pleasantly, it was going to mean big changes for him.

Their renewed friendship was probably related to his lack of money. If Rich was belatedly enlisting in the forces of responsible fatherhood, tightening the purse strings would be his weapon of choice. This would be quite a switch from his previous policy of using his son as a display case for conspicuous consumption.

Meanwhile, I caught Chief Jones giving me a speculative glance. He was obviously wondering where I fit into all this. The thought embarrassed me. Because I didn't fit in the situation at all. I wanted the chief to know that, though I wasn't sure just why.

"That is a surprise, Jeff," I said. "They'd

been divided — I mean divorced — nearly ten years, hadn't they? I know your dad had been single for a couple of years when I met him, and we were married five years."

Jeff scowled, making his eyebrow ring wiggle. "They split up when I was nine."

"I hope it all works out for them."

"Fat chance." Jeff's voice was bitter, but he didn't expand on the theme.

I looked at the chief. "Does that explain why Jeff decided that he needed to make a change in his life, even if it meant spending February in Michigan?"

"Maybe. But it still doesn't explain the second Texas car."

The chief let the silence grow, but Jeff didn't say anything more. After a couple of minutes that seemed like an hour, Chief Jones told Jeff he could go. Jeff and I walked back to the shop. Jeff said only nine words in the two blocks: "I found the gas money. I'll pay you back."

When we came in the front door of the shop I was surprised to see that Gail Hess was back. She not only was back, she was up on the step stool Aunt Nettie had been using the day before.

Aunt Nettie was behind the central counter, bent over and looking down. A pair of work boots was sticking out from behind the counter at an angle that showed their wearer was lying down on the floor.

"Not here," a muffled voice said. I recognized it as belonging to Joe Woodyard.

"Not here either," Gail said. Every strand of her frankly fake red hair was standing on end.

"If that doesn't beat all, I don't know what would," Aunt Nettie said.

"What in the world is going on?" I asked.

"One of the molds is missing," Aunt Nettie said.

"Missing? But I thought none of them was taken."

"Apparently one was," Gail said. "When I got them back to the shop I did an inventory. And one was missing. It's a Reiche mold, made in Germany sometime between 1912 and 1928."

"How valuable was it?" I asked.

"Oh, it's worth something. But it's not one of the rarest in the collection."

"What did it look like?"

Aunt Nettie answered. "It was that one that you thought looked so dirty, Lee. The one that was rusty."

"The mean-looking bear? The one with the muzzle?"

"Yes," Gail said. "Though I think he represented a dancing bear wearing a harness."

Joe crawled out from under the counter and stood up. "It didn't get knocked under there," he said. "Nettie, do you remember where it was displayed?"

"It was up there where Gail's looking. I thought maybe it was still there. It could have slid down. If it was lying flat, it could have been covered up some way."

"Well, it's gone." Gail got down and dusted her hands together. Maybe it was just the gesture, but she seemed quite self-satisfied. "I just wanted to be sure we hadn't simply overlooked it."

"That's crazy," I said. "Why would the burglar take just one mold?"

Gail answered. "Because you and Jeff disturbed him?"

"But why take that one? It was one of the hardest to reach?"

Gail frowned. "Was the step stool out?"

"No! I'm sure it hadn't been touched," I said.

Gail gave what looked like a delighted smile. "I guess that proves our burglar was tall," she said. "I couldn't have reached it without a stool or a chair."

I couldn't get over how calm she was about one of the molds being gone. Only her hair looked excited.

"Shall I call Chief Jones?" I said.

Her eyes narrowed. "Do you think we need to report it?"

"The insurance company will want a complete police report made, if nothing else."

"I'll take care of it." Gail spoke cheerfully and smiled again. "I've got to get back to the shop now." And she waltzed out the front door.

We all stared after her. Aunt Nettie shook her head. "Sometimes I think that messy hair of Gail's grows right out of her brain and proves that there's as big a tangle inside as there is outside," she said. "I don't understand her at all."

Nettie looked at Jeff. "I hope you've showed up to work, even though it's nearly quitting time. We need you." She hustled him into the back.

And Joe and I were alone.

I felt bad about our quarrel, although I didn't feel as if I needed to apologize for my feelings and opinions. Maybe I needed to apologize for the rudeness with which I had expressed them that morning. But I didn't know that Joe's unexpected appearance at TenHuis Chocolade had anything to do with our fight. I decided not to make an immediate reference to the quarrel.

"How did you get pulled into the mold hunt?" I said.

"I just came in to buy some chocolates," he said.

"Sure." I moved behind the counter. "What kind and how many?"

"Oh, I guess a pound."

"We have a bunch of prepackaged boxes, or I can do an individual selection."

"I think that's what I need. A specially packed box. I want three-quarters of the chocolates to be that hazelnut kind coated in milk chocolate and sprinkled with nougat."

"Frangelico truffles? Sure. And what do you want for the rest?"

"Dutch caramel."

"Yum! You're a good picker. That creamy, soft, gooey caramel is great. Do you want them in a teddy bear box?"

"No, just a regular box. Regular ribbon."

I folded a cardboard box and began filling it with two layers of chocolates. Twenty-six little milk chocolate balls — the Frangelico truffles — and eight square dark chocolate bonbons — the Dutch caramels. I was dying to ask Joe who he was buying chocolates for. But I didn't. I concentrated on the chocolates.

As I worked I tried to think of some way to smooth over how Joe and I had left things that morning — without apologizing. I couldn't think of anything. Joe didn't say anything either. The shop seemed awfully silent.

I was almost relieved when the bell on the front door rang, signaling the arrival of some new person. But I was surprised when I looked up and saw who the new person was.

Timothy Hart.

Oh, gee! All of a sudden I remembered I'd agreed to go out with his nephew the next evening. I hadn't told Joe, but he was bound to find out, Warner Pier being the size it is and the Dock Street Pizza Parlor being the community center it is.

Meanwhile, I had to remember that I sold chocolates for a living, and Timothy Hart was a potential customer. He stroked his dapper gray mustache and removed his Russian-style fur hat. "Good afternoon, Ms. McKinney."

"Good afternoon, Mr. Hart. I'll be with you in a moment. I hope you're doing well today."

"Better than I was yesterday." He gave an apologetic shrug. Then he gestured toward the door, still covered with plywood. "I'm sorry to see you received some damage last night."

"We're insured. But we're afraid that the

burglars were after the chocolate molds." I decided to let Gail Hess break the news that one was gone.

"Those molds! They've been a headache ever since our mother died."

"Oh?" I kept putting chocolates in Joe's box.

"First Olivia wouldn't let anybody touch them. Then she suddenly declared that the china cabinet they were in was an eyesore, and it was banished to the basement — molds and all. I don't know what finally became of that cabinet."

"Oh, really?" I stopped and checked the number of Dutch caramel bonbons I'd put in the box.

Timothy Hart kept talking. "Of course, after Vic's accident, Olivia shunned Warner Pier completely. Wouldn't come near the place."

"That's understandable." I tied a blue bow around the box of chocolates. "Here you go, Joe. Just a second, and I'll ring you up."

"Do you have a gift card?"

I took a plain gift card and a little envelope out of a rack behind the counter. "Will this do?"

"Great. Go ahead and help Mr. Hart while I write it."

I smiled at Timothy.

"I need something for a child," he said. "A chocolate toy?"

I showed him our molded cars, airplanes, and teddy bears, and he selected a ten-inch teddy with hand-detailed features. "An eight-year-old should like that, don't you think? I wanted to give one to the housecleaner's little boy. Can you send me a bill?"

"I'm sorry, Mr. Hart. We don't run non-commercial accounts." I wasn't about to give credit to a guy with a drinking problem, even if he was a member of a well-known family. "I can take a credit card."

"Oh, I think I have the money." Timothy Hart waved airily and produced a battered billfold. He found a twenty-dollar bill and handed it to me. I gave him change and he gave me a beaming smile.

He put on his furry hat and picked up the box that held his teddy bear. "Now, you tell that nephew of mine that he's to be a perfect gentleman when he takes you out to-morrow," he said merrily. Then he left.

I could have killed him.

I turned to Joe, ready to make the expla-nation I'd known I had to make, but before I could speak Joe shoved a credit card at me. His face was expressionless.

I took the card and swiped it through the appropriate gadget. I swiped a few remarks through my mind at the same time, but none of them seemed suitable. Then, as I handed Joe the credit card slip, Aunt Nettie came into the store.

"Lee," she said, "did you order the extra cream?"

I turned around and assured her that I had. She said something else, but before I could respond, I heard the bell on the door. Joe had opened it.

I turned around quickly. I needed to say something. "Joe!" Then I noticed that the chocolate he had bought was still on the counter. "Joe! You're forgetting your box."

"It's okay," he said. "I'm headed for Grand Rapids. I'll call you. Sometime." The door closed behind him.

I looked down at the pound box of chocolate. Why had he bought it, then left it behind? He had tucked the little white envelope under the ribbon, and now I saw that he'd written a name on it: Lee.

Joe had bought chocolates for me.

I pulled the envelope out and opened it. "Sorry," the message inside read. "Maybe things will change soon." Joe's name was at the bottom.

I didn't know how to react. One part of

me was really pleased. Joe had obviously meant the chocolates as a peace offering, and it was nice to know he wanted us to be friends. And that he knew my favorite chocolates, Frangelico and Dutch caramel. Another part of me was insulted. A gift of chocolates was just another example of his secrecy complex, and that complex was driving me crazy.

"Darn!" I said. "He could have sent me flowers." If he'd sent flowers from one of Warner Pier's florists it would have been all over town in ten minutes. For a moment I longed for a single yellow rose, delivered ostentatiously in a florist's van.

Then I opened the box of chocolates and took out a Dutch caramel.

Actually, it was nice to have a whole box of chocolates. Aunt Nettie's rule is two pieces per employee per day, and she and I are careful to stick to that, just the way we expect the other TenHuis staff members to.

I savored the Dutch caramel. Next I slowly ate a Frangelico truffle. Then I put the box in my desk. I tucked the note inside.

Aunt Nettie sent Jeff and me home at six. It was my turn to fix dinner, so I stopped and bought hamburger and buns to make sloppy joes. It used to be one of Jeff's favorites, and I figured he deserved a break.

He ate the sloppy joe appreciatively, then asked if we'd mind if he ate the leftovers later — "If I need a snack." We assured him that would be fine. The evening dragged. We built a fire, but nobody had much to say. Jeff and Aunt Nettie watched a little television, and I tried to call Joe. He wasn't home. Apparently he really had gone to Grand Rapids. I left a thank-you message on his answering machine.

At ten thirty Aunt Nettie went to bed, and Jeff said he was going up, too. When I went up at eleven, I could hear strange electronic noises from his room, and I deduced that he was playing games on his laptop. I put on a robe and went back down to the shower — our strange, old-fashioned shower that's so loud that it can be heard all through the house and keeps the person in the shower from hearing anything but running water.

When I got out of the shower and went back upstairs, I looked out the window. Jeff's car was gone.

Darn the kid! He'd sneaked out.

Well, at least he'd been smart about it, had waited until I couldn't hear him. And at least he had gas in his car. I dried my hair and went to bed. I meant to stay awake until Jeff got in, but I was too tired. I was sleeping soundly at two a.m., when Aunt

Nettie shook me awake.

"Lee! Lee!"

I sat upright. "What's wrong?"

"Mercy Woodyard just called. She says there's a big commotion down at the shop. She sounded really upset."

I jumped out of bed and ran across the hall. I gave a cursory knock at Jeff's door, but I wasn't surprised when he didn't answer. I threw the door open and turned on the overhead light. The bed hadn't been slept in.

"Where's Jeff?" Aunt Nettie said.

"I don't know," I said, "but I'll be dressed in a minute."

Aunt Nettie dressed even faster than I did, and we were at the shop inside of ten minutes. Mercy had been right; there was a big commotion. As we drove down Fifth Street, I saw flashing lights in the alley and spotted a Michigan State Police car back there. When we turned onto Peach, all three of Warner Pier's patrol cars were parked facing the shop. I parked at the end of the block, and Aunt Nettie and I ran toward the lights. Joe loomed up before we got there.

"What's happened?" I said. "Another break-in?"

"No, I don't think anybody got inside."

"Then what?"

Joe gestured at the nearest patrol car, and I saw a figure huddled in the backseat.

Jeff.

I gasped and stepped toward the car, but Aunt Nettie caught my arm. She pointed toward the door of the shop.

"What's that?" she said.

In the headlights I saw a heap of something emerald green piled on the sidewalk in front of the TenHuis Chocolade window. Nestled against it was a patch of something reddish, or maybe brownish. For a moment I thought of a red squirrel. Then the brilliant green became an object I recognized, and so did the patch of red. I was seeing Gail Hess's frankly fake hair and her bright green jacket.

"Oh, no!" I said. "What's happened?"

"Gail is dead," Joe said grimly. "And Mom found Jeff standing over her body."

Chapter 9

My stomach hit my feet with a thud. What was going on? Was Jeff under arrest?

I went to the patrol car and tried to open the door to the backseat. It wouldn't open, so I opened the door to the front seat, opposite the driver.

Jerry Cherry was behind the wheel. He turned and gaped at me. "Lee!" he said. "You can't get in."

"What is Jeff doing in a police car?" I said.

"We're trying to preserve evidence," Jerry said. "And the chief wants to question him."

"Is he under arrest?"

Jerry shook his head. "No. We want some lab work on his clothes and his hands."

Jeff looked miserable. He held up his hands, and I saw that they were stained. The light inside the car wasn't good, but the stains looked like blood.

"Does he need a lawyer?"

Jeff spoke. "I haven't done anything! I don't need a lawyer!"

I stood there, half in and half out of the patrol car, dithering. In spite of what Jeff said, I thought he might well need a lawyer. But that was not a realistic thing to want in the middle of the night in Warner Pier, Michigan. The nearest lawyer was at the county seat, thirty miles away.

Unless Joe . . . I glanced at him. Joe was a lawyer, true. He wasn't practicing, although as far as I knew he was still licensed in the state of Michigan. But his mom had discovered Jeff standing over Gail Hess's body, apparently with blood on his hands. Besides, Joe had been down on Jeff ever since he arrived in town. He wasn't the right person to involve.

Hart VanHorn was also a lawyer. I doubted that his fancy law firm practiced criminal law. He might recommend someone, but I couldn't call him in the middle of the night.

No, if Jeff needed help and advice right this minute, he might have to rely on his ex-stepmother. So I'd better figure out what was going on.

"Lee," Jerry Cherry said, "either get in or get out. The chief took Jeff's jacket, and I'm trying to keep the car warm."

"I'll be back," I said to Jeff. Then I slammed the door.

Joe was standing behind me. I grabbed his arm. "Okay," I said. "What happened?"

"I haven't the slightest idea, Lee."

"How did you get involved?"

"I got back from Grand Rapids about

151

twelve, and about one thirty Mom called me from her cell phone. She said she'd found Gail dead on the sidewalk. She sounded scared to death. I came right down. Maybe you'd better get the story from her."

He took my arm and led me across the street to Mercy's office. She unlocked the door as we approached, then locked it again as soon as we were inside. Only one dim light was on in the office, and Mercy looked pinched and scared.

I reminded myself to act sympathetic. "Mercy, what a terrible experience! What happened?"

"I'd been working late — in the back room, sorting some things. . . ." Mercy's eyes dodged away from mine. "When I started to leave, by the alley, sometime after one, I saw headlights down there by your aunt's shop. After the burglary last night, well, I thought I'd turn down and see what was going on."

I nodded. "Then what happened?"

"When I got around the corner I saw that Jeff's SUV was parked facing the shop. And I could see Jeff leaning over something on the sidewalk. When I pulled in beside his car — well, he took off running, Lee."

"He ran? Ran where?"

"Just down to the corner, I guess. He

didn't have anything on his head, and I'd seen him with Nettie yesterday afternoon, so I recognized him. I put the window partway down and yelled. Then he came back, and he told me he'd just found Gail lying on the sidewalk and asked me to use my cell phone to call 911."

"Did you look at Gail?"

"After I made the call." Mercy's teeth chattered. "There wasn't much point in calling the EMTs. But they came anyway, of course."

"When I saw Jeff — there in the patrol car — he seemed to have blood on his hands."

Mercy nodded. "I saw it."

"How did Gail die?"

Mercy put a hand to her lips and shook her head. Joe put one arm around her shoulders, then answered my question. "The medical examiner hasn't looked at her yet, Lee," he said.

I snapped at him. "Don't talk like a lawyer! Did you see her?"

"Not close," Joe said. "But her head — well, her head had been bleeding. Her hair was soaked, and there was a puddle on the ground."

"Then Jeff could have gotten blood on himself if he — oh, tried to see if she was still alive."

"Sure, he could have." Joe's voice was artificially encouraging.

"Jeff said he hasn't done anything."

Mercy spoke then. "I certainly didn't see him do —" she repeated the word — "*do* anything. But, Lee, why was he down here in the middle of the night?"

That was the question, of course. It was the question Jeff had refused to answer the day before.

The three of us stood silently, looking out through the broad front window of Mercy's office. The scene was busy. Warner Pier policemen and Michigan State Police were looking for evidence up and down the street. More merchants had turned up, afraid the previous night's burglar had hit their businesses.

As we watched, Aunt Nettie came across the sidewalk. Mercy opened the door and let her in, then locked the door again behind her.

Aunt Nettie looked like the Snow Queen, with her solid body covered by a blue ski jacket and her soft white hair peeking out like fur around the edges of her blue cap.

She spoke placidly. "The door to Gail's shop is open. The heat's all getting out. Maybe I should go and close it."

"No!" Joe and I spoke together.

"Better leave it to the police," he said. "It may be a clue."

"Oh," Aunt Nettie said. "I thought the police must have opened it. But why don't they take Gail away?"

"I think they want to get some pictures first," Joe said. "Was Gail a close friend of yours?"

"Not real close. But all the Warner Pier merchants know each other." She gestured toward Jerry Cherry's patrol car. "Why do they have Jeff in there?"

"He found Gail Hess," Joe said. "He'll have to explain why he was down here."

Aunt Nettie nodded. "Two nights in a row," she said.

Why had Jeff been roaming around Warner Pier — a town with nothing open after midnight, a town where he knew no one except me and Aunt Nettie — in the middle of the night, two bitterly cold winter nights in a row?

The night before I'd been afraid he was trying to buy drugs. Now I'd be relieved if that was the reason.

"We'll just have to wait until Chief Jones talks to him," I said. "He's got to have some kind of a story. Maybe they'll let him go then."

But Jeff's story, when he finally told it,

wasn't the kind that cleared him of all suspicion.

Chief Jones had asked to keep Jeff's SUV until the state police lab technicians had had time to check it over. I brought Jeff a change of clothes, and he washed up and changed. His first outfit was bagged as potential evidence.

I insisted that Aunt Nettie go home and stay home. Then I waited at the police station. Joe waited with me. He didn't seem to be worried about it starting gossip.

It was after six a.m. before the chief called me into his office and let me listen to a tape recording he'd made of his interview with Jeff.

He had simply been driving around in the middle of the night, Jeff said. He'd seen something lying on the sidewalk in front of TenHuis Chocolade, so he'd stopped to see what it was. He had realized it was a person, lying on the frozen sidewalk, so he jumped out of his car to see what he could do to help.

"But as soon as I touched her, I knew it wasn't any good," he said. "I was going to go call the police when Mrs. Woodyard drove up. She said she had a cell phone, so I got her to call."

"Why did you run when she called out to you?"

"At first I thought she was the killer! I thought he'd come back to get me! But when I got a look at her —" Jeff's voice cut off quickly.

"Then what, Jeff?" The chief's voice was silky.

"Nothing."

"You hadn't met Mrs. Woodyard, had you?"

"I'd seen her. Across the street. Mrs. TenHuis told me who she was."

"But you still ran when she called out."

"She scared me! It was the middle of the night. I'd just found a dead body."

"Okay, it made sense for you to be scared when somebody yelled at you. So, why did you come back?"

"Huh?"

"First you thought Mrs. Woodyard might be the killer, returning to get you, too. So you ran. Then you saw Mrs. Woodyard and you changed your mind and came back. Why?"

"Her coat was wrong."

"Her coat?"

"Yeah. The guy I saw earlier —" Jeff stopped abruptly.

"There was someone there earlier?"

Long silence. "Well, I drove by once, and I saw somebody outside the shop. That's why I came back to check."

"So you found Gail the second time you came by the shop?"

"Yes."

"And when was the first time, Jeff?"

"A little while earlier."

"How long is 'a little while' in Texas?"

Another long silence. "Maybe fifteen minutes."

"Then you did more than just drive around the block." No answer. "So you saw a guy there, and you were sure he wasn't Mrs. Woodyard. Were you sure it was a man?"

"No. It could have been a woman."

"Did you see the person's face?"

"No. It was just a shape. But it wasn't Mrs. Woodyard. Her coat was wrong."

"Wrong? What's wrong with her coat?"

"It's a coat — you know, long. And it's smooth. Some kind of wool. The other guy had a bushy jacket on. Shorter than Mrs. Woodyard's coat. And a bushy hat."

And that, basically, was all Chief Jones got out of Jeff. He'd been driving around Warner Pier in the middle of the night, and he'd seen somebody in front of the shop. He drove on. But about fifteen minutes later he got curious and came down to see what was going on. And he found Gail Hess dead.

"What does he mean by 'bushy'? What kind of a coat is 'bushy'?" I asked.

"He's a bit vague," Chief Jones said. "It was bulky, and it wasn't smooth. Not like Mercy's coat."

"Flannel," I said. "Mercy's coat is flannel."

"This guy's coat wasn't flannel. And it wasn't slick and bulky, like that down jacket you're wearing. It could have been a blanket type fabric, I guess."

"Or a fake fur," I said. I steeled myself and tried a finesse. "Now you've heard Jeff's exploration — I mean, you've heard his explanation. So, can I take him home?"

" 'Fraid not, Lee. A little more information is required."

"Chief, his story makes sense."

"Yes, as far as it goes. But he doesn't have any explanation for one important thing."

"What's that?"

"The baseball bat we found poked into the snowdrift at the end of the block. Right there at the corner Jeff ran up to."

"A baseball bat?"

"Yep. We haven't tested it yet, of course, but it sure looks as if it could be the murder weapon."

"Where would Jeff get a baseball bat?"

"In Gail's shop. It's an antique, endorsed

by Jackie Robinson. Quite a collector's item, I expect. Gail's assistant tells us it was part of a display of toys and sporting equipment at the back of the store. And the door to Gail's shop was standing open. We figure Gail and her killer had some kind of confrontation in her shop. She was chased across the street and killed. Or Gail might have seen someone across the street and stepped outside to hail them. Maybe she took the baseball bat as some sort of protection."

"Why did she have her jacket on?"

Chief Jones shrugged. "Who knows? She might have simply put the jacket on because the heat was turned down in the store, and she was cold."

The chief let me say good-bye to Jeff, and I assured him that I'd get him a lawyer first thing the next morning. He nodded dully. His tough exterior had worn pretty thin.

When I reached the outer office, Joe was standing there, staring at a map of Warner Pier.

"They're going to hold him," I said. I sat down in one of the plastic chairs they keep for visitors and cried.

For a minute I thought Joe was going to put his arms around me, but instead he pulled a chair around facing me. He took one of my hands.

"I've got to find him a lawyer," I said.

"I'll call Webb Bartlett in Grand Rapids just as soon as his office opens. He's good."

I felt grateful. "Tell him Jeff's dad has plenty of money. Tell him he'll pay any kind of a fee."

Joe squeezed my hand. "If I tell him that, he'll charge any kind of a fee."

"I don't care! I can't believe Jeff did this. He's just a kid!"

Joe's lips tightened. I remembered then that he'd been on the defense team for the Medichino case — a case in which two Detroit brothers admitted to killing their parents. He knew that kids can kill.

But he didn't say anything about the Medichino boys. He just pulled me to my feet. "Come over here and look at what I found," he said. He led me to a giant map of Warner Pier. "Now where did you first find Jeff last night? I mean, night before last, the night of the burglary?"

"At the Stop and Shop."

"Didn't you say his car was parked outside, but you couldn't see him inside?"

"Yes."

"And then he came out from the back of the store?"

161

"Right. So what?"

"Look at the map." Joe pointed to the top of the map. "Here's the Stop and Shop. And look at what's behind it, over on the next block."

"The Lake Michigan Inn. Again, so what?"

"Do you feel up to taking a ride out that way?"

"I don't think I could sleep."

I put on my jacket, and Joe and I went out to his truck. "Why are we doing this?" I asked.

"Maybe for no reason at all."

Despite its picturesque name, the Lake Michigan Inn is a fairly standard motel. It looks like the 1950s to me; cars with big tail fins would look right at home in the parking lot. That morning the parking lot was almost empty. An SUV was parked in a shed at the back of the lot, and all the rooms were dark. The only lights came from the motel's sign and from a light over the office door.

Joe parked under the office light — the winter sun was nowhere near the horizon, but the sky was growing light in the east — and we got out. Joe knocked on the office door. He knocked again. And again.

Finally the door opened and a bleary-eyed older man peered out. "Joe? What's going on?" He looked at me, then grinned slyly. "Don't tell me you want to rent a room?"

"Nope. But I've got an important question."

"It better be damn important and not hard to answer." When he spoke I saw that he didn't have his lower plate in. He motioned us inside.

"Lee, this is Tuttle Ewing," Joe said. "Tuttle, Lee McKinney."

Tuttle Ewing was a short bald guy. "How'ja do," he said. "You're Nettie TenHuis's niece." I nodded, and he turned back to Joe. "Wha'ja need to know?"

"Lee's stepson came to Warner Pier day before yesterday, and I wondered if he checked in here."

I almost gasped. Jeff hadn't checked in anyplace.

"Young guy? Kinda skinny? Glasses? Stud in his lip? Crazy earlobes?"

"Right. Driving a Lexus RX300 with a Texas tag."

"Yeah, he came by."

"Did you rent him a room?"

"Yeah. He paid for three nights. Off-season rate. Funny thing though. I haven't seen the SUV since."

"Is there somebody in the room?"

"I dunno. The Do Not Disturb sign has

been on the door ever since he checked in. So Maria — I've only got one maid, part-time, in the winter — she and I haven't disturbed him."

Joe and I exchanged looks. "I think we'd better disturb him now," Joe said. I nodded.

"I can't let you in the room."

"Just tell us which room it is."

"Twenty-three. Out back."

Tuttle Ewing let us out, and Joe and I walked along the covered sidewalk, toward the back of the motel.

"This makes perfect sense!" I said. "Plus, it explains the second car with the Texas tag. I should have realized that Jeff wouldn't have left college and come up here alone. He had some buddy with him, and he's been sneaking into town to see him."

"You knock at the door," Joe said. "Whoever's in there, a woman will seem less threatening. I'll wait down here." He positioned himself ten or twelve feet away, flat against the wall.

I had to knock several times before I even heard a movement inside. The door still didn't open. I pictured a scared kid standing on the other side.

"Hey!" I said loudly. "Jeff's in trouble. He needs help!"

Finally, the door opened a crack and one eye looked out.

"What is it?" The voice was a whisper.

"I'm Jeff's stepmom. Jeff's in trouble. I need to talk to you."

"Did he tell you about me?"

"It's a long story, and I'm freezing out here. Let me in, okay?"

The door closed, and I heard the clicking of the chain. When the door opened again, Joe suddenly appeared beside me. He pushed the door open wide, and we both were inside.

My impression was that we had started a bird from its nest. Something white flitted around the room.

"It's all right," I said. "We won't hurt you. We're just trying to help Jeff."

The white figure fluttered to a stop behind the bed. A high-pitched voice spoke. "What's happened? Where's Jeff? Did he tell you about me?"

The words came from a little bit of a girl. Her hair was tousled and her eyes swollen, but there was no missing one thing about her. She was a beauty.

CHOCOLATE CHAT

EYES LIKE CHOCOLATE

Although Janet Evanovich's Stephanie Plum books are not culinary crimes, they rely on food for atmosphere.

Early in the first book, when she describes Joe Morelli, one of the major series characters, we know immediately that he's a sexy guy.

"He'd grown up big and bad, with eyes like black fire one minute and melt-in-your-mouth chocolate the next," she writes.

Somehow we're not surprised a few paragraphs later, when Joe wanders into the Tasty Pastry Bakery, where the sixteen-year-old Stephanie worked, and buys — what else? — a chocolate chip cannoli. Later, "on the floor of the Tasty Pastry, behind the case filled with chocolate eclairs . . ."

Ah, that Joe, with those irresistible melt-in-your-mouth chocolate eyes. A girl doesn't have a chance.

Chapter 10

The girl was standing on the floor, of course, but she was so fluttery that she almost gave the impression she was perched on the headboard of the bed.

"Who are y'all?" she said in a chirpy little voice.

"We don't intend to hurt you," I said. "We're trying to help Jeff."

"He promised he wouldn't tell anybody I was here."

"He didn't. We figured it out. Who are you?"

The question seemed to be too hard for her to answer. She twisted her wings — I mean her hands — stood on one foot and lowered her lashes. Maybe it was just her tousled hair that made her look so birdlike, I decided. That and her size. She was tiny, with small, delicate features. She was wearing a white T-shirt, and the effect was of a cute little bird, maybe one of those Easter chickies. Then she moved, and I amended the impression. She looked like a cute little chickie with a cute little bosom.

Her short, spiky hair and the lashes against her cheeks were almost black. She had that fine-grained, pink and ivory skin that I personally would kill for. In fact, when I was sixteen and felt like a giraffe, I'd have killed to look exactly like her.

Finally the girl spoke. "I'm Tess Riley."

"You came up here with Jeff?"

"Well, sort of. Jeff met me in Chicago." She fluttered her eyelashes, then looked at us with bright black eyes. "Where is Jeff?"

I looked at Joe, wondering what I should tell her.

Joe didn't hesitate. "Jeff's in jail," he said.

"In jail!"

"Yeah. He may be charged with murder."

"Murder! Jeff would never kill anyone." Then the dark eyes grew wide. "Oh, no! He didn't!" She pressed her hands over her mouth.

"We're hoping you can alibi him," Joe said.

"Oh, yes! Anything I can do. Jeff was with me."

"Oh?" Joe said. "He was with you about eight p.m. last night?"

I drew a breath and looked at him. Joe touched my arm in what was obviously a signal for me to keep quiet.

Tess didn't hesitate. "Eight o'clock? Oh, yes! Jeff was here then."

I almost groaned. She not only looked like

a bird, she apparently thought like one. Just what we needed. A dippy little cuckoo who was willing to lie for Jeff.

She was warming to her theme now. "Right. Jeff came here a little before eight, and he brought me something to eat."

She gestured, and I saw one of Aunt Nettie's refrigerator dishes on the desk. Jeff had brought her the leftover sloppy joe. Joe and I looked at each other, but neither of us spoke.

Tess went on. "We watched television, and then we went out for a drive. Then we came back here. Jeff stayed until after midnight."

"But he came before eight o'clock?" Joe said.

"Oh, yes! I'm sure he was here by then."

"That's really funny," I said. "Since at my house Jeff was helping me with the dinner dishes at eight o'clock."

"Oh!"

"Why don't we all sit down," Joe said. "Tess, are you hungry? Lee? We could go out to breakfast. Maybe we could get acquainted a little. Then Tess might trust us enough to tell the truth."

"Oh, I wouldn't lie."

"You just did," Joe said.

"You tricked me!" Tess perched on the

169

edge of the bed and did the eyelash thing again. "When does Jeff need an alibi for?"

"I don't think we'd better tell you, Tess. If you feel sure that Jeff would never kill anyone . . ."

"Oh, I do. Jeff would never commit murder."

"In that case, all Jeff needs is the truth. He's obviously trying to keep you out of the situation. Why?"

"Because he's really a nice guy."

I was beginning to get a little impatient with Chicky Tess. "Jeff may be a nice guy," I said, "but most nice girls don't hide out in motels. Why is Jeff trying to keep you out of sight? Why didn't he just bring you out to my aunt's house?"

"He wanted to."

"Why didn't he?"

"I was afraid."

"Of us?"

"Oh, no! Not of you. Of . . . of . . ." She wasn't a very good liar. I could see the improvisation flitting around in her head. "I was afraid of . . ."

"Forget it!" Joe's voice was harsh. "We'll just call the police to come and get you."

"No! Then he'll find me!"

"Who?"

"My family! And if they find me, then . . ."

"Then what? What would happen?"

"If they find me, my dad's boss will find out, and then the police will think they know why Jeff might want to kill a guy!"

Kill a guy? That stopped me, and it seemed to stop Joe, too. Neither of us said anything, but we looked at each other.

It was beginning to sound as if Tess thought Jeff really might have killed someone. But she expected it to be a male person — a "guy." And you could call Gail Hess a lot of things, but no Texas girl would ever call her a guy.

Joe rephrased the question a couple of times, but Tess quit talking. Finally he sighed. "Look. Tess. You obviously don't know anything about the crime Jeff is suspected of committing. If you'll just talk to the police chief, then you may be able to straighten everything out. But you've got to tell the truth. You can help Jeff the most if you tell the truth."

"But I can't. . . ."

Joe went on. "Frankly, you're not a very good liar, and you'll get tripped up right away. So get dressed, and we'll take you over to the police station."

"The police station!"

"Yes. If you tell a straight story, maybe we'll get to take Jeff home."

"Yes. Come on," I said. "If you really want to help Jeff —"

"Oh, I do!"

"Then get dressed."

Joe moved toward the door. "I'll wait outside."

Tess gathered up an armful of clothes and disappeared into the bathroom. I sat down in the one chair. Obviously Joe was right not to question Tess further. She was willing to say anything, and she wasn't bright enough to tell a good lie. She'd sound coached if we talked to her too much before Chief Jones did.

I laid my head back in the chair and realized that I was tired right through to the bone. I had almost dozed off when I heard Tess give a yelp. Then I heard a sliding noise. In two leaps I was at the bathroom door.

"What's wrong?" I said.

"Nothing! Nothing!" Tess sounded like something had happened, but she didn't explain. I heard the sliding noise again. Then the door opened. Tess came out, pouting. Behind her I saw a window, the kind with clouded glass to keep people from looking in. It had been raised about an inch.

I almost laughed. The temperature in west Michigan that February morning was about fifteen. Nobody in their right mind was going to be opening a bathroom window for a little ventilation. Tess had obviously tried to open it with the idea of crawling out. I went into the bathroom and looked out through the crack. There was a storm window, of course, and the light outside was dim, but I could plainly see Joe standing about twenty feet away, with his back to the window. He'd been way ahead of me in anticipating that our birdbrained little Tess might try to flit.

Tess had put on an SMU sweatshirt and a pair of jeans that couldn't have been bigger than size three. She was wearing socks and tennis shoes.

"Why don't you pack up your stuff, Tess," I said. "You can move out to the house."

"I don't want to impose on you."

"Do you have any money?"

"Not a lot."

"Jeff says he doesn't have any either. And I can't afford motel rooms. If you don't want to contact your parents, I don't think you have a lot of choices. I assure you my aunt is perfectly respectable, and now that we know you exist, she'll worry a lot more about you being in a motel than being in her spare bedroom."

Tess didn't look convinced, but she put her few belongings into a backpack — she obviously hadn't been any more prepared for a long trip than Jeff had — and gathered makeup and toothbrush out of the bathroom. When she got to the stage of putting on her jacket, I went to the bathroom window, pushed it up, and looked out. Joe was still there. I rapped on the storm window, and he turned around. I waved, and he made a circular motion, pantomiming coming around the building. He was there by the time Tess and I got her stuff into the floor of the truck's cab.

"I told the manager you were checking out," he said.

Tess fluttered her eyelashes. "You're not really going to take me to the police chief, are you?"

"Not on an empty stomach," Joe said. "The Stop and Shop should have some fresh doughnuts by now."

Tess refused a doughnut, and she pouted all the way to the police station. She hung on to my arm, looking terrified, after we got out of the truck. She was so short I felt as if I were dragging her along.

Chief Jones was coming out as we approached the door.

"Hi, Chief," I said. "We found out why

174

Jeff kept coming into town in the middle of the night."

"Well, well." The chief looked Tess over. "I was gonna call all the motels after I had breakfast. I figured Jeff wasn't coming in to admire the quaint Victorian decor."

Tess cast imploring looks at us, but the chief escorted her into his office and left Joe and me in the outer room. I called Aunt Nettie to tell her the latest development.

"I should have known enough about human nature to figure that out," she said. "I'll change Jeff's bed. He'll have to sleep on the cot in the little room."

"I just hope he gets out of jail," I said.

I told Joe to go home, but he said he'd stick around.

"Thanks," I said.

He shrugged.

I sat down on a plastic chair, and I guess I fell asleep, because the next thing I knew Joe tapped me on the shoulder, and I opened my eyes and saw the chief coming out of his office. He motioned for Joe and me to come in. Tess was huddled in a chair. The four of us filled up the little office.

"Now, Miss Riley, I'm going to paraphrase your story," he said. "You correct me if I'm wrong."

Tess looked at him adoringly and

nodded. He smiled back. She'd found somebody who was susceptible to eyelashes. Good for her.

The story the chief told us was incomplete. Tess said she was from Tyler, Texas, and that she was a freshman at SMU. She had left her dorm room five days earlier and had driven north from Dallas. She had not really explained why she had taken a notion to do this.

When she got to Chicago, she'd seen she was going to run out of money pretty quick. So she called Jeff — "He's a good friend," she said when the chief got to that part of the story — and asked him to wire her money. Instead, Jeff got in his car and drove to Chicago to meet her. But Jeff hadn't had any money either. So early in the morning two days earlier they had headed for Michigan, apparently because Jeff thought I'd be a soft touch.

"So," I said, "you were the person in the second car with the Texas plates." I'd figured that out, of course, but I wanted to confirm it.

"Yes, I was," Tess said. She looked at the chief and fluttered her eyelashes. "Jeff said you'd towed my car."

"It's in the lot out back."

"I guess I can pick it up now."

"The gas tank is still close to empty," Chief Jones said. He continued her story.

When Tess and Jeff got to Warner Pier, Jeff rented a motel room, using almost the last of their pooled money, then went out to Aunt Nettie's house, where he was discovered by Joe before he fell in the window over the stairwell. Jeff had sneaked into town that evening and the next to see her.

"Tess says that Jeff was with her from eleven p.m. until around one thirty last night," the chief said. Tess nodded eagerly. "She was tired of being cooped up in the motel room, so they went out for a ride a little after one o'clock. After about fifteen minutes, Jeff suddenly said she had to go back to the motel, because he'd seen something he had to check up on."

"The person in front of the shop," I said.

"Maybe. But Jeff didn't tell her that. So her story substantiates Jeff's, sorta, but it's not really an alibi."

"Still, her presence in Warner Pier explains a few things," Joe said. "Now we know why Jeff was sneaking into town in the middle of the night. That fills the biggest gap in his story. Can you let him go?"

Chief Jones looked more Lincolnesque than ever. "Well, I'd like to wait until we see what the medical examiner says. And whether or not there are any fingerprints on that bat."

I started to speak, then remembered that Joe was the lawyer.

"We couldn't really expect any fingerprints when the temperatures are down in the twenties," Joe said. "Unless the murderer was too macho for mittens. And the medical examiner isn't going to be real specific about a time of death. After all, even when I got to the scene, Gail had only been dead a little while. Jeff must have stumbled across her body very soon after she died."

"I'm still going to hold on to him until I can run a couple of checks," the chief said.

Tess fluttered her eyelashes again. "What kind of checks?"

Joe spoke before the chief could. "He's probably going to see if Texas — or anyplace else — has outstanding warrants for you or Jeff. So if there's anything you want to tell us, now's the time."

Tess sighed and leaned back in her chair. "No, that's okay."

Tess asked to see Jeff, but the chief told her to come back later. Tess produced her car keys, and the chief escorted us out to the City Hall parking lot, where Tess's car occupied a corner. Joe brought Tess's backpack around from his truck, and I began to give Tess directions to Aunt Nettie's. "We'll stop at the Shell station, and I'll buy you some gas," I said.

But Tess wasn't paying any attention to me. She was staring at her car.

"What's wrong?" I said.

Tess pointed. "My taillight. How did it get broken?"

Chapter 11

I stared at the broken taillight, trying not to panic. It was the left one, like on the car Jeff and I had seen. Would Chief Jones think that Tess had been in the car that sped away after the burglary? Would he think Jeff had tried to cover up her connection with the crime?

I tried frantically to picture the car Jeff and I had seen. I simply didn't care enough about cars to remember it. My dad was an auto mechanic, so you'd think I would have been raised knowing one taillight from another, but Rich's view of cars solely as status symbols had made me lose interest in the whole subject. If a vehicle moved when I pressed the accelerator, that was all I asked.

Tess's car was an inexpensive Ford. But Jeff had said the fleeing car had been some sort of sports car. Had he recognized it as a sports car? Or had he simply been leading us astray?

Joe and Chief Jones had also been staring at the broken taillight; and it was Tess who spoke first. "I certainly hope the city of Warner Pier will pay for that light," she said. "Those things are expensive to replace, and I'll get a ticket if I drive without it."

I bent over to look more closely, and both Chief Jones and Joe knelt behind the car.

"You won't be driving it for a few days," Chief Jones said. He and Joe looked at the snow under the rear of the car.

"Maybe you could scoop the snow up and melt it down," Joe said. "See what you find."

"It had to happen here," the Chief said. "We were looking all over for broken taillights. If we'd found an abandoned car with one, we'd have noticed. Besides, if one of my guys puts a car in the lot without making a note of anything that's wrong with it, I'll have his uniform. There was nothing on the record sheet."

"What are they talking about?" Tess said to me.

"They're saying the light wasn't broken when the car was towed in."

It made sense. If the police impounded a car, they'd be responsible for its condition when it was picked up by the owner. They couldn't leave themselves open to the kind of demands that Tess had just made, that they pay for damage that occurred while the car was in their lot.

The chief stood up. "Guess I'd better ask around, find out if anybody unusual was seen in the city lot."

"But who's going to take care of getting this fixed?" Tess said. "If it was all right when it was towed in . . ."

"For the moment, we're going to keep the car, get the crime lab to look at it," the chief said. "We'll try to find out just what happened."

"I haven't got the money to repair it," Tess said. "And my dad doesn't either." Her face was all screwed up. Tess obviously didn't come from a wealthy family. Jeff would have shrugged off the damage.

"Come on, Tess," I said. "We'll worry about getting the taillight fixed after Chief Jones investigates. Right now we're heading for the house. I've got the wonderful job of trying to track down Jeff's dad."

"Oh, no! You can't call him. He mustn't find out I'm here."

I sighed. "Come on," I said.

Joe handed Tess her backpack. He grinned at me, I guess because I was the one stuck with Tess and he wasn't. "I'll call Webb Bartlett," he said. "His office ought to be open by nine."

"Who's Webb Bartlett?" Tess was still pouting.

I started shoving her toward my van, parked around the corner. "Webb Bartlett is the lawyer Joe is going to call and ask to represent Jeff. That's why I have to get hold of Jeff's dad."

"But I can't let anybody know where I am."

"Jeff needs a lawyer," I said. "His dad is going to have to pay the bill."

"But surely there's some way . . ."

"Look, Tess! Jeff may be accused of a very serious crime. I may feel sure he didn't commit it, and you may feel sure he didn't commit it. But that doesn't count. If he doesn't have the right legal representation, he may go to prison for years!"

"But I can't let anybody know where I am!"

At that I lost what temper I had left. "Oh, yes, you can! You can quit running away like a little kid. You can tell me why you and Jeff left college and came up here. You can tell me — and Chief Jones — why you were hiding out in that motel, why Jeff wouldn't tell us you were with him. Why you abandoned your car in the parking lot of a grocery store."

"No! No, I can't!"

"Okay! Don't tell us. Stand around saving your cute little butt and let Jeff be convicted of murder!"

"Murder?" Tess gave a sob, and when she spoke her voice was just a whisper. "Murder is what we were trying to avoid."

I stared at her, and she stared back, and suddenly I was cold clear through. And only part of it was because it was dawn on a winter day in Michigan.

What had Tess meant? Murder was what she and Jeff had been trying to avoid? I wasn't sure I wanted to know, but I asked her. All she did was cry.

Tess had scared me into regaining control of my temper, I was able to talk more calmly. "Let's go out to Aunt Nettie's. Maybe she can inject a little common sense into the situation."

We walked around the corner and got into the van, and I started the motor. "I'm exhausted," I said. "Whatever you and Jeff and the Warner Pier burglar are up to, it's sure kept me from sleeping the last couple of nights."

I started to pull out from the curb, but lights flashed in my rearview mirror, and I stopped to let a car pass. It didn't pass. It stopped, blocking me. Its door opened, and the driver jumped out. "Lee!" he yelled. "Lee!" He ran around the front of the car — it was a big Lincoln — and I saw the shock of beautiful hair. It was Hart VanHorn.

I rolled my window down. "Hart?"

"I hoped that was you. I saw the Dallas

Cowboys sticker on the van yesterday."

"It's me. My dad put the sticker on, so I wouldn't forget my origins. What can I do for you?"

"A reporter I know called to find out if I'd heard anything about a murder here in Warner Pier."

"Oh, it's a regular mess," I said. "And it looks like my stepson is in the middle of it — I don't mean he did it! But he found the body, and the police are holding him."

"That's what Mike Herrera said."

"Mike Herrera? How'd he get involved?"

"As the mayor of Warner Pier, he knows most things that go on around here. So I called him."

I should have figured it out without asking. Hart VanHorn was important; a state legislator and a possible candidate for Congress. That meant he would have lots of contacts. He could probably find out anything about anybody in the entire state of Michigan with one phone call.

"Mike said the victim was Gail Hess," Hart said. "That's why Mom and I came down to find out what's going on."

"I'm sorry to say I haven't given poor Gail a thought," I said. "I've been too worried about Jeff."

"Does he need a lawyer? I could call —

well, nobody in my old firm handles criminal matters, but I know people who do."

"Joe Woodyard was here — his mom was the second person on the scene. Joe said he knew somebody. Webb Bartlett?"

"Webb's a good choice." A smile flickered over Hart's face. "Joe and Webb were a year behind me in law school. Joe knows a lot more about defense attorneys than I do."

Neither of us needed to go into the reasons Joe knew a lot about defense attorneys. But Hart had brought up another point.

"Did you say a reporter called you?"

"That's right. A political reporter from the *Chicago Tribune*."

"Chicago! Oh, no!"

"He's a nice guy. We've dealt with each other before. Why does that upset you?"

"Because Chicago is a long way from the *Warner Pier Gazette*. That means the reporter got a tip. And that means somebody from Warner Pier called him. Or called somebody."

"So?"

"So, somebody around here is still in contact with the reporters — maybe the tabloid reporters — who had such a great time in Warner Pier when Clementine Ripley was killed."

"Not good."

"No." I dropped my voice. "Listen, Hart, let's forget that pizza for now."

"But I'm not afraid for the press to know I have a date with an attractive —"

"That's very chivalrous, but this is not the time."

Hart looked as if he were going to argue, but before he said anything someone else spoke. "Hart? Were you able to find out anything?"

Hart moved, and for the first time I realized that his mother was in the car behind him.

"Oh! Mrs. VanHorn," I said. "It's a real mess."

She raised her well-bred eyebrows. "Is it true that Gail Hess has been killed?"

"I'm afraid so." As Olivia and I peered at each other through our car windows, Hart stood in the street between us and Tess huddled in the seat beside mine. I sketched what I knew about the situation, worked in a casual introduction of Tess, identifying her as a friend of Jeff's, and described the discovery of Gail's body.

Olivia frowned. "This is very shocking."

"It's certainly shocking for Warner Pier," I said. "Frankly, once the tourists go home, we have almost no crime. But after the wild events of last summer" — Olivia nodded to indicate that she remembered the murder of Clementine Ripley — "this could turn into another invasion of the tabloid press."

"Yes, Mother." Hart's voice sounded mocking. "It could mean a big scandal."

Olivia shot him what — in a less-refined woman — could have been a dirty look. "I didn't know Gail very well," she said. "Had she mentioned any personal situation that might be linked to this? Any quarrels? Any threats? Family problems?"

"Family problems are the most frequent cause of murder," Hart said. "That and psychological problems." He almost sounded amused.

Was I imagining the mockery in his voice? I glanced at him, but his face was bland. "Gail hadn't said anything to me," I said. "I had only seen her a few times recently, when she came over to see the display of molds and when she came to pick them up. Then, of course, she came back when she discovered that one of them was missing."

Hart spoke then. "One was missing?"

"Yes. We hadn't realized it at first."

"She called and told me about it," Olivia said. Her voice sounded a little short.

"She and Aunt Nettie searched everywhere," I said. "It was the trained bear in the harness. All we could conclude was that the burglar took it. But we don't know why — it was up on a top shelf. That was the last time I saw Gail. Maybe she did have some personal problem. She seemed to see some big significance in that particular mold being missing. And she seemed fascinated by the sports car Jeff and I saw. Her reaction was really strange. I'm trying to figure it out."

"Strange?" Hart said. "Strange in what way?"

I opened my mouth to describe Gail's triumphant behavior, but Olivia spoke. "Lee and Jeff's friend must be freezing, Hart. We should get home."

I realized that Olivia was right about the temperature. Tess's teeth were chattering. Hart said good-bye; he and his mother drove on, and I pulled out behind them, following them across the Warner River bridge and down Lake Shore Drive, since their house was maybe a quarter of a mile beyond Aunt Nettie's. The taillights of the Lincoln kept going as I turned into the drive.

I escorted Tess inside and introduced her to Aunt Nettie. Aunt Nettie had moved Jeff's things out of the extra room and changed the bed for Tess. She'd tossed Jeff's sheets and towels into the washing machine; it was quite homey to come into the old house and find it smelling of laundry soap, bacon, and coffee. Aunt Nettie was going to have Tess eating out of her hand by lunchtime.

After breakfast I did the dishes, Aunt Nettie went back to bed, and Tess took a shower. By then it was after ten o'clock, which meant it would be after nine a.m. in Dallas. Rich's office would be open. I couldn't put off that phone call any longer. This time I had to explain the entire situation to someone who knew how to get hold of Rich — in Mexico, or wherever he was. Even if it was Miss Brit.

The receptionist with the British accent answered again, and once again she assured me that Rich was unavailable, and that his personal assistant was, too. I took a deep breath, then asked for Alicia Richardson.

"Tell her it's Lee McKinney," I said.

That put a little excitement into Miss Brit's clipped tones. We might not have met, but after my repeated phone calls I was willing to bet she had found out I was Rich's ex. If he was off on a trip with his first wife, having the second one turn up — even on the telephone — was sure to put the office on its ear.

Almost immediately I heard Alicia's soft Texas voice. "Accounting."

"Alicia, it's Lee."

"Lee? Lee McKinney?"

"Right!"

Alicia actually sounded glad to hear from me. She began a flurry of questions. "Where are you, Lee? We heard you'd moved to Michigan."

"I'm fine, Alicia, and I did move to Michigan. And I want to know all about your family. But first, I've got an emergency up here, and I need to find Rich ASAP. Can you help me?"

Alicia's voice became cautious. "Well, Lee, Rich is on a trip to Mexico. And he's deliberately out of contact with the office and —"

"I know he's with Dina, Alicia. I wish them luck."

"Oh." Alicia sounded relieved.

"But Jeff is up here, and he's in bad trouble."

The conversation went on about fifteen minutes. Alicia had worked for Rich for years — she was an old hand when Rich and I got married. She knew all the dirt on him, and she almost ran his business.

"The problem is," Alicia said, "Rich promised Dina he wouldn't be calling the office three times a day, the way he usually does when he leaves town."

"Don't I know!"

Alicia laughed. "And this time he's actually sticking to it."

"He must be serious."

"I think he is, Lee. So he and Dina may be hard to find. But I'll get on the phone and start trying."

"Thanks, Alicia. In the meantime, we're hiring Jeff a lawyer up here. And I'm assuring that lawyer that he'll be paid."

"Right. Rich is still solvent." Alicia hesitated. "And you say Jeff hasn't given you any explanation of why he came to Michigan?"

It was my time to hesitate. Should I tell her about Tess?

I thought of the possibility that Miss Brit was listening in. "Jeff hasn't explained a thing," I said. It wasn't a lie. He hadn't. Joe and I had found Tess without a hint from Jeff.

I asked a couple of questions about Alicia's family, then hung up. When I turned around, Tess was standing in the doorway that led to the back hall and the bathroom.

"You didn't tell her about me," she said.

"There didn't seem to be any need."

"Thanks." Her voice was calm, and if she blinked back tears, at least she wasn't hysterical.

"Tess, the press is going to get hold of this," I said. "Even if I don't say anything, even if Chief Jones keeps quiet, word is likely to get out. Think about calling your parents later today."

She nodded miserably and went upstairs.

I almost went up, too. But I'd had to pump myself up to call Rich's office. Now that I could go to bed, I discovered I was too wide awake to want to. I decided to walk down to get the newspaper from the delivery box at the end of the drive.

I put on my jacket and went out onto the porch, and I entered a new world. When Tess and I had come home about eight-thirty, the sun had been coming up. The day hadn't looked too promising, but it had been only partially overcast. Now it was snowing and the large flakes were being driven at an angle by the wind. The drive was rapidly being covered. It was mighty cold to a Texas girl.

I paused and looked the situation over, and I almost went back inside. Then I remembered that I was determined not to be a wimpy Texan who was afraid of a little snow, and I zipped up my bright red jacket, pulled my white knitted hat down over my ears, and started down the drive.

Earlier, one of the snowmobile jerks had

been cruising around the neighborhood, but now things were silent — silent except for the occasional faint moan of the wind, and the scrunch of my boots as I walked through the fresh snow.

It was cold, true, but it was also pure, somehow. As soon as I was twenty-five or thirty feet down the drive, the house disappeared, hidden by the blowing snow. There was quite a bit of undergrowth in the patch of trees between the house and Lake Shore Drive, so the hundred feet or so that I had to walk became like a hike into the deep forest. The bare limbs of the trees lifted up into an icy fog, and the swirling eddies of snow isolated me. I might as well have been alone in the big woods. I felt that I'd left all my problems back at the house or downtown at the police station. I could have simply walked on into the woods and left the world behind. I might have been the only person left on earth.

Lake Shore Drive, which even in the winter has some traffic, was empty. I crossed to the clump of mailboxes and newspaper delivery boxes, then pulled the rolled newspaper out of the delivery tube. I took the newspaper out of its plastic sack and stuffed the sack in my pocket. Then I simply stood there, enjoying the woods and the snow, the silence, the loneliness, and the loveliness, and wishing I didn't have to return to real life.

A snowmobile's motor started, close to me. Resentfully, I turned toward the sound. And from the drive of the Baileys' summer cottage — a house I knew was empty that time of year — a purple snowmobile came barreling out onto the road.

It headed straight toward me.

Chapter 12

The next thing I knew, I was behind the row of mailboxes.

I will always half believe a guardian angel threw me there, because I have no recollection at all of jumping, sliding, or stepping aside. But suddenly I was behind the mailboxes, and the snowmobile — after almost running over my right snow boot — had gone by me and was disappearing into the blowing snow.

I was furious. I stepped into the road and shook my fist at the snowmobile's driver, a shapeless blob in a furry jacket and a helmet like a black bowling ball. "Hey! Are you nuts?" I yelled loudly, though I knew the rider couldn't hear me over the roar of the engine.

The snowmobile was just a faint outline in the gloom, but I could see it slowing down, and for a moment I thought — maybe a tad self-righteously — that the rider was coming back to apologize.

The snowmobile turned, chewing up the frozen slush alongside Lake Shore Drive with the tractor tread that pushed the thing. It swung back to face me — looking like a giant praying mantis with skis for front legs — then headed right at me again.

I jumped back behind the mailboxes. But the snowmobile had figured that one out. This time it left the road and went behind the mailboxes, heading for my hiding spot.

The driver was trying to kill me.

That realization got my adrenaline in gear. I ducked, curled myself into an egg and scooted under the mailboxes, as close as I could get to the poles that held them up. The snowmobile came right for me. It knocked one mailbox askew, but it missed me by six inches as it went by.

I huddled under the mailboxes. I had to find a better shelter than a few fence posts. I was across the road from Aunt Nettie's house, on the lake side of Lake Shore Drive. All the houses on that side were summer cottages. And in mid-February every one of them was probably locked up as tight as the bank the day after Jesse James left town. Not only were they locked, but they had heavy shutters on the windows.

I could run into the underbrush, but I wouldn't be able to run fast, and I'd risk tripping and breaking my neck. There was no help on that side of the road.

No, I had to get across Lake Shore Drive to the inland side. Aunt Nettie's house was my nearest haven.

The snowmobile had almost disappeared in the swirling snow, but I could see the purple lump turning around again. And if I could see purple, I knew that the rider could see red. I cursed the color of my vivid jacket, but I didn't dare take time to snatch it off.

The snowmobile was coming back — and this time it might simply mow those mailboxes down. I dashed across the road, toward the house. The snowmobile came roaring right after me.

Merely running up the driveway, where I'd be an easy target, was not my plan. I made it across the road six inches ahead of the snowmobile, veered into the woods, pivoted, and jumped behind a large maple tree.

The snowmobile went up Aunt Nettie's drive, then slowed and turned around, coming back. The rider was getting better at those quick turns. The machine lay in wait in the driveway, between me and the house.

For a moment I considered just staying there, clutching my maple, in a standoff situation. But there was no permanent safety in that. I had no way of knowing if the snowmobile rider had a gun, for example. The furry jacket and helmet might disguise some kind of monster; he could get off, catch me with his bare hands, and break my neck.

No, my best bet was to try to get back on the drive, where I could run. But for now I had to stay in the underbrush, where branches and logs on the snow-covered ground would keep the snowmobile from following.

I edged forward, toward a new tree, one that was closer to the drive. But I got too close to the drive, and the snowmobile moved toward me. I leaped back toward a tree, tripped over one of those hidden logs and fell flat on my face.

For a moment I thought I was dead. I rolled into a ball, pulled my arms over my head and got ready to be run over and chewed up by that snowmobile. Its roar grew louder and louder.

Then it was past me. The log that had tripped me had also saved me. I had rolled close to it, and the snowmobile had not been able to pull in near enough to run over me.

I scrambled onto my hands and knees. The house was still a long way off, but I was within a couple of steps of the drive. I got out there and started running.

It was no good. A glance over my shoulder confirmed what my ears told me. The snowmobile was coming back. A giant cedar tree was looming up on my right.

Aunt Nettie hated that tree. It followed the usual habit of cedars, so its branches only had needles on the outer edges. The whole interior of the tree was bare and ugly. But right now I thought it looked beautiful. I lowered my head and dived in among the lower branches.

That saved me from the next pass of the snowmobile, but it wasn't a good place to be. I was stuck in there. It was going to be a lot harder to get out than it had been to get in. I tried to spot another tree I could hug, one closer to the house.

In the meantime, the snowmobile was turning around again. The black helmet had a reflective visor that turned the rider into an anonymous force and made the whole apparatus look more like a man-eater than ever.

I crawled out of the cedar and ran into the drive, daring the snowmobile to come toward me. It moved slightly, and I jumped behind another maple on the other side of the lane.

I was still about fifty feet from the house, with at least twenty feet of driveway before the stretch of beach grass Aunt Nettie and I called the lawn. And the snow on that lawn was deep; it would suck at my feet. The lawn might as well be quicksand.

The snowmobile had stopped, its motor still roaring, between me and the house. I jumped forward, but the engine gunned. The snowmobile seemed to be pawing the ground, like a bull waiting to run at the bullfighter. And I jumped back behind my tree like a toreador who forgot his cape.

Rats! The snowmobile was moving toward the house. As I watched, it came to the corner where the trees ended and the beach grass began. There it waited, ready for me to try to cross the cleared area.

Well, I didn't have to do that. Pretty soon Aunt Nettie, no matter how soundly she was sleeping, was going to notice all that roaring in her yard. She'd look out. She'd see what was going on. She'd call the police.

All I had to do was stay put, and the cavalry would arrive. I contemplated that possibility, and I almost began to breathe normally.

But when it came, the cavalry was going to have a hard time catching that snowmobile. Police cars can not go down the footpaths that link the houses in Aunt Nettie's neighborhood, but the snowmobile could. It could speed off into the woods and never be seen again.

Chief Jones was going to be asking me what that snowmobile had looked like. I peeked around my tree. The snow was still swirling, and my pursuer was just a dim shape. The snowmobile's purple looked dull, a sort of eggplant. I could see the skis at the front and the heavy springs that linked them to the body of the snowmobile. Now I made out the slick plastic — fiberglass? — body, the swept-back windshield. And I could see the storm trooper who was riding it. His jacket was some dark color, black or navy, and it had a lot of texture.

The motor gunned again, and the snowmobile moved forward.

It was coming in. Maybe it planned to pin me to my friendly maple. I marked another tree a few feet closer to the house and jumped for it.

I got to that tree, huddled behind it, and put my head around to look at the snowmobile. It went by so close that I could have touched the faceless creature riding it. But he missed me. As he went by I ran closer to the house, to another maple — one tree nearer to safety. I peeked around my tree and decided I had enough time for one more dash.

And that dash took me to the tree closest to the house. Not that I could see the house very well, but this big elm, maybe sixty feet high and eight feet around, was on the edge of the lawn. The lawn was covered with several feet of snow. If I cut across the lawn, I'd cut a hundred feet or more off my dash to safety. But it wasn't going to be easy running.

The snowmobile veered out onto the beach grass and swung around. Screaming wasn't going to do any good. The snowmobile's noise was deafening. I muttered under my breath. "Aunt Nettie, wake up and call those cops."

What was I going to do? Throw snowballs at the snowmobile?

I looked at my hands helplessly. And for the first time I realized they weren't empty. I was still holding a rolled-up copy of the *Grand Rapids Press*. Fat lot of good that was going to do.

I decided to feint. I'd jump out and entice the snowmobile into making another pass. Then I'd jump back behind my tree. After the snowmobile had passed me, I'd run for the back porch. I knew the back door was unlocked.

I took a deep breath and jumped out. But the snowmobile didn't bite. It stayed on the drive.

I stepped forward one more step. Then another. Had it given up?

Suddenly the engine revved, and it came at me.

I was still out from behind my tree.

I ran back toward the tree. And that deep, horrible snow pulled at my feet every step. It was like slogging through mud, through five feet of water, through a vat of chocolate.

The snowmobile was nearly on me. I wasn't going to make it. I was going to die. Desperately, I threw the rolled-up newspaper. It hit the swept-back windshield.

And the snowmobile veered, went by me, hit a tree and tipped over. It lay on its side, its front skis sticking out helplessly, its back tread churning in the air.

I stared. Then I ran for the house.

I'd been told that snowmobiles tipped over easily. But I'd also heard that they were easy to get back upright. So I didn't wait around to check on the rider.

I didn't look back. I slogged through the snow to the back walk, skidded over the new snow that was rapidly covering the flagstones, and jumped onto the porch. I didn't stop. I charged right into the kitchen, slammed the door, and locked it. Then I took two deep breaths before I ran into the back hall, which had the closest window that looked over that side of the lawn.

For a moment the blowing snow almost kept me from seeing anything. Then I saw a purple form. And a woolly jacket and bowling-ball head. The rider was pushing the snowmobile upright. As I watched he got aboard and took off across the lawn and down the drive, leaving nothing behind but a chewed-up patch of snow. In less than a minute there was nothing to see but the snow, nothing to hear but the swish of the falling flakes.

I stood there, looking out the back window, and the whole episode seemed unbelievable. Had I really run through the snow, dodging a man-eater? I stood there in that odd little back hall — part pantry, part corridor between Aunt Nettie's bedroom and the bathroom — and for a moment I actually doubted the chase had happened.

Then the door to Aunt Nettie's bedroom opened, and she looked out. She wore a blue robe, and her hair was messed up, and I was so glad to see her that tears began to trickle down my face.

"I called the police," she said firmly. "I don't know who's riding that snowmobile around here, but I'm really tired of it. I guess they think we're at work this time of the day and won't know about it. But there is a limit!"

Then she looked closely at me. "Heavens! Lee, have you been outside? And what happened to your jacket?"

The jacket looked as if I'd been rolling in the snow. Dirty snow. The cedar had ripped a sleeve. I'd tracked snow all over the kitchen floor and into the back hall. I went back to the kitchen door, the assigned spot for taking off outside clothes, and told Aunt Nettie what had happened. I tried to laugh it off. I didn't want to frighten her.

But her round face screwed up into an angry apple. "Oh, Lee!"

"I'm not hurt," I said. "It was pretty exciting. But the police will be here soon, and I'll tell them about it. Maybe they can identify the snowmobile by its tracks."

"I doubt it." Aunt Nettie looked out the kitchen window. "It's snowing harder."

She called the police again, telling the dispatcher that the snowmobile rider had not only trespassed, but had actually chased her niece.

"Please tell whoever is on duty to get right out here," she said. "Maybe they can still tell something about the snowmobile."

"Maybe they could even follow it to its lair," I said.

But it was no good. Jerry Cherry showed up within a few minutes, quickly followed by the chief. They tramped through the yard and looked at the piled-up snow along Lake Shore Drive, but when they came inside to report, the chief said the new snow made tracking the snowmobile impossible.

"I guess my messed-up jacket is the only evidence I can show you to prove the whole thing even happened," I said.

"Did you see the rider?" Chief Jones asked.

"I could tell that somebody was guiding the darn thing," I said. "But he had on a helmet. It made his head look like a bowling ball, and it had a guard over the face. It could have been anybody."

"How big did the guy look?"

"Enormous! But that may have been the jacket." I described the jacket, saying it was made of some woolly fabric. "It could have been fake fur," I said. "Or Polartec. Something with a lot of texture."

The chief frowned, and his frown made me furious.

"You'd better not say you don't believe this happened," I said.

"Well, after the burglary night before last and a killing last night . . ."

"This was more than trespassing by a snowmobile. Trying to kill me is a major crime."

"It sure is," Chief Jones said. He was drawling, pulling his words out long. "And adding it to what Jeff said . . ." He paused again.

"What Jeff said? This is one thing you can't blame on Jeff, Chief."

"But if it was the killer of Gail Hess coming back. . . ."

"That's silly! Why would the killer hang around here?"

"I don't know, Lee. But I do know that, except for the helmet, your description of the snowmobile rider is a lot like the description Jeff gave of the person he claims to have seen minutes before Gail Hess's body was found."

Chapter 13

That remark seemed to have knocked me out. The next thing I knew I was tucked into my own bed, the clock radio read 2:30 p.m., and someone was tapping at my door.

"Ms. McKinney? Lee?"

I rolled over, barely catching my head before it fell off my shoulders. "Tess? Come in."

She peered around the door, looking as if she expected to need a whip and a chair. "I'm sorry. I know you haven't been asleep long enough. But that Joe guy called."

I groaned, sat up, and discovered I was wearing my underwear and no pajamas. The jeans and sweatshirt I'd had on when the snowmobile chased me were tossed on the back of a chair. I guess I had simply pulled them off and crawled under the covers.

I held on to my head. It wouldn't do to allow it to roll under the bed. "Is Joe still on the phone?"

"No. He said not to get you up, but if you woke up to tell you that Jeff's attorney is going to be meeting with him at four p.m. Your aunt went to the chocolate shop."

"Thanks, Tess." I yawned so widely I nearly dislocated my jaw, got out of bed, and headed for the shower.

By four o'clock I'd poured hot water outside me and coffee inside me and had dragged myself — and Tess, who didn't want to stay at Aunt Nettie's alone — to the police department in time to meet Webb Bartlett before he saw Jeff. The day was still gray, but the snow had stopped, and the streets had been plowed.

Webb might have been Joe's age, but a bald spot and a paunch made him look older. His eyes were shrewd, and he didn't bluster. I liked him, and I hoped Jeff would.

Webb didn't ask me any questions before he saw Jeff, and he told Tess she'd have to wait until he and Jeff had conferred before she could go in. So Tess and I moped around the police station. The chief was out, but the part-time secretary took me into his office and quietly told me that the chief had run a check, and neither Jeff nor Tess seemed to be in trouble with the law, either in Texas or in any state between there and here. I was almost ashamed of how relieved I was to hear that.

When Webb came out, Tess went in, armed with the clean clothes, toothbrush, comb, and razor we'd brought for Jeff. The

Warner Pier Police Department doesn't really have a jail, just a holding cell, which is usually empty. But I appreciated the chief's keeping Jeff there, instead of booking him into the county jail thirty miles away. I pictured Jeff in with hardened criminals and shuddered. He might have a stud in his lip, but he was just a baby.

Webb and I sat down to talk. He brushed aside my assurances that his fee would be paid. "I'll take my fee out of Joe's hide if Jeff's dad balks," he said. "Now, the police have to charge Jeff within forty-eight hours or let him go. Maybe he won't have to go before the judge at all. What do you know about the victim, this Gail Hess?"

"Not a lot. Her antique shop is across the street from TenHuis Chocolade, but — well, in the summer we were all too swamped to socialize, and during the fall I was trying to get my job figured out and didn't get around much. I didn't really get acquainted with her until this Teddy Bear Getaway campaign started."

"She was the campaign chair?"

"Right. Aunt Nettie wasn't planning to do much with the campaign, but Gail insisted that we should take part."

"Your aunt opposed the campaign?"

"No, she thought it was a good idea, but

it's not really key to our business. Most of the retail merchants in Warner Pier are completely dependent on the trade of tourists and summer residents. Some of them close up after Labor Day, and the ones who stay open, naturally they'd like to increase their winter sales. But TenHuis Chocolade has built up quite a mail-order business. Our retail shop pays for itself in the summer, but it doesn't make a lot of difference to our overall profit picture. This time of year we're busy shipping Easter and Mother's Day orders. We don't care much about retail sales. The shop's only open as a sort of courtesy. Of course, that attitude shocked Gail."

"Was she a Warner Pier native?"

"I don't know, but Aunt Nettie will. We could go over to the shop and ask her."

I spoke briefly to Jeff. Then Tess, Webb, and I left the police station and walked toward the shop.

Webb took a deep breath and gestured at our surroundings. "This is marvelous! Marvelous to be able to walk anywhere in the business district. And in a beautiful little town like this. I see why Warner Pier is such a tourist attraction."

"It is really pretty," Tess said. "In the daylight." She obviously felt like she had been let out of her motel-room jail. When Jeff had been locked up, she'd been released.

Webb Bartlett was gesturing again, this time at the upper stories of the buildings along Peach Street. "What's up there?" he said.

"Mostly apartments."

"Apartments! Maybe there were witnesses to Gail Hess's killing."

I frowned. "I doubt it. Aunt Nettie has an apartment upstairs in her building, but it's only occupied when the summer workers hit town. I think that's the case for nearly all the buildings. The downtown is deserted on winter nights."

"There's the skating rink man," Tess said. "Jeff and I saw him when we went out. That would be an awful job."

I explained to Webb that the Warner Pier tennis courts are transformed into skating rinks every winter, and that one city employee had the job of maintaining them in the depths of the night. "There are people who run snowplows, too," I said. "But I don't think they would have been out last night. The snow didn't start until this morning."

"Finding a witness would be an extra added attraction," Webb said. "I guess we'd better not get our hopes up."

By then we had reached the store, and I was pleased to see that the glass in the door had been replaced. I took Webb back into the shop to meet Aunt Nettie, who was draining milk chocolate from the thirty-gallon vat where it was kept already melted. She took a work bowl full of the ambrosial stuff to a table and began to ladle it into plastic molds shaped like the back halves of teddy bears. Without stopping her work — pour a ladleful of chocolate into the mold, tip the mold this way and that to make sure the inside was properly coated, pour out the excess, weigh the mold to make sure she'd used the right amount of chocolate, then put it aside on a tray — Aunt Nettie greeted Webb. Then she asked Tess if she'd like to make a little money by taking over Jeff's job packing chocolates. When Tess agreed enthusiastically, Aunt Nettie called to Hazel, the chief hairnet lady. Hazel escorted Tess back to the packing area for her first lesson in the shipping and handling of the fragile molded chocolate.

Aunt Nettie took her tray of hollow chocolate teddy bear halves to the cooling tunnel and started the batch along the conveyor belt.

Webb was bug-eyed. "That's fascinating," he said. "But why are you making the back half of a teddy bear?"

Aunt Nettie showed him the matching molds that were the front halves of the teddy bears, plus the miniature chocolate toys — tiny cars, tops, balls, and drums — that would fit inside the two halves. "The fronts of the bears are already decorated," she said, displaying the bears' happy white chocolate grins and dark chocolate eyes. "When these backs I'm making are firm, we put the little chocolate items inside, then we glue the halves together with chocolate. They're a special item for the promotion, but Marshall Fields is taking two hundred and fifty of them."

"It must be the dickens to get those dark and light designs on there!"

"The designs are part of the mold," Aunt Nettie said kindly. "We do that first. Then, after the design is set, we pour the milk chocolate in. It's not that hard." She smiled a little smugly. The truth is that it is hard. But Aunt Nettie has developed her own secret technique — which I won't describe — for making the designs quickly. Or a skilled person can make them quickly. I can't.

"I'd like to buy one for my daughter."

Aunt Nettie presented Webb with a teddy

bear that had already been assembled and given its special Teddy Bear Getaway wrapping. He held it like a treasure. I could see that we'd gained a customer.

I asked her about the apartments. She agreed with me that nearly all the downtown apartments were empty in the winter.

"Most of them are rented to summer workers," she said. "Just a few are occupied. Gail's, of course."

Webb looked surprised, and I'm sure I did, too. "Gail lived over her shop?" I said.

"Yes. She said she couldn't pay a mortgage on the shop and another one on a house. You know how expensive it is to rent or buy a place to live in Warner Pier."

I knew. With people building million-dollar homes in Warner Pier and leasing houses and condos for thousands and thousands of dollars each summer — well, I knew I was lucky to live with Aunt Nettie in a house that had been in the family for a hundred years. It was that or commute from someplace way back off the main road or from Holland or Grand Rapids.

But learning that Gail lived over her shop was real news.

"I'd been wondering how she happened to cross paths with the killer," I said. "I thought maybe she'd been lying in wait for the burglar and had caught him breaking in over here again."

"She wouldn't have needed to set an ambush," Aunt Nettie said. "She would have only had to look out her front window."

I walked to our show window and looked over at Gail's shop. "It's covered with crime scene tape at the moment," I said. "I guess her apartment is, too."

Webb turned to Aunt Nettie. "Was Gail a native of Warner Pier?"

"No, but she'd lived here nearly twenty years."

"Did she have any family?"

"She was single, and I never heard her mention having been married. She never talked about any family, but that doesn't prove anything. I know who might know, though. Mercy Woodyard."

"That's Joe's mom," I said to Webb. "She has an insurance office here. She insures practically all the local businesses. I'll call her and ask."

Mercy Woodyard told me she had sold Gail a small life insurance policy. Her beneficiary was a sister, Nancy Warren. "She's a teacher in Indianapolis," Mercy said. "I gave Chief Jones her name, and he contacted her. She's due in any moment. The chief doesn't want her staying in Gail's apartment, so I made her a reservation at the Inn on the Pier. It's practically the only place open this time of year."

I didn't remind her that the Lake Michigan Inn was open, too. Mercy obviously meant that the Inn on the Pier was the only picturesque place open. And it definitely looks picturesque, though in February, when it could be called the Inn on the Ice, it also looks darn cold. It sits right on the edge of the river. In the summer boaters come up the Warner River and tie up at the inn's dock, then check in as if they'd parked their Chevys outside the Holiday Inn.

"Thanks for the information, Mercy," I said. "Jeff's attorney wanted to know."

"Webb Bartlett? Is he there? Joe wanted to see him."

"I'll have Webb give him a call."

"Joe's here. I'll tell him to drop over."

I had a slanting view of Joe's mom's office — across the street and three doors down — from my desk. Joe was already coming out the door. Something about the way he held his head told me he was mad.

"What's Jeff done now?" I may have muttered the question. It was the first thought that popped into my head.

But when Joe got to the shop, he didn't

display his anger to Webb. No, he gave him the old college greeting — handshake and poke in the gut — and asked him about his session with Jeff.

I was still convinced he was mad, but he got the whole Jeff session thrashed out with Webb before he turned to me. When he spoke, he sounded accusing. "What's this about somebody chasing you with a snowmobile?"

Webb's eyes popped, and he gave a surprised, "Huh?" Aunt Nettie blinked and looked from Joe to me, frowning.

"He didn't catch me," I said. "I hit the guy with a newspaper and he fell over."

"A newspaper!" Joe still sounded angry. "Why did you hit him with a newspaper?"

"I didn't happen to be carrying a two-by-four," I said. "What's the matter?"

"The matter? You could have been killed!"

"I am well aware of that, Joe. I didn't deliberately seek the experiment — the experience."

"What were you doing out in a snowstorm, battling snowmobiles with a newspaper?"

"I was proving to the people of western Michigan that Texans aren't wimps."

"Well, that's for damn sure! When people

around here go hunting snowmobiles, they use rifles. But Texans go after them with newspapers! Did you roll it up like a stick? Or throw it over the guy like a blanket?"

Aunt Nettie began to laugh. Webb joined in. Then I laughed. And finally, Joe laughed, too.

"Joe," I said. "I've been trying to take a walk, just a short one, every day, so that people around here would quit telling me that Texans are afraid of cold weather. I had walked down to the road to get the newspaper, and the snowmobile roared out of somebody's driveway and chased me back to the house. It finally got so close I threw the newspaper I had in my hand at it, and that distracted the rider, and he veered off and fell over. I got to the house before he got the snowmobile upright again."

Now Webb was frowning. "Did you call the police?"

"Yes. But, as Joe says, it was snowing when it happened. The snow covered most of the tracks before the police could get there. There are snowmobiles all over Warner Pier, and, as you'd expect, the rider was wearing a helmet with a reflective face-plate and a bulky jacket. I didn't get a good look at him."

"Do the police think this was linked to the

killing of Gail Hess?" Webb said.

I sighed. "Maybe. The description of the rider's jacket matches the description of the jacket on the guy Jeff says he saw last night, when Gail Hess was killed."

Joe and Webb looked at each other. It wasn't just a glance. This was a significant exchange.

"What's the problem?" I said.

"I guess Webb and I were just thinking how that would strike a prosecutor," Joe said.

"A prosecutor? It didn't seem to concern the chief."

"Yeah, but the chief knows you. That makes him more likely to believe you."

"I hope so. But are you saying a prosecutor might not believe me?"

"Well, imagine you're presenting the case to a jury," Webb said. "Jeff says he saw this mysterious figure in the woolly jacket. Nobody else saw him."

"Right, there's nobody to back up his story," Joe said.

Webb nodded. "Then somebody else sees this figure — is actually chased by him. Voilà! Another witness. But —"

I saw what was coming. "But the other witness is Jeff's stepmother, and she's committed to proving that Jeff is innocent. And any tracks in the snow or other evidence that proves she was chased by the snowmobile were covered up before anybody else saw them."

Joe and Webb both looked glum.

"Well," Aunt Nettie said. "I saw Lee when she ran into the house, and she'd better not have tracked up the kitchen floor like that just so she could tell the police a lie."

That made us all smile again, and the atmosphere lightened.

"How did you hear about the chase?" I said.

"The chief came in asking Mom if she had any kind of list of snowmobiles insured in the area."

"Apparently the chief is trying to check my story." I turned to Webb. "My story is not going to change. So I guess we might as well move on. Is there anything I can do to help Jeff?"

"You could check these buildings along here," he said. "It sounds unlikely, but there could be someone living upstairs. I'm sure the police will be checking, too, but there's no reason our side can't ask a few questions."

"Okay," I said. "I'll ask all the business owners if anybody's living upstairs."

"It's just about closing time," Joe said. "We'd probably better wait until to-morrow."

"I can try to catch some of them. I'll call them after dinner if they've already left."

Joe looked at the floor. "You're busy to-night, aren't you?"

I felt blank. Then I gasped. I'd completely forgotten my date with Hart VanHorn — the date I'd broken at dawn that morning. But Joe hadn't forgotten. That was grati-fying.

"That was called off," I said. "This trouble over Jeff. Besides — well, I was afraid the tabloids were coming back."

"The tabloids!" Joe looked wary.

I told Joe, Aunt Nettie, and Webb about the call Hart had received from a Chicago reporter. "So somebody tipped him off," I said. "You were right, Joe. The tabloids are probably still with us."

Almost on cue car lights hit the shop's front window. For a panicky moment I felt as if the four of us were on display. I went to the window to pull the shade. When the car lights died, I saw Mercy Woodyard getting out of the passenger side. She circled around the car and waited for the driver, a short woman wearing a knitted cap and dark-colored jacket. They crossed the sidewalk toward the shop, and I opened the door for them.

"Hi, Lee," Mercy said. "Sorry to come in right at closing time."

"Aunt Nettie and I will be here for a while."

Mercy and her companion came in. The second woman's face was pinched; she looked like one of the dried-apple dolls Gail Hess had sometimes displayed.

Mercy seemed quite uncomfortable. "This is Nancy Warren, Lee. She's Gail Hess's sister. She arrived right after you called. She's moving her car over to the Inn on the Pier, but she wanted to see the place where the tragedy occurred."

I gasped and made gibbering sounds, but Aunt Nettie met the occasion. She took Nancy Warren's hand. "We're so sorry about Gail," she said. "We want to help you in any way we can."

Nancy Warren's dried-apple face screwed up even tighter. "Thank you," she said. "Everyone's being so kind."

Mercy gestured toward Joe. "This is my son," she said. "After I found Gail I called him, so he was one of the first people on the scene of the . . . the death."

Joe looked even more uncomfortable than his mother, but he managed to shake Nancy

Warren's hand and mumble something sympathetic.

Mrs. Warren looked miserable. "It was outside here?"

"Yes," Joe said. "She was lying on the sidewalk."

He walked outside with Mrs. Warren. I got my jacket, then went out as well. They were standing silently, looking at the spot where Gail's body had been.

"Did you talk to Gail often?" I said.

Nancy Warren shook her head. "No. We'd almost lost touch. It's my fault, I guess. Anyway, we didn't talk more than a couple of times a year."

"So you hadn't talked to her recently?"

"A couple of months ago. At Christmas. She was all excited about the possibility of handling some big estate sale." Then she gestured at the sidewalk. "I thought . . . Don't the police draw a chalk outline?"

"That's only on television," Joe said. "In real life they usually take photographs."

Mrs. Warren turned to me. "Mrs. Woodyard said your stepson was found standing over her."

I tried not to sound too defensive. "Jeff says he had just driven by and saw her body on the sidewalk. He stopped to see if he could help her. The police are holding him,

225

but we hope to get him released quickly."

"This stepson . . . ?" She stopped talking.

"He's actually an ex-stepson," I said. "My ex-husband's son. Jeff has never been in trouble before. He'd only been in town two days." I left out any reference to the ear-lobe eyelets.

"Then he didn't know Gail?"

"They may have met briefly, when she came by about the Teddy Bear Getaway."

"Teddy Bear Getaway?"

"Yes. Gail was chairing the Merchants' Association midwinter promotion."

"Oh!" Mrs. Warren's voice rose to a wail. "Gail wasn't handling money, was she?"

CHOCOLATE CHAT

THE *SWEET AND LOW* DOWN

It takes John Putnam Thatcher, the urbane banker created by Emma Lathen, to solve a case involving machinations on New York's Cocoa Exchange.

In *Sweet and Low*, published in 1974, Thatcher — senior vice president and trust officer of The Sloan, third largest bank in the world — is named a trustee of the Leonard Dreyer Trust, a charitable foundation established by the world's largest chocolate company. The Dreyer Trust is a major stockholder in the Dreyer Chocolate Company, manufacturer of the most famous chocolate bar in the world. Thatcher gets involved when one of Dreyer's cocoa buyers is murdered on the eve of a meeting of the trust and the company's chief cocoa futures trader is killed on an elevator in the Cocoa Exchange itself.

The book is typical Lathen, giving an inside look at a particular corner of the financial world, in this case the commodities market. It's a painless way to get a whiff of economics. For many mystery fans, John

Putnam Thatcher — whose deductions rival Hercule Poirot's and whose witty observations are often hilarious comments on America and American business — is one of the finest detectives.

Chapter 14

That was a strange reaction. I'm sure I gaped before I replied. "Gail had a lot to say about how the promotional budget was spent. But there's a board that approves everything."

Nancy Warren seemed to be struggling to contain herself. "I'm sure it's all right," she said. She bent over, once again examining the sidewalk she'd already looked over carefully.

I thought about Jeff sitting in the Warner Pier lockup and I decided she needed to explain. Did Gail have some secret in her past? Something to do with money? Would knowing whatever it was help Jeff?

"Why did you ask that?" I said. "About handling money?"

"Oh, no reason."

"That's hard to believe, Mrs. Warren. Had Gail had trouble over finances before?"

"No. Well, it seems she was always complaining about not making enough money. . . . I mean, if she was worried about her own finances, I'm just surprised that she took on other people's money." She laughed, but it sounded forced. "You know, the shoemaker's children run barefoot."

"Is there some reason that Gail should not have been handling money?"

"Oh, no! No. Gail had a business degree. She had operated her own business since she was thirty. I'm sure it would be perfectly all right." She produced a tissue from her pocket and dabbed at her eye. "And now, I guess I'd better get over to the bed-and-breakfast."

Joe and I gave her directions, and since it's impossible to get lost in Warner Pier, we waved her off satisfied that she would get there.

As her car disappeared down the street, Joe gave a sort of grunt. "What did you think of that?"

"She makes me wonder why Gail left Indiana."

"Right. Maybe Chief Jones knows somebody in Indianapolis."

"And maybe Aunt Nettie or your mom could suggest that the Merchants' Association audit the festival accounts."

Joe and I went inside and reported our conversation with Nancy Warren to Webb, Aunt Nettie, and Mercy. Webb was noncommittal. Mercy lifted her eyebrows and admitted that Gail's insurance had nearly been cancelled a year earlier because of a late payment. Aunt Nettie clucked and assured all of us that Gail's reputation had been fine. Then she went to the phone to call the vice president of the chamber of commerce to suggest that the accounts be checked. Joe promised to call Chief Jones and ask him to check the Indiana situation.

Mercy Woodyard left, saying she'd walked out without closing up her office. Webb shook hands, asked me to thank Aunt Nettie for his chocolate teddy bear and left. Aunt Nettie was still on the phone in the office.

Joe and I were alone in the shop. There was a moment of stiff silence. Then we spoke at the same time.

I said, "I loved the chocolates." He said, "I can help you find out about the downtown apartments."

We both looked at the floor. I felt awkward, and Joe looked as if he felt awkward. Then we did our unison speech act again.

He said, "It was kind of a dumb thing to get you." I said, "I can call everybody."

We both laughed. Joe opened his mouth, but I held up my hand like a traffic signal. Then I put my elbows on the counter and leaned over. "I'll go first," I said. "It was very nice to have a box of chocolates all my own. How did you know my two favorite flavors?"

"Then they were right? I try to listen, but

sometimes I forget and talk." Joe took my hand and held it gently. "Now, how about letting me help you call the downtown property owners?"

"It'll only be this block. I can do it."

"I'll be glad to help. You take the river side, and I'll take the Orchard side."

In Texas everything is north, south, east, and west, but that doesn't work in Warner Pier. Because it's laid out parallel to the Warner River, which runs southwest into Lake Michigan, you would have to say "It's a block northeast," or "I live on the west corner." So Warner Pier's directions are divided into lake, highway, river, and Orchard, as in Orchard Street. It sounds silly, but it works.

Joe gave my hand a final squeeze, and we left it that way, with me to call property owners or merchants on the river side of the street, the side where TenHuis Chocolade was located, and Joe to call those on the Orchard side, the side where his mom's office was. We didn't need a list; we knew everybody on both sides of the block. Besides, about a third of the shops weren't open in the wintertime.

Aunt Nettie called out, saying she and Tess were leaving by the back door. Joe said good-bye and went across the street to his truck, which was parked in front of his mother's office, then drove off. I picked up some paperwork to take home. I hadn't done a stroke of work that day. I left by the street door, since I'd parked in front of the shop.

The picturesque streetlights of downtown Warner Pier don't exactly shine like spotlights, so the block was fairly dark, as well as deserted. I was locking the door to the shop when I heard a banging noise.

This was followed by someone calling out, "Gail! Gail! I'm here! Let me in!"

I whirled toward the sound. Someone was standing in front of Gail Hess's antique shop — inside the crime scene tape. All I could make out was a bulky coat, but I could tell the voice belonged to a woman.

A dim light shone in Gail's window, but nothing stirred behind the curtain. Or behind any other window on the block. The streetlights puddled on the slushy snow along the curb. When the woman stopped knocking and yelling, the whole street was silent.

The woman called out again. "Gail! I'm freezing!"

Someone was trying to rouse Gail Hess, to rouse the dead.

It was spooky. A rabbit ran over my grave,

making me shudder, and I fought an impulse to jump into my van and tear out of there.

But that wouldn't do. I sternly curbed my imagination, and called out, "Hello! Can I help you?"

The woman turned toward me. Now I saw an oval of white face, topped by dark hair. "I hope you can," she said. She stepped across the yellow crime scene tape and moved toward me. "Gail Hess invited me to stay with her. She knew when I was to arrive. But she's apparently not there. Has something happened? I didn't understand all this yellow tape."

Great. I was going to get to tell one of Gail's friends that she was dead. I decided I'd better not yell it out. I jaywalked across the empty street, meeting the woman near the opposite curb.

"I'm sorry," I said, "I'm afraid I have bad news."

"Bad news? Has something happened to Gail?"

We stood there in the slush, and I told her about Gail. As far as I could see in the faint light, the woman looked shocked, but she didn't burst into tears.

"Good heavens!" she said. "Do they know who did it?"

That was a trickier question. I decided to level with her. "No," I said. "They're holding my stepson as a witness, but I'm convinced he didn't have anything to do with it."

The woman lifted her eyebrows. "And you are?"

I introduced myself and pointed out TenHuis Chocolade. "Are you an old friend of Gail's?" I asked.

"Not really. My name is Celia Carmichael. I'm the author of a book on chocolate molds."

"Oh, yes. Gail mentioned that a well-known expert on antique molds was coming to take a look at the Hart collection. But she hadn't said when she expected you."

"Are the molds in her shop?"

"I suppose so."

"I'd still like to get a look at them."

"That would be up to the police." It occurred to me that Celia Carmichael might be worth questioning. She hadn't been in Warner Pier the night Gail was killed, true, but she knew a lot about chocolate molds — if that was what our burglar had been after — and she had obviously talked to Gail recently.

Celia Carmichael sighed deeply. "I suppose I might as well drive on to Chicago.

There's probably no place to stay here. Gail said most of the inns and motels were closed."

"A few are open, and they're certainly not crowded. Besides, Chief Jones might want to talk to you."

The woman's eyes narrowed. "The police chief? Why would he be interested in me?"

"I expect he's interested in anybody who talked to Gail during the past few days," I said. "Come into the shop and I'll call him."

"I don't know anything about this. I barely knew Gail. I'll just drive on. I only came to see the molds."

"The molds may be involved in Gail's death."

"How could that be?"

"She had displayed some of them in our shop, and someone broke in there two nights ago. One of them was stolen."

"One was stolen? Only one?"

"My stepson apparently interrupted the burglar, and he ran out the back way."

"What would this have to do with the attack on Gail?"

"I consider it a strong possibility that the burglar came back for the rest of the molds, not knowing my aunt had insisted that Gail take them back to her shop. If Gail came out and confronted him, he might have killed her. Please wait while I call the chief."

Ms. Carmichael frowned. "It's late, and it will still take me more than three hours to get to Chicago. I'd better go on."

I was becoming more and more convinced that she should talk to the chief. "It will take you even longer if he asks you to drive back tomorrow. After I tell him you were here."

She moved toward her car. "Look, I hardly knew Gail."

"Then why were you coming to stay with her?"

"I wanted to see the molds."

"Well, apparently the molds are still there. Stick around and maybe the chief would let you in to look at them. Maybe he'd even want you to look at them. Give him an expert opinion."

"I get paid for that sort of work."

"Not if you're subpoenaed." I tried to say that confidently. I had no idea whether or not it was true. I wasn't even sure if you could subpoena a witness for questioning, or just to testify in court.

"I'll leave my card. If the chief wants to talk to me, he can call." She pulled off one of her gloves and started scrabbling through her purse.

I didn't want her to leave without talking

to the chief, but I was beginning to be afraid I was going to have to wrestle her into TenHuis Chocolade like a rodeo cowboy with a steer. "This is a small town," I said. "The chief can be here within a few minutes."

She handed me a card. "I don't want to wait."

I took the card, but I decided to try one final, desperate bit of arm-twisting. "I don't understand. You say you drove all this way to see the molds, but you won't wait ten minutes to ask the chief if he'd let you see them."

"Examining them would take longer than ten minutes. I was going to combine seeing the molds with a visit to Gail."

"But you said you and Gail weren't close friends."

"We weren't! I was only coming because . . . well, because she talked me into it."

I'd hit a nerve. "Was Gail paying you for an expert opinion?"

"No."

"Then why were you coming? And coming to spend the night? If your home base is Chicago, you could drive up, spend several hours checking the molds, then drive back the same day."

Celia Carmichael stood silently for a long

moment before she spoke again. "Look, apparently you knew Gail fairly well. Did she ever try to talk you into doing something you didn't want to do?"

"Well, she wanted my aunt to display the antique molds in her shop, and Aunt Nettie wasn't crazy about the idea."

"Did Gail give up?"

"No. She kept coming around. She brought the molds over. She was pushy."

"Well, that's the way she was about my coming by here. She found out I was going to a sale in Saginaw, and she became convinced I should drive back — way out of my way — and stop to see the molds. She just pushed and pushed until it was easier to come than to argue anymore."

"You seem like a fairly strong-minded person, Ms. Carmichael. It's surprising that Gail could push you around like that."

"She must have taken lessons from you! Is everybody in this town this aggressive?"

"If we need to be. Look, just walk across the street with me and wait — in our nice warm office — while I call the chief."

She glared.

I made one final push. "It will be even more annoying if I call the chief and he asks the state police to pick you up ten miles outside of town."

She gave an exasperated growl. But she walked across the street, toward TenHuis Chocolade.

I let us into the shop, then went into the office and called the police station. The dispatcher said she'd find the chief and send him over. Then I turned around and got my first good look at Ms. Carmichael.

She looked just like Gail Hess. That rabbit ran over my grave again.

Chapter 15

As soon as my shuddering had stopped I realized that my first impression wasn't really right. The resemblance between Gail and Celia Carmichael was superficial. But it was certainly startling.

Celia Carmichael was probably fifteen years older than Gail. But like Gail, her most striking characteristic was frankly fake red hair, cut short and tousled. Her features were nothing like Gail's, but the two women were much the same height. The down coat Celia wore was bright green. Gail's coat had been almost exactly like it.

I decided I'd better act like a hostess. "You must be frozen. Can I Gail you something?" I bit my lip. "I mean get you something?"

Ms. Carmichael was scowling. "I don't look like Gail," she said angrily. "She looked like me. She used to imitate everything I did."

"What's the saying? The sincerest form of flattery?"

"It may have been sincere, but it was extremely annoying. Every time I wore something to an antique event where Gail was, the next time I saw her, she'd have something like it. When I decided to become a redhead, I thought that would stop her. But, no! She got the same haircut and colored her hair exactly the same shade."

"I can see it would be embarrassing. How long had you known her?"

"Too long!" Celia Carmichael clamped her jaw shut. She sat down in one of our straight chairs, folded her arms and glared. She declined a chocolate and refused to take her coat off. She just sat there. I called Aunt Nettie to tell her I'd be home a little late. Then Celia Carmichael and I waited silently until Chief Jones came to the door.

I'd expected the chief to ask her to go down to the station, but he merely pulled up our second chair and talked to her in his casual way. I guess it worked. He did get a bit more information out of her.

I went into the office and pretended to work, but neither Chief Jones nor Celia Carmichael lowered their voices, so I could hear every word. The tale she told the chief was the same one she'd told me, and the chief responded with the same question I'd asked her.

"If you and Gail weren't friends, why did you agree to come here and spend the night with her?"

"Gail simply nagged me until I agreed to stay over. Plus, I did want to see the molds. She wanted me to advise her about selling them. They're quite famous, you know."

"No, I wasn't really aware of that."

"Oh, yes! Matilda Hart — I guess that this Olivia VanHorn is her daughter — was one of the earliest collectors of Americana. The chocolate molds were only a part of her collection. She snapped up butter tubs, pie safes, wonderful furniture — lots of real treasures — back in the thirties and forties, when most people thought that sort of thing was just junk. Some of her collection is on permanent loan to the Smithsonian."

The chief whistled, and Celia nodded firmly. "That was why the idea of Gail handling a Hart estate sale was so silly. She didn't have the contacts, the organization. The entire Hart Americana collection is going to be worth something over a million."

"But wasn't Gail talking about an auction of things here at the Hart-VanHorn summer cottages? The valuable stuff would have been at Mrs. VanHorn's permanent home."

"Perhaps that's what the VanHorns had in mind. But Gail was thinking big."

The chief mulled that over a moment. "You say she e-mailed you. Do you still have those messages?"

"I may have killed some of them, but most should still be there. My laptop's in the car. Or I could pull them off any computer with Internet access."

The chief asked if she could use my computer, and Celia logged on and pulled up her e-mail messages. She had a half dozen from Gail, and she allowed me to print all of them out for the chief. Celia was right about one thing: Gail had definitely been thinking big about the Hart-VanHorn sale.

All the messages were gushy, in typical Gail style, but the final one really outdid itself. But gush was all it contained; no facts.

"Celia!" it began.

> *You will NOT believe what has happened. I'm not saying anything until it's all settled, but I've stumbled across a MAJOR OPPORTUNITY. You'd never believe how much old glass — or even plastic — can be worth. ☺ LOL!!!!!*
>
> *Hopefully, I'll be able to TELL ALL when I see you.*
>
> *Bye-bye,*
> *Gail.*

Celia Carmichael swore she had no idea

what Gail had been talking about. "She was always full of big plans," she said. "But none of them ever came to anything. And I know nothing about glassware. If she'd stumbled across some exciting piece of glass, she wouldn't have been telling *me* about it."

"There's no indication that this had anything to do with the Harts and VanHorns," Chief Jones said.

"No. In fact, I interpreted it as meaning she'd come up with some new project, gotten some new bee in her bonnet, maybe forgotten all about the VanHorns. That's the way Gail operated."

That ended the conference. The chief told Celia she could go on to Chicago if she wanted, then mentioned the motels and a couple of B&Bs that were open. He escorted both of us outside. But I grabbed Celia for one more question before she drove off. "Do you know anything about why Gail left Indiana?"

"No!" She snapped the word out, got in her car and slammed the door. But as soon as she started the motor her window came gliding down.

"Anything I've heard about Gail and Indiana is gossip," she said. "Ask the Indiana Association of Antique Dealers for the real story. If the executive director doesn't know, she'll be able to find someone who does." Then Celia Carmichael drove off.

Chief Jones and I walked back across the street together.

"Are you sure I can't take Jeff home with me?" I said.

"Not tonight, Lee. But I've got a few more hours before I have to charge him. Maybe I won't have to." He patted my shoulder. "And I'll run down that Indiana Antique bunch first thing tomorrow."

His promise was cold comfort. I thought about it as I got into my van. Whatever had happened to Gail in Indiana, it seemed unlikely that it would have any connection with whatever had happened to her in Michigan. The chief drove away, and I left, too. I needed to get home and start calling the merchants along Peach Street, as I'd told Joe I would.

Then, when I was nearly to the end of the block, I saw the light, both literally and figuratively.

The light in this case was in a third-floor window over Mike's Sidewalk Café, at the corner of Peach Street and Fifth Avenue. And behind the lighted window I saw our mayor, Mike Herrera, in his apartment above one of the restaurants he owned. He was pulling down the window shades.

When Joe and I had divided up the block into river side and Orchard Street side, we'd ignored the cross street, less than half a block from TenHuis Chocolade. Some of those buildings also had apartments upstairs. In fact, two months earlier Mike Herrera had astonished his son and daughter-in-law by selling his house and moving himself into the apartment on the third floor of his building. Now one of his restaurants, the Sidewalk Café, was on the first floor, his office was on the second, and he lived on the third.

And at that moment Mike was in his apartment, just waiting for me to quiz him. I parked, jumped out of the van, ran across the sidewalk and began ringing the bell beside the inconspicuous door marked OFFICE – HERRERA ENTERPRISES. I knew that door led to the apartment as well as the office, because I'd seen Mike and Tony carrying a mattress up those stairs.

It took a few minutes, but I heard footsteps coming down the stairs. Mike opened the door. "Lee! My Texas friend. What are you up to tonight?"

"I'm trying to help my stepson, Mike. Can I ask you a question?"

"Of course, of course!" Mike escorted me

up one flight, opened the door to his office and turned on the lights. The office was a utilitarian affair of metal desks and filing cabinets. He waved me toward a chair that had apparently been rescued from one of the more downscale of his four restaurants.

Mike pulled up another chair, a straight chair with a metal frame and ripped upholstery. "What can I tell you?"

I swiftly explained that Jeff's lawyer had suggested that we question all the people who lived in Warner Pier's downtown apartments.

Mike shook his head. "I saw nothing of the murder, Lee. My bedroom is at the back, you see. I knew nothing about it until I was awakened by the commotion after one thirty. Then I saw the reflections of the lights, and I got out of bed and looked out the front windows."

I sighed. "I was afraid that would be the case. I guess that one thirty on a winter morning in Warner Pier is a good time to do something you don't want witnesses for. I hoped — well, we hope someone saw a car or something."

Mike's eyes widened slightly. "I didn't see a car. Not after one a.m."

For some reason he had emphasized the time. I decided to press him a little.

"Actually, Mike, Jeff says he first saw something suspicious about half an hour earlier, a little before one a.m. He had this silly girl, Tess, with him. He took her back to the motel where she was hiding out, then returned to check on the shop. That's when he found Gail's body. But Jeff says there was a prowler of some sort earlier."

"At one?" Mike shook his head. "No. I saw nothing at that time."

Mike's voice had become singsong, molding his Texas-Michigan accent into something with a Spanish sound. I'd noticed this about Mike before; when he got excited or upset, he reverted to the Spanish of his youth.

But what would Mike have to be upset about?

I decided not to say anything, but just to look at him expectantly, silently.

And in the silence, I heard a noise outside the office.

It was just a little creak, a shuffling sound. The back of my neck prickled for a second. I wondered if the sound had been my imagination.

Mike began to stammer. "I, I, I . . ."

If he hadn't reacted so guiltily, I might have convinced myself that the little noise I'd heard had merely been the old building creaking. But his confusion convinced me that someone was outside the office.

Suddenly I was crazy to see who was there.

I stood up. "Well, Mike, if you didn't see anything, I might as well get out of your hair." I whirled around and in three long strides I was at the office door.

"Lee!" Mike's voice was anguished.

I didn't say a word. The door was already ajar, and I simply snatched it wide open. The light from the office fell out onto the landing and splashed up the stairs.

And, there, partway up to the third floor, stood Mercy Woodyard. Mike's mom had changed from her business suit to a beautiful golden velvet robe and embroidered slippers.

She and I stared at each other. Then Mercy smiled and shrugged. "Hello, Lee," she said.

"Hello, Mercy," I said. I was embarrassed. After all, we'd all known that Mercy Woodyard and Mike Herrera had the occasional dinner date. If their relationship had progressed to a more intimate level, it was none of my business.

I wondered if Joe knew.

"I'd come down," Mercy said, "but there are no shades on the office windows, and

Mike and I still make some effort to be discreet. Maybe you and Mike better come upstairs."

Now I began to stammer. "No, no! I didn't mean to interrupt —"

"You're not interrupting anything more exciting than a drink before dinner," Mercy said. "Anyway, Mike is going to have to go to Hogan Jones with what he saw. No later than tomorrow."

I looked at Mike. He shrugged and motioned toward the stairway. We both followed Mercy up a floor.

Mike's apartment was not fancy — it featured mass-market furniture in styles and colors from around twenty years earlier — but it wasn't bad, particularly considering it belonged to a man who was largely immersed in his business affairs.

Mike waved me to a chair, gave a deep sigh and spoke. "It was around twelve forty-five," he said. "And it wasn't out on Peach Street or on Fifth Avenue. It was in the alley between Peach and Pear."

You can't see the alley between Peach and Pear from Mike's office or apartment. I started to point that out, but I thought about it again and snapped my jaw shut. The alley between Peach and Pear Streets runs behind Mercy Woodyard's office.

"It was a car," Mike said. "A small car. It was driving out the other end of the alley, onto Third Avenue."

"What kind of car? Could you see the license plate?"

"No, no, no!" Mike sounded exasperated. "I didn't get a good look at it. But . . ." He sighed. "But the left taillight was out."

That was about all I got out of Mike. He refused to guess at the make of the car. "Small. Yes, it could have been some kind of a sports car." And there had not been enough light for the color to be seen.

"It was dark," he said. "Maybe there was something wrong with it. The motor sounded funny."

Mike couldn't explain just what "funny" meant. The engine hadn't been missing or running roughly. He didn't think there had been anything wrong with the muffler.

"It just sounded different," he said.

But at least Mike had seen enough to link the mysterious car Jeff and I had seen the night of the burglary to the second crime. I'd already assumed that might be the case, but I was relieved to have some evidence.

Anyway, Mike promised to call Chief Jones the next morning. He walked me down the stairs and over to my van. As I opened the door, he spoke.

"Mercy didn't see the car," he said. "I'd like to keep her out of this."

"I won't mention seeing her," I said. "To anybody." I let him read the name Joe into that comment.

Mike nodded. "I love Warner Pier," he said. "But it sure can be . . . small." Mike was already back inside by the time I reached the corner.

I drove home. Aunt Nettie had made hot German potato salad and bratwurst — a sausage they really do right in Michigan — but none of us had much appetite. I left the dishes to her and Tess, perched at the end of the counter, and rehearsed how to tell Joe what Mike had told me without telling him his mother had been in Mike's apartment looking cozy. I had a feeling my tongue was about to twist into a knot. When I dialed Joe's number, I was almost relieved to get a busy signal.

I started phoning people who owned property in our block. If I couldn't remember who owned a particular building, Aunt Nettie could. Periodically I tried Joe again, but it was ten o'clock and both Aunt Nettie and Tess had moved into the living room before I caught Joe.

Joe said he had found that only one of the apartments on the Orchard side of the street was occupied, and the guy who lived in it hadn't been home. I described my conversation with Mike Herrera — omitting any mention of Mercy — with only one bobble. I stumbled over where Mike had seen the car, describing it as "the alley between Parch and Peer." Joe didn't laugh, but maybe that distracted him. Anyway, he didn't ask what the heck Mike Herrera had been doing in that particular alley shortly before one a.m.

The unusual sound of the motor interested him. "I wish I knew more about sports cars," he said.

"I could call my dad," I said, "but he mostly works on pickup trucks. He rarely gets a sports car in his garage."

"You don't see the real old-time sports cars much anymore," Joe said. "Not since the SUV became the macho car of choice. Actually . . ." He paused for a long moment. "Actually, that reminded me of something odd."

"What's that?"

"The most striking sports car I ever saw around Warner Pier . . . but that was fifteen years ago. I'm sure that car is long gone by now. But its motor sure did have a distinctive sound."

"What kind of car was it?"

"It was a 1968 MGB. A real classic. It used to park outside The Dockster in the summertime. Back when I was in high school."

I decided to cut off his reminiscences. "Well, like you say, that was a while back. If you haven't seen the car recently, we need to think about current cars."

"Yeah, that's probably right. It's funny though. That car belonged to Timothy Hart."

Chapter 16

Joe and I were both silent for a moment.

"That's an odd coincidence," I said. "But Timothy told me he hadn't driven in years."

"I know he lost his license. But I wonder if he sold the car around here."

"Even if he did — Joe, that's too far-fetched."

"Yeah. You're right. Though Timothy Hart — well, he's an odd duck. Tomorrow I'll ask Mom if she's insured any kind of a fancy sports car for anybody. Though she probably hasn't. A car like that would probably belong to some summer person, and it would be insured somewhere else."

Joe and I hung up, but I walked into the living room still wondering about Timothy Hart. Aunt Nettie was sewing a button on one of her white cook outfits, and I sat down beside her.

"Tell me about Timothy Hart," I said.

Her eyes grew even rounder than usual. "Every family has some sort of problem," she said.

"He described himself to me as an 'embarrassing limb' on the Hart family tree."

"That about sums him up, I guess. He's

256

never been in any trouble that I know of. Not around here."

"Does he have a profession?"

"I really don't know, Lee. I've never taken any particular interest in the Harts."

I laughed. "And one of them was a congressman. Warner Pier amazes me. There are so many rich and well-known people around here that they're almost invisible. The CEO of this company, the president of that university, the candidate for vice president — they all hang out here, and nobody even notices them! Nobody's even mentioned to me exactly where this Hart-VanHorn property is located."

"Oh, it's on our end of the shore road. That place with the big stone gates."

"With the line of Japanese lantern-type lamps? The white frame house close to the road and the Craftsman-type house back toward the bluff?"

"There are a couple of newer houses, too," Aunt Nettie said.

"Wow! I thought that was some sort of subdivision. Is it all one piece of property?"

"I believe so, but I'm not really sure. If you really want to know, you can pick me up a bottle of vitamins tomorrow."

"Vitamins?"

"The generic senior vitamins in the drug

department at the Superette." Aunt Nettie nodded. "That's the cheapest place to get them."

"The Superette drug department?" I looked at Aunt Nettie narrowly. Was she scolding me? The druggist at the Superette pharmacy was notorious as the biggest gossip in Warner Pier. Aunt Nettie did not approve of him, and she generally avoided his department. A reference to pharmacist Greg Glossop — known around Warner Pier as Greg Gossip — might be her way of letting me know I'd moved from friendly interest in my neighbors over the line into nosiness.

But Aunt Nettie was smiling. "If you really need to know more about the VanHorns, you might as well take advantage of our natural resources," she said. "Go straight to information central. Greg Glossop knows everything."

So when I walked into the Superette pharmacy department the next morning, I did so with Aunt Nettie's approval.

Greg Glossop bustled out from behind his high, glassed-off area, as I had thought he would. I knew he'd expect me to trade information, to give him the lowdown on Gail's death. I'd figured out a few harmless tidbits to use as bait, and I turned them over in my mind as he approached, almost rubbing his hands together in anticipation of the gossip goodies he was about to reap.

Glossop's comb-over failed to cover his scalp, and his lashes and brows were thin and colorless. This, added to his broad face and plump body, seemed to give him an abnormal amount of skin. As he greeted me, his round belly bounced with what could be excitement.

"Good morning, Lee. How are you coping with the current emergency?"

"Trying to hang in there, Mr. Glossop." I decided to get my licks in early. "I'm entirely convinced of my stepson's innocence, and I think Chief Jones is, too. I hope Jeff will be released today."

Glossop danced on his toes. "But if the chief doesn't think he did anything, why is he holding him at all?"

"Because Jeff found Gail's body. He stopped to try to help her, and now he's being held as a witness. It doesn't always pay to be a good Samaritan."

"Tsk, tsk." Greg Glossop was the only person I knew who actually clicked his tongue that way. "Then these wild stories about your stepson breaking into the shop . . ."

"Absolutely untrue," I said. "He could

have taken a key from Aunt Nettie or me if he wanted to get into the shop. Besides, Jeff knew there was nothing valuable there."

Glossop's eyes sparkled. "What about the Hart-VanHorn chocolate molds — weren't they supposed to be quite valuable?"

"They were taken back to Gail's shop after the burglary. And Jeff knew that. As far as I know, they're still over there. I hope they're returned to the VanHorns soon. Mrs. VanHorn has been very gracious. I certainly don't want to cause her more problems."

There. I'd introduced the VanHorns into the conversation. "Apparently she's had more than her share of problems in the past," I said.

"Ah, yes. The tragic death of her husband."

"Yes. And her brother seems to be a worry."

"Timothy Hart? Oh, yes. He's been in treatment several times."

"Treatment?" It didn't take much encouragement to keep Greg Glossop talking.

"Yes." Glossop lowered his voice. "Alcoholism. But he always falls off the wagon as soon as he's on his own. In recent years, I believe the family has simply given up."

"He's a pleasant person. Does he have a profession?"

"Luckily, he has a trust fund — or so I'm told. Actually, I've heard he graduated from college with high honors." Glossop leaned forward and dropped his voice even lower. "Perhaps he is a belated casualty of Vietnam. He served there with Congressman VanHorn."

"I didn't know either of them had served in Vietnam."

"The congressman had quite a record — not the Congressional Medal, but some very high honors. He and Timothy were in the same unit, or that's the story."

"So Timothy introduced his sister to her husband?"

"Oh, yes! Congressman VanHorn came from a working-class background. He went to law school on his military benefits. Of course, I gather he was always ambitious."

I didn't want to talk about Congressman VanHorn. I wanted to talk about his brother-in-law. "So the congressman had remained friends with Timothy?"

Glossop raised his eyebrows. "Drinking buddies."

"Oh!" I tried to sound startled.

Glossop nodded and winked. "Both of them were steady customers for the Superette's liquor department."

"Oh, my," I said. "Mrs. VanHorn *has* had problems." Back to Timothy, I reminded myself. Drunk or sober, Congressman VanHorn had been dead fifteen years. "Where does Timothy live in the winter?"

"He lives here year-round."

"At the Hart compound? But they're talking about selling it!"

Glossop's eyes sparkled. Apparently we'd reached the juicy bit. "Yes. I think there are three year-round houses and the summer cottage in the Hart-VanHorn compound, plus several garages, barns, and such. Timothy Hart has always lived in what they call the 'little house.' Now Olivia VanHorn is apparently planning to sell her brother's home to finance her son's political career."

"Perhaps Mr. Hart wants to leave. It must be lonely there in the winter."

"Oh, Timothy has lots of friends. He entertains a lot." In Glossop's mouth the word "entertains" took on a sinister meaning, hinting at drunken revels. I decided to ignore his implication.

"It can't be easy to live out there. It's almost outside the city limits, and Mr. Hart told me he no longer drives."

"Did he, now?"

"That's what he said."

"I know he says he doesn't have a driver's license." Glossop chuckled.

Now we were down to what I really

wanted to know. I decided it was time to be overtly nosy. "Does he drive? Even without a license?"

"I don't know that he ever leaves the property," Glossop said. "But there are fifteen or twenty acres down there, you know. Lots of drives and paths. I delivered a prescription to him last spring, and when I arrived he met me at the gate in that old sports car of his."

It was all I could do not to grab his arm and blurt out a question: Did it have a broken taillight? But even if Timothy's old car hadn't had a broken taillight last spring — nearly a year earlier — it might have one now. Besides, the last thing I wanted to do was alert Greg Gossip to the importance of what he had told me. He would spread the word all over town within minutes, and Timothy Hart's old sports car might disappear before Chief Jones could check on it.

So I did my best not to react to this news. Instead, I paid for Aunt Nettie's vitamins, discouraged Glossop from telling me a tidbit about someone I'd never heard of, told him the two pieces of news that I'd previously prepared, and left the Superette headed for the police station and ready to solve the murder of Gail Hess.

After all, we all knew Timothy Hart was an unstable character. He had given the molds to Gail for sale without telling his sister what he had done. Olivia had probably scolded him. He must have broken into TenHuis Chocolade to get them back, though I had no explanation of why he would have taken only one hard-to-reach mold unless Jeff had interrupted him from taking them all.

But Gail must have suspected Timothy. Perhaps he even tried to break into her shop and get the molds back. Timothy must have quarreled with her, lost his temper, picked up the baseball bat from the display in her shop, chased her down the street — and killed her. I felt sure I was right. I went straight to the police station.

I was rather let down when Chief Jones didn't see the situation quite the way I did.

"Now, Lee," he said, leaning back in his desk chair and stretching his long legs across the office. "Let's not let our imaginations run away from the facts."

"Has Mike Herrera been in here?"

"Yep. Mike was here early this morning. He told me about seeing some sort of sports car in the alley behind Gail's shop."

"And now we discover that Timothy VanHorn still has a sports car, or at least he still had it last spring. You've got to admit there's a possibility that he's involved."

"I'd have to see the car first."

"You're the law! Go look at it."

"I'd need permission from the property owners."

"I'd hate to give Timothy that much warning."

"It's either that or a warrant. And I think it very unlikely that any judge would issue a warrant based on a story from Greg Glossop."

I growled. Then I sat down and glared at the chief. Neither action seemed likely to change the situation. What could I do? An idea appeared in the back of my mind.

But before I could focus on it, the chief spoke. "I was going to tell you what I found out about Gail's problems in Indiana."

"What? Was she wanted?"

"Hardly. Apparently there was some discrepancy in the accounts of a big antique show she helped organize. But the Indiana antique dealers decided it would be too embarrassing to have a full investigation. Gail 'found' the missing money, and no charges were filed."

"Then she moved to Michigan. Does this tell you anything?"

The chief shrugged. "It tells me that I

might not want to elect Gail treasurer of anything."

"It tells me she might have a very unusual and creative idea of right and wrong."

"True. But Gail's not a suspect. She was the victim."

I thought about that for a minute. "How about that antique dealer who showed up last night?"

"Celia Carmichael? She's still here. The lab people didn't want anybody in Gail's shop until this afternoon, and Ms. Carmichael decided to wait and take a look at the chocolate molds."

I got up. "Well, what about Jeff?"

"Webb Bartlett has already called me," the chief said. "This is the day I've got to charge him or let him go."

"Can I see him?"

"Sure. He's bored out of his skull."

Neither of us mentioned that Jeff was lucky to be sitting in the holding cell at the Warner Pier Police Department, instead of the Warner County Jail.

Jeff didn't see it that way, of course. When the chief opened his cell and waved me inside, Jeff greeted me with a glare. "I've just got to get out of here," he said. "I didn't do anything!"

I sat down next to him on the bunk. "Unfortunately, we can't prove that, Jeff. But Webb Bartlett is working on it. And so am I. Plus, I'm trying to get hold of your mom and dad."

For the first time Jeff didn't snarl at me when I mentioned his parents. He looked down and blinked. Darn! He was just a kid. He needed his mother, for heaven's sake. I wanted to hug him.

So I did. I put my arm around his shoulder in a half hug, and Jeff didn't pull away. He dropped his head and stared at his feet.

"We're all doing our best for you, Jeff. Alicia Richardson is on the job. If anybody can find your folks, she will."

Jeff nodded. One or two wet drops appeared on the floor beside his feet. In a minute, I eased off on the hug, and Jeff took his glasses off and rubbed his eyes on his sleeve. "I guess I'd really like to see my folks," he said. His voice broke on the last word.

I promised him they would be there soon. "And maybe you'll already be out of here," I said.

We exchanged good-byes, and I got up and left. It wasn't going to do Jeff any good if I began crying, too. I collected my belongings and made it out of the police station and into the city clerk's office before I bawled like a baby. Pat VanTil gave me a tissue and the same kind of hug I'd given Jeff.

In a minute I pulled myself together. "I've got to get to work. Thanks for the emotional first aid, Pat."

Pat waved her hand. "Bring me a chocolate teddy bear next time you come, and I'll let you have a whole box of Kleenex."

I took a deep breath, walked out into the crisp winter sunshine — the temperature was up to twenty-eight — and went down to the shop. On the way I made up my mind about my next step. I was on the phone before I even took my boots and jacket off.

The phone was picked up after the fourth ring. "Vintage Boats."

"Joe, I hear that there's a big boat-storage building down at the Hart-VanHorn compound."

"So?"

"What'll you bet they've got some antique wooden speedboats down there?"

Joe thought a moment before he spoke. "You want to nose around at the Hart-VanHorn place."

"Yes. Will you help me?"

"I'll be on my way in fifteen minutes."

"I'll be ready."

"You can't go," Joe said.

268

CHOCOLATE CHAT

CHOCOLATE AND ROMANCE

Many mainstream novels use chocolate as a symbol or a plot device. Two major novels of the 1990s, both of which also became romantic films, were *Chocolat*, by Joanne Harris, and *Like Water for Chocolate*, by Laura Esquivel. Both use elements of magic realism; in them food makes magical things happen.

In *Chocolat* a young woman and her daughter come to a small French village just as Lent begins. The young woman, Vianne Rocher, opens a shop offering the most enticing chocolates the villagers have ever seen and plans a chocolate festival for Easter Sunday — much to the annoyance of the puritanical village priest. Vianne's chocolate becomes a symbol of everything pleasurable about human life, contrasting with the narrow life espoused by the priest, Francis Reynaud.

Like Water for Chocolate tells the story of the youngest sister in a Mexican family, Tita, who is told that she can never marry — despite her great love for her sweetheart,

Pedro — but must stay home to cook and take care of her mother. The water of the title refers to a method of melting chocolate, and the hot water needed becomes a metaphor for sexual excitement. The food Tita cooks changes in magical ways the lives of those who eat it.

Chapter 17

I started to argue, but Joe kept talking.

"First, Lee, you don't buy boats. Second, Warner Pier — and that includes Timothy Hart — knows about your determination to get Jeff released. There's no way anybody would believe you'd stop in the middle of that effort to go look at antique boats. Not just out of curiosity. Even Tim's pickled brain would figure out that you were up to something the minute you got out of the truck."

Joe shut up then, without mentioning that there were a couple of more reasons I shouldn't go, but I thought of them. Third, I had accepted a date with Hart VanHorn, even though the date had been cancelled. So if I casually showed up at Hart's house in the company of Joe Woodyard, it was going to look kind of funny. Rude? Brazen? I wasn't sure, but it was going to look odd.

Fourth, Joe still didn't want to be seen in public with me. That reason rankled, but since Joe was doing me a favor I wasn't in a position to argue about it.

So I breathed deeply a couple of times, but I didn't object out loud.

"Okay," I said. "As long as you understand what you're really looking for."

"A 1968 MGB with a broken taillight."

I had to be content with that. I hung up, reminding myself that Joe might not even get on the property. There was no real reason any member of the Hart-VanHorn clan should allow an unauthorized visitor.

So until noon I stared at the computer screen, pretending to work, and chewed my nails. The hands of the clock on the workroom wall had just reached the twelve when the phone rang.

It was Joe. "You want to see a movie?" he said.

"A movie?"

"A video. I took Mom's camera along when I went boat scouting."

"Where are you?"

"Mom's office. Come on over."

I picked up a couple of papers, hoping to look as if I had business with Mercy Woodyard, put on my jacket, and jaywalked across the street. Joe beckoned me into his mother's private office, then closed the door.

"Did you have any trouble getting on the property?" I said.

"No. Poor old Timothy was glad to see a friendly face." Joe took my jacket and pointed me toward a leather couch. After we'd both taken a seat, he gestured at the television set with a remote and punched the button to start the VCR. Immediately an overall view of the Hart-VanHorn compound appeared on the screen.

I'd driven past the compound dozens of times, of course. I'd walked past it on the lake side, for that matter, so I'd probably seen the Hart-VanHorn houses from the beach. If you have lakeshore property — which is worth a small fortune per square foot around Warner Pier — the normal thing to do is build a house overlooking the beach, a house with picture windows and a deck or porch designed for keeping an eye on the kids as they build sand castles, and for watching the sunset, or for simply sitting and looking at the water, the trees, and the sand. If you have enough land for garages, boathouses, and storage sheds, those can go up near the road, where they won't obstruct the view of the water.

The Hart-VanHorn property followed this pattern. A big barnlike building was near the road, and this, plus some huge trees, meant the houses were largely hidden from passersby. Also, this was the first winter I'd spent in Michigan, so I'd never seen the property with no leaves on the trees. Now, with Joe's video, I had a clearer idea of the layout.

The compound had two sets of stone gates, one where the blacktop drive went in and one where it came out, and the video showed that a snowplow had cleared the drive. The blacktop looped through the property, passing each of the four houses.

Easiest to spot was the "little house," the one Greg Glossop had said was the permanent home of Timothy Hart. It was too close to the road to have a view of the lake, and it was an L-shaped white clapboard 1890s farmhouse — a smaller version of the one Aunt Nettie and I live in. It probably had a kitchen, living room, and a dining room downstairs and two bedrooms upstairs. One room, which I was willing to bet was the living room, stuck out as a one-story wing, and the house was sure to have a Michigan basement, which has stone or concrete walls and a sand floor. It must have central heating, or Timothy wouldn't be likely to live in it year-round, but it didn't look as if it had been modernized in any other way. It was probably the first house the Hart family had built on the property. It might well have already been there when they acquired the land.

Behind it, closer to the lake, was a low

bungalow of stone and shingled siding, a prime example of the Arts and Crafts style and a generation younger than the farmhouse. Its front door faced the drive, so its side was toward the lake. The video showed glimpses of a large porch on that side, a porch that was now shuttered for the winter. Beyond the porch there seemed to be a deck or a patio, and I thought I saw a chimney out there, evidence of a built-in barbecue pit. This house must be the one Greg Glossop said was not winterized. It must have been the cat's meow in the twenties and thirties.

Beside it, and squarely facing the camera, were two houses designed to present blank walls to the road. I was sure, however, that their back walls would be entirely of glass.

One house was brick and one stone, and both had nearly solid front walls — only one or two windows — centered with heavy, grandiose doors that wouldn't have been out of place on medieval castles. In fact, the front door of the stone house was approached over an ornamental bridge that crossed a miniature moat, almost like a drawbridge. The house looked as if it could have been held against an army. But both houses were huge, twice the size of the bungalow and four or five times the size of the farmhouse. They both had a 1970s look.

It was a very impressive layout.

"Wow!" I said. "Have all those houses been sitting empty for fifteen years?"

"Except for Timothy's."

"Seems as if they'd rent them out or something. Who built the stone and the brick ones?"

"I'd guess that the VanHorns built the stone one when Hart's dad began to have political ambitions. Anyway, that seems to be the one Mrs. VanHorn and Hart are staying in. Mom says the brick house was built by Olivia VanHorn's sister, but she moved to California and quit using it a long time back. I don't know who used the bungalow. Olivia and Timothy's parents, probably."

"Are there boathouses?"

"Nothing down on the lake. There's a big storage shed near the road. See, the red barn at the left."

"The red barn? Did you get a look inside?"

"Sort of."

We continued to watch the video. Now the scene shifted. Timothy was opening his front door.

"How did you hide the camera?" I said.

"I just tucked it under my arm and left it running."

On the video Timothy was greeting Joe effusively and inviting him in. Joe answered, telling Timothy he bought and restored wooden speedboats, and that he was scouting for likely projects.

"Well, there's my dad's old boat, over in the barn," Timothy said. "I don't know if Olivia wants to sell it. It hasn't been in the water in twenty years."

"Could I take a look at it? Maybe get some pictures? Then if you and Mrs. VanHorn put it on the market later, I'll know what we're talking about."

"I'll go back to the kitchen and get the keys and my jacket."

Joe turned around while he waited, and the video camera swept around the compound. I found myself admiring the landscaping. The snow might have covered the flower beds, but it couldn't hide the hedges, the trees, the stone walls, the tennis court. It was a beautiful property.

Apparently Joe had thought so, too, because when Timothy reappeared in a heavy red Pendleton jacket, Joe commented on the compound. "The property is in top-notch shape. Do you take care of all this?"

Timothy gave a tipsy laugh. "I'm not what you'd call handy. But I'm in charge of making sure the key's in its usual hiding place when the handyman and landscapers come."

Joe followed Timothy's red jacket across the snow. They seemed to be breaking a trail around the end of the tennis court that centered the compound. In a few minutes they reached the second part of the drive — the exit, I guess you'd call it — coming out on the blacktop near the big storage building that resembled a red barn.

"This hasn't been opened this winter," Timothy said. "We may find a squirrel's nest."

"Don't Hart and Mrs. VanHorn park over here?"

"No, there's a garage in the basement of the stone house. The barn door is around at the side."

Timothy fumbled with a lock and opened a small door. The video went dark as Joe entered the building, then brightened as Timothy turned on a glaring overhead light and the camera's automatic lens adjusted. I leaned forward, eager to see what was inside the barn.

For a moment it looked like a morgue. Then I realized that everything inside was shrouded in canvas dust covers. Timothy led the way past a couple of hulking objects; one obviously was a boat, and the other might have been anything. Then he pulled the canvas back to reveal a mahogany prow.

"This was Dad's boat," he said. "It's a Chris-Craft. He was very proud of it. It was 'postwar,' if that means anything to you. He got it when he came back from World War Two."

Joe evidently laid the camera down on the lumpy item next to the Chris-Craft, because I could see him and Tim folding the cover back. "It's a beauty," Joe said. "A seventeen-footer, I think. One of the first ones made after the war."

At that point the conversation deteriorated to a discussion of boats. Joe raved about the Chris-Craft. Timothy preened. They moved away from the camera, and I couldn't hear much and got only intermittent looks at the two of them.

"The Chris-Craft is the only wooden motor boat here," Timothy said. "Of course, there's our mother's canoe."

Joe gasped. "Where is it?"

He did remember to pick up the camera then, and he swung it around the barn, which seemed to be about the size of a four-car garage.

The canoe was up in the rafters, upside down. "A bit hard to get it down, I'm afraid," Timothy said.

"No need," Joe said. He aimed his camera up at the canoe.

Then a new voice was heard on the tape. It was muffled, but I understood the words. "What are you two doing?"

Joe swung around, or at least the video camera did, and a figure appeared silhouetted in the open door. It was just a fuzzy outline for a moment, as it moved inside and closed the door. Then it became Olivia VanHorn.

She looked as much the grand dame as ever, wearing her casual mink jacket and a wool scarf — I was willing to bet it was cashmere — draped around her head. She approached the camera, smiling graciously. "Tim? What are you doing out here in the cold?"

"Just showing Joe here Dad's old boat," Tim said. "I didn't think you'd mind." Suddenly he seemed to lack confidence.

"It's a honey," Joe said. "I'm Joe Woodyard, Mrs. VanHorn. I was in law school with Hart. But now I'm restoring antique power boats."

"Oh, yes. Your mother has an insurance agency."

The social chitchat went on between Joe and Olivia VanHorn for several minutes. Neither of them made any reference to Joe's ex-wife, though Olivia obviously knew who Joe was. Joe kept his attention on the postwar Chris-Craft, enthusiastically telling Olivia and Timothy what a nice boat it was.

"If you decided to put it on the market," he said, "I'd definitely want to make an offer."

He had tucked the camera under his arm again, so I couldn't see Olivia as she replied. But her voice sounded slightly sardonic. "If you really want to make an offer, Joe, shouldn't you be telling us it isn't worth very much?"

Joe laughed. "Oh, I think you're smart enough to get an appraisal before you sell it, Mrs. VanHorn. I don't think you'd be easy to cheat. Are there other old boats around? Mr. Hart showed me the canoe."

"No, there's the ski boat, but it's less than twenty years old."

"Then it's probably fiberglass. Not my thing. However —" Joe gave a boyish chuckle "— Mr. Hart, you may not know it, but you had a piece of fiberglass that caused me to commit the sin of envy in a big way, back when I was in high school."

Timothy Hart gave a snort. "I can't believe I ever aroused envy in anyone."

"I assure you that every guy at Warner Pier High School envied you that sports car you had. An MGB with a fiberglass top."

Joe moved the camera, and now I could see Timothy's face cloud up. He looked stricken. But I couldn't tell if he was feeling sorrowful or angry.

He spoke. "The MGB. . . ." Then he stopped and glanced at his sister. "I l-l-lost the MGB. . . ."

Olivia VanHorn jumped in to smooth over an awkward situation. "Tim doesn't drive these days," she said. "In fact, Tim, I was making a grocery list, and I wondered if you wanted anything."

Joe was being dismissed. He and Timothy replaced the canvas cover on the Chris-Craft. He swung the video camera around as he was escorted out, but the chitchat became innocuous. I was barely listening as Olivia herded the two men back toward the door.

Then I saw it.

It was the lumpy thing that had been next to the Chris-Craft. Compared to the boats, it was small, maybe ten feet long and four feet high. Its canvas cover shrouded it completely — except for one corner.

Joe probably didn't see it himself, but the camera, now held down at his side, picked up the key detail.

A ski. A ski just a few feet long. And above

it, a shiny purple surface.

"Joe! Stop the tape!" I shrieked the words.

"What's wrong?"

"Look! Look under that cover. It's purple!"

Joe nodded. "Yeah. I see it."

"Joe, it could be that snowmobile. The one that chased me."

Joe and I looked at the flickering video. "It's hard to believe," he said. "I can see Timothy arguing with Gail. But why would he chase you with a snowmobile?"

My heart was pounding. Suddenly I covered my eyes. "Turn it off. That snowmobile — it was horrible! I don't want to think about it."

The next thing I knew Joe had taken me in his arms. "It's okay," he said. "I'm not going to let anything hurt you."

I got a big handful of his flannel shirt, and I hung on for dear life. I didn't say anything. I buried my head in Joe's shoulder, and I just sat there and trembled.

It was wonderful to have Joe hold me, to have him act as if he cared about what I was going through. It didn't matter if he wouldn't take me out in public. I didn't care if he was mixed-up and didn't know what he wanted, even if he ran for cover every time he saw someone who looked like a tabloid reporter. His arms were so comforting that I could have sat there all day.

I don't know why I didn't cry. I think I simply didn't dare — if I'd started I wouldn't have stopped for days.

In a few minutes I sort of pulled away and said, "I guess that I've been so worried about Jeff that I just haven't reacted to being chased by that snowmobile. I can't break down yet, Joe. But I'm beginning to think this mess will never end."

He pulled me closer and kissed my forehead. "It's going to end, and it's going to end happily. And happy or unhappy, you're going to handle it."

Then he kissed me. On the mouth this time.

As I said, Joe and I had mostly had a telephone relationship. Until our necking party a few days earlier, he'd only kissed me a few times, and those kisses had been — well, exploratory.

This one was the real thing. He was kissing me, and I was kissing him, and neither of us wanted to stop. If the phone hadn't rung, I don't know what would have happened next.

But it did ring, and it distracted both of us enough that Joe relaxed his grip and quit kissing me, and I moved away slightly. So we were looking fairly decent when Joe's mom rapped on the door, then opened it and looked in.

"It's for you, Lee," she said. "It's your aunt."

I took a deep breath, thanked her, and went to the extension phone on her private desk.

"Lee!" Aunt Nettie sounded excited. "A woman called from Dallas. She said she works for Richard Godfrey Associates."

"Alicia Richardson?"

"Yes, that was the name. She said to tell you she finally got hold of Jeff's mom and dad."

"Wonderful! Where are they?"

"I don't know that, but she said to tell you they are on their way to Michigan. They're flying into Chicago this afternoon."

Chapter 18

My first reaction of relief at the prospect of handing over the responsibility for Jeff quickly turned to dread. I hadn't seen Rich in two years; I didn't want to face him when he'd just learned that his son might be accused of murder. I had a feeling that he was going to think the whole thing was my fault.

I saw only one flimsy hope. "Wouldn't it be wonderful," I said, "if this case is solved and the right person is under arrest by the time Rich and Dina get here?"

"That doesn't look likely," Joe said. "We haven't even figured out what was really behind all this, and I don't think Hogan Jones knows either."

I sat down again. "That's right, I guess. Though obviously the burglary — the one Jeff stopped Tuesday night — had something to do with those molds. After all, the molds were at TenHuis Chocolade Tuesday night and at Gail's Wednesday, when she was attacked."

I'd almost forgotten Mercy Woodyard was standing in the doorway. "I haven't figured out why anybody would want to steal those molds," she said. "They look pretty ordinary to me."

"They're worth quite a bit," I said. "And they made a nice decoration for the shop." Then I realized something. "Mercy, you were never in the shop while the molds were on display. When did you see them?"

"They're over in Gail's storeroom in a box. I looked at a few of them when I was over there this morning."

"Is the shop no longer considered a crime scene?"

Mercy shrugged. "The tape's still up out front, but the chief told Nancy Warren she could have access to her sister's property. Nancy gave me a key, so I could keep an eye on things until she gets through the funeral and gets a lawyer to settle the estate. I let Celia Carmichael in and checked the place over earlier."

I sat up straight. "Do you think the chief would mind if I took a look?"

"Apparently not. I'll get the key and take you over."

Joe went with us, and we ducked under the yellow tape and went in Gail's front door. Going into the shop felt spooky, but there was actually nothing gruesome about the scene. The state police crime lab had taken anything gory away — if there'd been anything. After all, the chief thought Gail confronted her killer in the shop, because that's where the baseball bat had been, but he believed she was chased across the street before the deathblows were struck. Or maybe Gail saw someone at TenHuis Chocolade, decided to confront them, and took the baseball bat with her.

"The molds are in the back room," Mercy said.

Joe and I followed her through the shop, which was the junky type of antique store. Everything was jumbled together and nothing looked too valuable. In Jeff's mom's shop in Dallas only a few pieces were out, and each one was carefully displayed, often with accent lighting and carefully draped backdrops. Gail's shop was set up to make the buyer think each piece was a bargain; Dina's shop was designed to make buyers think they were getting something rare and worth the prices she charged. I guess I prefer the more carefully arranged shops; the clutter in shops like Gail's makes me feel as if I'm about to bump into something or step on something or break things in some other way.

But I got through the shop without demolishing the Depression glass, upending an urn, or tripping over a table. As Mercy entered the storage room, she pointed to a huge cardboard box. Bold letters on the side, made with a black marking pen, identified its contents: "Hart-VanHorn collection."

Inside the box, a lot of bits and pieces were tumbled together.

"What a mess," I said. "This is obviously junk from the cellar. If getting a box like this on consignment made Gail think she was going to get to run a sale for an estate like the Hart-VanHorn compound, she was the most optimistic person I ever ran into."

"This stuff may have been tossed in the box like junk," Joe said, "but apparently the molds were in the lot." He pulled a couple of the molds out of the top of the box. "Here, lay these out on that worktable, and we'll look at them."

Mercy went back to her office, and Joe handed the molds to me. They'd been wrapped in tissue paper, and I unwrapped them and laid them in rows on Gail's table. Joe heaped the other items from the box on the floor.

I examined each mold as I put it out. The bears we'd had in the shop were on top, of course. There were seated bears and standing bears and a walking bear and an acrobatic bear who wore a funny hat and was apparently about to do a cartwheel. But there was no mean-looking bear with a harness on its snout. That one was still missing.

"It was the rusty mold, too," I said. "And Gail said it wasn't the most valuable bear in the collection. That really mystifies me."

"Huh?" Joe said.

"Just thinking out loud."

Next Joe handed me other animals. There were dogs — a funny little Scottie, a dachshund, a comical bulldog. There were elephants doing tricks, elephants trumpeting, stylized elephants and realistic elephants. Then came birds — storks, ducks, even a peacock. These were followed by dozens of molds of children — Kewpie dolls, children dressed as brides and bridegrooms, a New Year's baby.

"I seem to be down to the Santas and Easter bunnies now," Joe said.

"I had no idea how extensive the collection was," I said. "I guess it nearly filled up that big box."

"There was a lot of old kitchen stuff in there, too. I guess it's worth something, because I saw similar things out in the shop as we walked through. And there are a few pieces of wood at the bottom. And some broken glass."

Joe handed the rest of the molds up to me, and I kept laying them out in rows and examining them. They were fascinating.

And they were all in perfect condition, though some had traces of chocolate, as Aunt Nettie had said they should. Even after being stuck in a basement — ever since Congressman VanHorn died, according to Timothy — there was no sign of rust on any of them.

"That's so weird," I said.

"What is?" Joe was bent over, with his head down in the box. His voice was muffled, though I heard the occasional thump, and I decided he must be digging the pieces of wood out of the bottom of the box.

"All these molds are in perfect condition," I said. "Or I think they are."

"So?"

"The one the burglar took wasn't. In perfect condition, I mean. It was rusted."

"What are they made of? Tin?"

"They're tin-plated. I think the basic metals varied, according to the time they were made. But the outer surfaces were tin."

"Tin will rust. Or a tin can will."

"Yes, but this was a valuable collection. And judging by the condition of these molds, it had been carefully preserved. But that one mold was rusted. That particular one had been treated carelessly."

"So had this. Look."

I turned around. Joe was still kneeling on the bare wooden floor of Gail's storeroom, but he had laid some bits of wood out on the floor in front of him. He had arranged them into some sort of order, but they were still just scraps of wood with hunks of broken glass sticking out here and there. In the center were two small brass knobs.

"They were doors!" I said.

"Right," Joe said. "The stuff in the bottom of the box seems to be the glass doors of a china cupboard."

I knelt beside Joe and gently touched the glass. "It was a nice piece, too. That glass was curved. I don't know too much about old furniture, but I think china cupboards with curved glass are often considered quite valuable. Lots of people want them."

"Well, somebody didn't want this one." He fingered a two-inch gouge. "I'd guess that this had been broken up with an ax."

"That's impossible! Even if you wanted to get rid of something like this, you wouldn't break it up with an ax."

Joe shrugged. "The rest of it probably is in some Hart-VanHorn basement. The doors were in a dozen pieces."

We stared at the doors. Then I stood up. "Well, I've looked at all the molds, and you've assembled the doors. And I'm more mystified than ever."

Joe began to put the pieces of wood back in the box. "I left the broken glass in the box," he said. "I wonder what Gail made of it."

"Do you think she saw it?"

"She must have, if she dug all the molds out."

"I wonder what happened to the china cupboard?"

"If you have a live-in alcoholic, Lee, anything can happen to your furniture."

"You think Timothy got drunk and broke up the furniture?"

"Something sure happened to that china cupboard. And I don't think it was hit by a car."

"I guess we could ask the chief if there's any record of a police call out there."

Joe looked at me. He didn't need to say a word.

"Okay," I said. "I admit that Olivia would let Timothy smash up the entire house before she'd call the cops."

We looked through the rest of the shop, but we saw nothing worth getting excited about. It would have taken an army of technicians to do a complete search.

A smashed china cabinet and a rusty

mold. What significance could they possibly have?

I started for the door, then turned to Joe. "Has Timothy always lived at Warner Pier?"

"I don't think so, but Mom will know. Why?"

"I agree that Olivia VanHorn would never have called the cops on him. If he lived in Grand Rapids or Ann Arbor or someplace, though, and if he has a history of breaking up furniture or doing other violent things, somebody else might have called the cops about him sometime."

"You could ask the chief to check."

I went back to TenHuis Chocolade feeling let down. I finally decided it was because I liked Timothy Hart. I didn't want him to be guilty. But I felt that the VanHorn collection just had to be connected with the burglary, and hence with Gail's murder. And Timothy seemed to be the only Hart or VanHorn unstable enough to get into such a mess. Now that his "drinking buddy," Congressman Vic VanHorn, was gone.

It was a real puzzle.

When I got to the shop, the situation there was even more depressing. Aunt Nettie and Tess were in the office, sitting in my two visitors' chairs. Tess was crying.

I hovered at the door, wondering if I

should stay out, but Aunt Nettie motioned for me to come in.

"Tess is fearful about what may happen after Jeff's folks get here," she said.

"I feel so selfish," Tess said. "I know Jeff needs their help. But I'm so afraid!"

I pulled my chair around the desk, and I sat down beside Tess. Now she had Aunt Nettie on one side and me on the other. She was effectively boxed in.

"Tess, why are you so frightened of Jeff's parents?" I had a sudden thought. "Tess, you're not pregnant, are you?"

"Oh, no!" It was almost a wail. "Jeff and I don't sleep together. I mean, I've never slept with *anyone!*"

Aunt Nettie patted her hand. "It's hard for us to understand, Tess. Obviously, something very frightening happened to you in Texas. But you and Jeff don't seem to be involved in any sort of crime."

Tess shook her head vigorously.

"Your problems seem to be more serious than something like grades."

Tess nodded.

"Yet you ran away from college, and you seem terrified that someone from Texas will find you. You're even afraid of Jeff's parents, whose help he needs very much right now."

"I know. That's why I feel so guilty. But I'm so afraid they'll find me!"

"Jeff's parents?"

"No! My parents! My dad's boss."

Aunt Nettie patted again. "Why are you so frightened of your father's boss?"

"It's not him." She sobbed two more sobs, looked around the office desperately — as I said, we had her boxed in — and finally spoke. "It's my dad's boss's son!"

Tess seemed to feel that she'd explained everything that was necessary, but I was still clueless. Luckily, Aunt Nettie was beginning to get a glimmer.

"Tess," she said, "did you date your dad's boss's son?"

"Only once. Only because I thought my dad wanted me to."

Now I was beginning to get the picture, too. "He came on a little too strong, huh?"

"Oh, yes. He parked way out in the back of the Wal-Mart parking lot. It was really late. I barely got out of the car. I had to walk home."

"And then he wouldn't leave you alone."

She nodded miserably. "He kept calling. I told him I wouldn't tell his dad, but he kept calling me anyway. He kept driving past the house. I thought that when I went away to college he'd forget about it, but he didn't!

He came over to Dallas and got a job. He used to cruise around the campus."

"Did he threaten you?"

Another nod. She pulled her arm out of the sweatshirt she wore and pulled up the sleeve of her T-shirt. "The marks are almost gone," she said.

True, the bruises on her upper arm were faint, but they were there. And they definitely had been made by fingers.

Aunt Nettie hugged her, and I patted her shoulder.

And another part of the picture came into focus. "You came up here to get away from this guy, right?"

Tess nodded.

"But you were afraid he'd follow you. Am I right again? Maybe even afraid he'd kill you?"

Another miserable nod.

"Tess, that morning when Joe and I came to the motel — were you afraid Jeff had killed him?"

This time she sobbed. When she could talk again, she said, "I knew it didn't make sense. But I've been scared for so long. It seemed like Jeff was the only person who would help me. If he tried to protect me . . ." Then the tears really ran.

Aunt Nettie hugged her.

"Tess, you know there are laws against this kind of thing," I said. "You could send that guy to jail."

"But my dad! His job! Wally says he can get my dad fired."

"If he does, his dad will be very sorry," I said. Maybe I spoke more firmly than I should have, but I felt that I had to calm Tess's fears. "There are laws about that, too, Tess. If this guy's dad fires your father because you won't have sex with his son, your dad could sue the pants off him. He could wind up owning his boss's business."

Tess's eyes got big. "But my dad would never sue anybody!"

"You'd be surprised what dads will do when their girls are threatened," I said. "You haven't told your parents all this, have you?"

She shook her head.

"That's the first thing you must do. Can you call them now?"

"No! I mean, both of them would be at work."

Aunt Nettie spoke gently. "You must call them tonight, Tess. I'm sure they're worried sick." She hugged Tess again. "Let them have an opportunity to back you up."

Tess still looked miserable, but she

seemed calmer. After a little more reassurance, she left the office, telling Aunt Nettie she'd go back to work as soon as she had washed her face.

"What do you think?" I said. "Does that explain why Tess has been in such a state? Why she ran away from college?"

"It certainly seems to explain it, Lee. Violence against women is such a hard problem to deal with. A lady named Rose worked here for a while. She used to come in all black-and-blue. She finally got the nerve to leave her husband, but she wound up having to move clear across the country to get away from him. Hiding out sometimes becomes the only defense." She sighed. "It's really sad."

I had tossed my jacket on a chair when I'd come in. I stood up and started to hang it up on the coat tree in the corner of the office. I heard a clunk, and looked down to see a key on the floor.

"Rats! I forgot to hand Joe the key to Gail's shop. I'll have to take it over to Mercy." I put the jacket back on and stomped out the front door, unhappy at the interruption.

As I crossed the street I noticed that Joe's truck was still sitting in front of his mom's office. When I went inside Mercy beckoned me into her private office. Joe was in there, too. He was on the telephone. He nodded, but he didn't speak into the phone. I decided he was on hold.

"I forgot to give the key back," I said. "Plus there's been a new development, though I'm not sure that it means anything."

I repeated Tess's story. Halfway through it Joe turned his back on us and began to speak into the telephone receiver.

I kept talking. "It's hard to believe that Tess would be so scared she ran away from college, instead of telling her parents and getting a lawyer."

"Tess is just a young, inexperienced girl," Mercy said. "And some women never get up the nerve to confront these situations. It can become an insurance problem — health coverage, even death benefits and liability. That's one of the reasons our state organization took it on as a project."

I edged toward the door. I didn't have time to listen to a speech. "I know it took a lot of women speaking out to begin to make a difference."

"Oh, yes! Violence against women was definitely a crime that was hidden away — along with insanity, incest, and even cancer. But it covers all segments of society from the poorest to the richest. Why, a few years back the ex-wife of the CEO of a blue-chip company wrote a book describing years of abuse by her husband. She would hide in the closet when she heard him come in from a board meeting, afraid he'd come upstairs and beat her!"

"That's terrible."

"Even today it's hard to get legislators involved. That's why we were so lucky to get the support of Hart VanHorn." She smiled. "I guess most of us fail to get interested in other people's problems unless we have some sort of vested interest."

I stared at her. "Are you saying Hart has personal experience with wife beating?"

Mercy gave a little chuckle. "He's never been married, so I don't think he's ever beaten anybody or been beaten. But he speaks very emotionally about the issue, and the episodes he describes from his years as a prosecutor . . ."

I was still staring at Mercy. Hart had a personal interest in spousal abuse. He had an alcoholic uncle. And according to Greg Glossop — who occasionally was right, darn him! — his father had been a drinking buddy to that uncle. Could Hart's father have been a wife beater?

But that was silly. Who would have the

courage to abuse a woman with a personality as strong as Olivia VanHorn's? Plus, Olivia was old money. Why would she put up with a situation like that? She could walk out. Olivia was afraid of nothing.

Well, she was afraid of one thing. The conversation I'd eavesdropped on had revealed that. She was afraid of damaging Hart's political career. Had she been just a little too emphatic when she denied that there was any scandal in Hart's past?

Before I could complete the thought, Joe spoke. He had hung up the phone. "The librarian's going to fax something you might want to see."

"The librarian?"

He nodded impatiently. "Yeah, after you wondered if Timothy had ever been accused in any sort of assault — a barroom brawl or anything — I decided Webb might be able to find out."

"Jeff's lawyer?"

"Sure. Webb's one of these guys who knows everybody, and Mom said that Timothy lived in Grand Rapids before he moved down here full-time."

I was still confused. "Webb knows a librarian?"

"At the newspaper. He called down there and got me in touch with the person who's in charge of the archives. She's faxing me a story about Timothy. It seems he once punched out his brother-in-law at a Grand Rapids banquet."

Chapter 19

I was definitely interested in that, so I hung around until Mercy's fax began to groan. A client came in, and Mercy had to go back into the front office, but Joe and I stood over the machine, reading as a copy of a newspaper clipping slid out. It wasn't a long story, but the headline spread over three columns:

CONGRESSMAN ATTACKED AT BANQUET;
BROTHER-IN-LAW SHOUTS THREATS

The date was only a few weeks before Vic VanHorn had died. The gist of the story was that U.S. Representative and Mrs. VanHorn had been attending a political dinner, and Timothy Hart had been seated next to his sister. The word "drunk" was never used, but witnesses reported that just before the baked Alaska was served, Timothy got to his feet, went around his sister, and accosted her husband, "calling him names." At first he demanded that Van-Horn accompany him outside. When the congressman refused, he threw a punch. Bystanders pulled Timothy away from the table and removed him from the dining room. Timothy continued to yell, but the newspaper did not quote any of his shouts.

The congressman apparently had not been seriously hurt.

"Wow," I said. "I bet Olivia was frosted."

"There's another sheet coming," Joe said.

He pulled it off the fax machine. This headline was much smaller, probably one column. It had run the day after the first story:

CONGRESSMAN
ASKS LENIENCY
FOR OLD FRIEND

That story reported that Representative VanHorn told the prosecutor that he had not been injured and pled the case of his brother-in-law, citing him as a Vietnam veteran. Since the congressman did not want to file charges, the prosecutor had agreed to release Timothy Hart, "one of the heirs to the Hart food-processing fortune."

And that was all the *Grand Rapids Press* had in its files on Timothy Hart.

"They hushed that up in a hurry," Joe said.

"I can see why," I said. "I guess Chief Jones ought to see these clippings. This definitely shows that Timothy has a history of violence."

Joe offered to take the faxes down to the police station, and I went back to the chocolate shop. I sat in my office and stared at my computer screen, feeling unhappy about the situation. In spite of his problems, Timothy Hart was a likeable old guy. I wasn't pleased with the thought of him as a killer. Of course, I liked the thought of Jeff as a killer even less. Yes, the more Timothy could be made to look like a possible killer, the more likely it would be that Chief Jones would release Jeff.

And the closeness of Timothy's attack on his brother-in-law to the death of that brother-in-law was interesting. Had Timothy still been angry the night Vic VanHorn wandered out into a heavy rainstorm and stood too close to the bank that overlooked Lake Michigan?

Chief Jones would say I was letting my imagination run away with me on that one. Olivia VanHorn would do a lot to avoid scandal, but it was hard to believe she'd cover up a fight between her husband and her brother if it made her a widow.

The whole situation made me feel miserable. I opened my desk drawer and had a Dutch caramel from the box Joe had given me. It didn't make me feel better, but it did remind me that I hadn't had lunch. I admitted to myself I wasn't getting any work done, stood up and put on my jacket, then told Aunt Nettie I was going down to the

Sidewalk Café for a sandwich.

At least the weather was pleasant that day. The sun was shining, and I tried to cheer up as I walked down the block. But the thought of Jeff in the Warner Pier Police Station was like a heavy weight on my shoulders. I was sure he was innocent. But all Joe and I had been able to do was dig up another suspect. We had no real evidence against Timothy.

Then there were Gail's actions right before her death. She'd acted crazy. Why had she been so pleased when the mold turned up missing after the burglary? What had she meant when she e-mailed Celia Carmichael and told her she'd found a piece of valuable glass, "or even plastic"? Didn't she know which it was?

Darn it! Joe had gotten so close to finding out whether Timothy still had his old sports car — and checking to see if it had a broken taillight. . . .

I stopped dead in my tracks, right in front of Downtown Drugs. Old glass or maybe plastic! Could Gail have been referring to the taillight of a car? Could she have been aware that Timothy's car was still around, and that it had a broken taillight? Could she have tried to blackmail Timothy over the broken taillight?

Suddenly it became very important to find out whether that classic sports car still existed. I half turned, ready to go down the street to the police station.

And at that moment Hart VanHorn walked out of Downtown Drugs and almost bumped into me. He smiled.

"Oh!" My squeal sounded guilty to me, but I guess I sounded thrilled to Hart.

He beamed at me. "Listen, I'm still eager for us to go out sometime."

"That sounds supper, Hart." Supper? Had I said supper? "Super!" I said. "It sounds great. But right now things are in tumult. I mean turmoil."

"The police are still holding your stepson?"

"Yes. But we did find his parents. They'll be here tonight."

"Good. Then all the responsibility won't be on you."

"All the blame may be."

I was aware that I sounded glum. Hart looked sympathetic. "I wish I knew something to do to help."

I thought briefly of suggesting that he turn his uncle in for killing Gail. But I quickly faced the fact that even if Timothy was involved in Gail's death, Hart probably knew nothing about it. Timothy, even with his pickled brain, would be unlikely to confess to his nephew.

"Webb Bartlett seems to know what he's doing," I said. "And Jeff has confidence in him." It was time to change the subject. "You're bustling about today."

"I'm off again. Some vacation." Hart gestured, and I turned and saw his mother's Lincoln parked by the curb. "Mother and Uncle Tim are with me. We stopped to pick up a prescription, and I've got to talk to a guy in Grand Rapids."

I waved at Timothy Hart and Mrs. VanHorn and said good-bye to Hart. I went on toward the Sidewalk Café but I didn't go inside. When I got to the restaurant I turned and looked back. Yes, the VanHorn car was turning the corner, headed toward the highway to Grand Rapids.

I lost interest in eating lunch and formed a new goal.

Running into Hart might seem coincidental, but in a town of twenty-five hundred, coincidences like that happen all the time. You can't go to the grocery store, or to the drugstore, without running into someone you know. But this particular meeting seemed to be full of meaning.

If Hart, Olivia, and Timothy were all going to Grand Rapids — driving time at least an hour up and an hour back — then the Hart-VanHorn compound would be deserted, possibly all afternoon.

It was the ideal time for a burglary.

I took two deep breaths and made up my mind. I would break into that barn-garage where the Harts and VanHorns stored their vehicles, and I would check under every canvas cover until I made sure that a 1968 MGB wasn't there. And I'd check out the snowmobile.

I made a swift U-turn and went back to the shop. I stuck my head in, told Aunt Nettie I was going to be gone for a while, then got into my van and drove off. I tried to do it all without hesitation. I knew that if I thought the situation through, my law-abiding nature would pop back into control, and my career as a burglar would be over before it started. So as I drove to the Hart-VanHorn compound, a quarter of a mile south of Aunt Nettie's driveway, I concentrated on how to accomplish the task at hand.

First, I needed a place to hide my van. That was no problem. I decided to leave it in Aunt Nettie's driveway and walk to the Hart-VanHorn place.

I took a flashlight out of the glove compartment and went back to Lake Shore

Drive. I stepped along briskly, trying to look as if I were just out for some exercise, and walked down Lake Shore Drive to the big stone arch that marked the Hart-VanHorn entrance.

The white gate was closed, but it was only designed to keep out cars. A pedestrian could climb right over, and I did.

The compound's drive had been carefully plowed, so what snow was there was hard-packed and would not show footprints. I might be determined to become a house-breaker, but I wasn't particularly eager to pay a penalty for my actions. I'd been careful to wear my gloves — slick leather ones that wouldn't leave fuzzies behind — and to cover my hair with a stocking cap I kept in the van. My red jacket was a problem, but it was too cold to leave it in the van. Anyway, the neighborhood wasn't ex-actly thronged with people that time of the day and that season of the year.

As I walked I decided that the simplest way to break into the barn was to first break into Timothy's house and find the key to the barn. That barn was solid metal, with metal doors and no windows. It would be much easier to break into the old farmhouse.

Timothy's walk had been neatly shoveled. I followed it to the front porch. I knocked on the door, just in case. Then I tried the handle. No luck. Timothy's brain wasn't so addled that he went off and left his door unlocked. I shrugged. But what had he said on the tape? He was responsible for leaving the key in the usual place for the handyman and landscapers.

Timothy routinely left a key outside his house. Where?

A quick look showed me that it wasn't under the mat. And the mailbox was back on the road, so that wouldn't be a good place to leave it. My grandmother had always wired an extra key to a bush outside her house, but all of Timothy's bushes were bare of leaves. I would have seen a wired-on key in a minute.

Well, there are a few advantages to being tall. I pulled off one of my gloves and felt the top of the door frame. Nothing. I wiped any fingerprints away with my balled-up glove.

Maybe the key was at the back door. I hopped over the edge of the porch into the snow and headed around the house. I did try to swish my feet around, hoping to obliterate my footprints. Timothy had old-fashioned wooden storm windows, the kind with ventilation holes along the bottom. I tugged at a couple, but they were in solidly. I was prepared to smash one out, but I hoped it wouldn't come to that.

I tracked snow onto the back porch and tried the kitchen door. Locked. Then I reached up and felt the top of that door frame. And my fingers felt something furry.

I nearly jumped out of my skin. And as I did something flew through the air and landed on the porch floor with a kerplunk.

It was a strip of fur with a key ring attached. And that key ring held a key.

My heart began to beat faster as I used my glove to erase any fingerprints from the top of the door frame, then slid it back on. I was about to break and enter.

It was a big disappointment when the key didn't fit the back door. It was much too small. Now what? There must be dozens of locks on the four houses and assorted outbuildings of the Hart-VanHorn compound. Which one would this key open? Or did it open a door at all? It really was tiny.

I looked over the edge of the porch and saw an old-fashioned cellar door. The "slide down my cellar door" kind. By all rights it should have been covered with snow, but Timothy had apparently opened it recently and it was fairly clear. And like most of its kind from around 1900, it was kept closed by latch and a padlock.

In a split second I was off the porch and

trying that little key on the padlock. It opened. I pulled open the cellar door, grabbed my flashlight out of my pocket, and was down the stairs and into the house. My career as a burglar had begun.

As I'd guessed, Timothy had a Michigan basement. Most older houses in our area, including Aunt Nettie's, have them. I flashed my light around. All I could see were boxes and heaps of the kind of stuff that accumulates in basements. The stairway was along the right-hand wall.

I went back and wrestled the cellar door shut. Then I crossed the sandy floor to the stairway, stamped my feet to remove what snow and sand I could on the bottom step, and went up to a closed door. The door opened into the kitchen. I looked around. It was a very ordinary kitchen. Judging by the red-and-white color scheme, just like my Texas grandmother's, it had probably been updated sometime in the 1950s. As I walked across the floor, I left sandy tracks. Tough. Maybe I'd have time to sweep before I left.

"I'll go back to the kitchen and get the keys." That's what Timothy had said on Joe's videotape. I was in the kitchen. So, where would Timothy Hart keep keys? In a drawer?

It took me maybe three minutes to find

the keys. They were in the broom closet on a key rack made of varnished wood with little brass cup hooks screwed in a row. A child's wood-burning set had obviously been used to cut the word "Keys" into the top of the rack. The rack had such a Boy Scout-project look about it that it summoned up a picture of Hart as a dark-haired twelve-year-old making a Christmas present for his favorite uncle.

The key rack made me feel like an interloper. But I reminded myself that Jeff had been a cute little twelve-year-old, too, and I looked at the keys.

Luckily, most of them were labeled, and I found one that said Garage and one that said Barn right away. Since I wasn't positive what Timothy called the big storage building, I took both of them. Then I went on through the house, unlocked the dead bolt on the front door, and left it unlocked. Again, I might need to get back through that door in a hurry. I left via the front porch.

I followed the path Timothy and Joe had taken that morning — it was pretty well trampled down by their traipsing back and forth — and went over to the big storage building. The Barn key fit the side door, the one Joe and Timothy had entered by. I closed the door behind me and used my flashlight to find the light switch. There before me were all those shrouded mounds I'd seen on the video.

I didn't fool around looking at wooden boats. I began nearest the door and moved from mound to mound, yanking up the canvas covers.

The first thing I found was that purple snowmobile. I pulled its cover all the way back and looked it over as well as I could. Of course, snowmobiles all look pretty much alike to me. Unless I found newsprint from the *Grand Rapids Press* on the windscreen, I wouldn't be able to tell if this was the one that chased me. But it sure did look like it.

I found the model and serial numbers and committed them to memory, one advantage of being a number person. I shuddered and pulled the canvas back over it.

Then I looked under the other covers. I found the newer boat, the one Joe had sneered at as fiberglass; the old wooden Chris-Craft; a big riding mower; a garden tractor; and a small camping trailer. And at the end of the row, exactly opposite a closed overhead door, was an empty space.

It was obviously the place where a car could have sat.

But there was no car there.

I stared at that empty space. I'd convinced myself that Timothy still owned his MGB. Greg Glossop had seen it just a year earlier.

But it wasn't there. Tears welled up in my eyes, and I stood there blinking.

Then I spoke sternly to myself. "Cry later, Lee," I said aloud. "Right now you're trespassing. Get out of here. Then you can bawl all you want."

I walked clear back to the end of the barn, making sure there were no more rooms to it. But it was just a big, empty shell. There was a loft over half of it, true, but I didn't think Timothy Hart was strong enough to toss a sports car up there. Just to be sure, or maybe just out of curiosity, I ran up the little stairway and shone the beam of my flashlight around.

Old furniture and boxes. I could see why Gail had been so eager to handle any estate sale the Hart-VanHorn clan planned. There was enough old stuff out there to stock a dozen shops the size of Gail's.

But there was no MGB. I had broken and entered for nothing.

Now to get out. I hurried back to the door and peeked out, almost afraid I'd be facing some law officer summoned by a neighbor. But there was no one in sight. I stepped outside and pulled the key out of my pocket.

And a second key dropped into the snow.

I scrabbled around until I found it. It was the key marked Garage. I locked the barn door, then stared at the second key.

"Garage." Hmmm. On the videotape Timothy had said that his sister had a garage in her house. As a matter of fact, the other house, the brick one, probably had a garage, too. Of course, it was unlikely that Timothy's car would be parked in either of his sister's garages.

But as long as I had the key, I thought I'd better look.

I trotted down the drive, toward the stone house with the little bridge leading to the porch. The drive, of course, was well cleared down that way, too, and it led around the end of the house and curved down a slope. As soon as I went around the curve, I saw a three-car garage.

The garage was under the house, in the basement, and it had two overhead doors, a double and a single. The Garage key didn't fit either of them. Perhaps the key fit a garage in the brick house instead.

I stood in the driveway and stared at the key stupidly. Then I noticed a sidewalk that led to the back of the house. It was covered with snow, but its outline was clear. I followed it, doing the foot-twisting trick I hoped would keep my boot tracks from being identified. And there, under a deck overlooking the lake, was another door, an ordinary door, not an overhead door. And the Garage key from Timothy's kitchen fit.

I went inside and groped for a switch. There was none near the door, and I had to use my flashlight to find a way to turn the overhead light on. And when it came on, I saw another of those canvas-shrouded mounds the VanHorns were so fond of.

This one was long, but not too tall. I was afraid to lift the canvas. It seemed to be my last chance to clear Jeff.

I forced myself to grab the canvas sheet and throw it back.

And there, dirty and mud spattered, was a black sports car.

My heart nearly stopped.

I yanked the cover completely off. I walked down the side of the car, leaned over, and examined the left taillight.

It was broken.

"Yee-haw!"

I'm not a Texan for nothing. I jumped up and down. I crowed with delight. I howled like a coyote.

Jeff was going to get out of jail. Before Rich arrived!

"Yee-haw!"

I was still yelling and jumping when a motor clicked on and the double garage door began to go up.

CHOCOLATE CHAT

JUST A LITTLE BITE

Many short stories have used chocolate as a prop.

- The ultimate story focusing on chocolate may be "Of Course You Know that Chocolate Is a Vegetable," by Barbara D'Amato. Published in 1998 in *Ellery Queen Mystery Magazine*, the story won the Agatha, Anthony, and Macavity Awards for Best Short Story in 1999. It was anthologized in *Crème de la Crime* in 2000. And what is the exotic murder weapon used in the story? I'll never tell!

- Agatha Christie wrote a story called "The Chocolate Box," published in the United States in *Hercule Poirot's Early Cases* in 1974. It's typical Christie, expertly using sleight of hand to confuse the reader. In it Hercule Poirot describes a case of political and religious intrigue that he investigated as a young detective in Belgium. And the key clue turns out to be not the chocolates, but the box they are in.

- Lee McKinney also made her debut in a short story. A look at Lee when she was sixteen and first worked at TenHuis Chocolade was the background for "The Chocolate Kidnapping Clue," published in 2001 in the anthology *And the Dying Is Easy.*

Chapter 20

I nearly wet my pants.

The dirty cheats! Less than an hour earlier, Hart had told me they were headed to Grand Rapids. They couldn't possibly have driven all the way up there and back again already.

I left the dust sheet off the sports car and the garage light on, and I ran out the door I'd come in. I made a sharp right turn and ran along under the deck. There was a little snow there, but I didn't worry about making tracks. I was making time.

My troubles began when I got to the end of the deck and came out at the other end of the house into hip-deep snow. Not only had the snow been piling up there since November, but the ground also rose steeply. I slipped and slid as if I were climbing the Matterhorn without a safety rope.

But I kept going, slogging through the snow, trying to get around the side of the house, out of sight.

Then I heard a voice. "Lee! Lee! What are you doing? It's only me. Olivia!"

Just as she yelled my feet went out from under me. I landed on my fanny and slid halfway down the slope. I could hear Olivia laughing, though she didn't sound terribly amused.

"Lee," she said. "Come here. I'm not going to hurt you."

I'd been caught. But I hadn't been caught by Timothy. Timothy, who'd already killed. It was very likely that Olivia didn't know that her brother had sneaked his car out to make clandestine trips into town to commit crimes. I'd realized that I'd have to confront her sometime. I'd planned to have Chief Jones there, but it now seemed I was going to do it alone.

I got to my feet and came back, feeling really stupid. Olivia VanHorn was her usual poised self, stunning in winter-white slacks, polished boots, and her casual mink.

"I owe you an apology," I said. "I'm trespassing."

"Now you're not. Now you have my permission to be here. Were you looking for the MGB?"

I nodded. "Yes. I've simply got to get Jeff out of jail. And that meant I had to find that car. The taillight is broken. It's going to implicate your brother."

Mrs. VanHorn's eyes widened. She made a noise that could only be described as a ladylike grunt. Her mouth twitched. Then she led the way into the garage and went to the back of the sports car. "I had suspected Timothy had taken the car out," she said. "I guess I lacked the courage to check the rear end, even after I heard the police were hunting a sports car with a broken taillight."

She leaned over and looked at the taillight closely. Then she sighed. "We might as well call the police."

"I can drive back to the station and talk to Chief Jones."

Mrs. VanHorn shook her head. "No, I have to face it. You're quite right about your stepson. We can't let that innocent young man remain under suspicion any longer. Come into the house with me, and I'll call Chief Jones."

I was amazed at how calmly she was taking the whole thing. I followed as Mrs. VanHorn went to a door in the center of the back wall, then led me up a stairway that ended in a beautifully decorated kitchen. "Take your coat off," she said. "There's a coat rack behind the door. Just let me put my boots away, and then I'll telephone the police."

She walked on through a foyer and down a carpeted hall. I was a little surprised that she didn't take her own boots off before she stepped onto the carpet. Then I realized that Olivia hadn't been running through the snow the way I had. Her boots were dry.

I found a small rug near the back door, and I stood on it, stamping the snow off my feet, trying to keep from spotting the tile. I unzipped my jacket, but I didn't take it off, though I saw a navy blue Polartec parka hanging on the rack Olivia had mentioned. I wondered if Timothy had worn it when he chased me with the snowmobile.

I was still standing there, feeling ill at ease, when Olivia VanHorn came back down the hall. I was surprised to see that she hadn't taken off her boots, or her coat either.

I was even more surprised when she pulled a pistol from behind her back.

I gave a yelp. "What's going on?"

Olivia sighed. "You're a burglar, Lee, and I'm going to shoot you."

"Shoot me!"

"Yes. Young woman, you are simply too nosy. I must protect my family."

"But Timothy — he'll get off with diminished responsibility. I can't believe you would kill to protect him!"

"Timothy? Don't be silly. Timothy wouldn't kill anyone. He passes out by nine o'clock every evening. He couldn't possibly get out in the night, meet people, do the things I had to do to protect my son."

"Your son!"

"Certainly. You can understand that — after all the trouble you've taken to protect a boy who's merely your stepson."

"Hart? You're trying to protect Hart?"

"It's imperative, I'm afraid. I really have no choice. If this story comes out, it will ruin his political career. Please step a little further into the kitchen."

I ignored her request. "Did Hart kill Gail Hess?"

"That wretched blackmailer? Of course not!"

"Then how will killing me protect Hart?"

"We won't go into that. Please, step a little further into the kitchen."

I didn't budge. "Why?"

"So it will be clear that you were an intruder, that I surprised a burglar who was actually in the house. Then it will be legal to shoot you."

I backed up a step.

"No, no!" Mrs. VanHorn spoke as if I were a backward child. "Don't move away. Come forward."

I stared at her. This situation was unbelievable. This ladylike, gracious woman was going to kill me. And she had invited me into her home so that it would look legal. It was like the advice of a cynic — if you shoot a burglar on the porch, drag him inside the house to make it look legal.

The whole thing was so absurd I was tempted to laugh. But the pistol in Olivia VanHorn's hand and the calm resolve on her face kept the situation from being funny.

I put my hand behind me and touched the doorknob. To get out I'd have to open the door and run all the way down the narrow stairway. Mrs. VanHorn would have plenty of time to shoot me as I ran.

Or I could rush forward and try to slam into her. She'd have plenty of time to shoot me that way, too.

But either fate would be better than standing there and letting her kill me, then pass my death off as the shooting of a burglar.

Now Mrs. VanHorn's eyes narrowed. "I'm tired of waiting," she said. "Move forward!"

My fingers gripped the doorknob. Getting shot in the back would be the best way, I decided. That way she wouldn't have such an easy time passing my death off as the murder of an intruder.

I shrank back against the door.

"Very well," she said. "I'm not waiting any longer."

She raised the pistol. I turned the door handle.

And the doorbell rang.

Mrs. VanHorn and I both froze, and in the awful silence I heard Timothy Hart's voice coming from outside. "Olivia? Olivia! Someone's broken into my house! There are tracks all over the kitchen floor and the front door's unlocked! I called the police!"

Olivia's head whipped toward his voice.

I whirled, yanked the door open, and plunged down the steps to the garage.

Thumpety thumpety! My boots hit every other step. Then a louder thump drowned them out. A shot! I didn't think it had hit me. I fell down the last three steps, but I caught myself with the door handle. The door into the garage swung open, and I stumbled out and ran headlong into Hart VanHorn.

I screamed like a Texas banshee.

Hart grabbed me. He screamed, too. But the sounds he made produced words. "What's wrong? What's happened?"

At first I could only point at the door and shriek. Then I managed, "A gun! She's got a gun. She's going to kill me!"

Olivia came rushing out. She was still brandishing her pistol, and she aimed it at me.

Hart's grip on my arms tightened, and for a second I thought he was going to hold me still so his mother could shoot me. Then he slung me around.

He shoved me behind him. He put his body between me and his mother. He yelled, "No! Stop!"

Olivia looked like a madwoman. Her calm façade had completely collapsed. "Get out of the way!" she screamed.

"No!"

"She's a burglar! I'm going to shoot her!"

"No!" Hart let go of me, and I staggered against his mother's car. A shot echoed thunderously, bouncing off the garage walls.

Hart jumped toward his mother. They were both yelling. He grabbed at the pistol, and it went off again.

Blood spurted. I shrieked. Hart growled.

Olivia screamed. "I've shot you!"

The "you" was Hart. He clutched his arm and leaned against the fender of his mother's Lincoln. I realized he was still trying to stay between me and the gun.

Olivia dropped the pistol to her side and stared at him. Fear, horror, shock, and anger washed over her face.

In the sudden silence, Hart spoke quietly. "Mother, no matter how many people you kill, I'm not going to run for Congress."

Now the emotion on Olivia's face was agony, and her voice was a whisper. "Hart, Hart. I love you. I wanted to protect you."

"I know, Mother. But I can't hide behind you any longer."

"Does it all have to come out?"

"Yes. This can't go on."

Olivia sobbed. After all the screaming, the yelling, and the shots, that simple sound may have been the most soul chilling of all.

Then she turned and ran back into the house.

Behind me I heard Timothy Hart's voice. "What on earth is wrong with Olivia?"

"I'm not sure," I said. "But call an ambulance. Hart's been shot."

I heard a piercing, shrill sound. A siren. The cavalry — personified by the Warner Pier Police Department — had arrived.

I saw a box of what looked like clean rags on a shelf near the door to the kitchen stairs. I grabbed a handful. I went to Hart, helped him out of his jacket and applied pressure to his arm. Timothy was disappearing up the driveway, I assumed to direct the police car to Olivia's garage. In a few seconds I heard him speak. "Thank God you got here so fast. Olivia's gone berserk. And we need an ambulance."

Right at that moment I heard a far-off, muffled thump from inside the house. Hart closed his eyes and groaned, way down deep in his chest.

I was using both hands to hold the rags on his arm. "I'm so sorry, Hart," I said. "I'm so sorry."

It didn't seem adequate, but what else was there to say?

Faced with an armed suspect, Jerry Cherry followed procedure and called for a backup. Chief Jones and a Michigan State Police car were there within minutes. The chief and the state cop entered the VanHorn house through the garage while I sat in the patrol car, shaking. Olivia did not challenge them or answer the questions they called out to her.

They found her in the bathtub, dead, still wearing her fur coat. There was a note on the bathroom counter, which the chief let me see later. "I killed Gail Hess," it read. "She was a filthy blackmailer, and she had found out I broke into the TenHuis shop and took the mold. Fifteen years ago, I killed my husband. Hart had nothing to do with it."

As usual, word of what had happened at the Hart-VanHorn compound spread through Warner Pier rapidly. By the time I got to the police station to make a statement, Joe was on the spot. He met me with a big hug, a hug I deeply appreciated, and he didn't reproach me for breaking and entering.

We were sitting on a bench in the main room, holding hands, when Hart VanHorn and Timothy Hart came in. Hart's arm was in a sling.

Timothy gestured at Hart. "He should have stayed in the hospital."

Hart shook his head. "My arm's not that serious," he said. "I need to talk to Chief Jones, and I want to do it now."

"It's all my fault!" I didn't know the words were coming out until I'd spoken them. "I suspected Timothy of being our burglar, because I learned he'd still owned his MGB as recently as a year ago. So I — I admit it — I broke into the storage barn at the compound looking for that car. When it wasn't there, I looked in your mother's garage."

"And you found the MGB," Hart said.

"Yes. And the taillight was broken. I was desperate to get Jeff out of jail."

"I could have told you the car was there, but I didn't know about the taillight."

I decided to ignore that. "I thought your mother and Timothy had gone to Grand Rapids with you."

"No, they went only as far as Holland. I had to pick up my SUV at the dealer's there, so they dropped me off and came back. None of us went to Grand Rapids."

"You said you had to see a man in Grand Rapids."

Hart smiled gently. "I didn't deliberately mislead you, Lee, but what I said was that I needed 'to talk to a man in Grand Rapids.' I never intended to go there to talk to him. I — well, I knew Mother was up to something, though I wasn't sure just what. I wanted to talk to my psychologist about it. I called him from Holland because my cell phone works better up there."

I clutched Joe's hand, but I spoke to Hart. "Your mother caught me in the garage. First she acted quite friendly. She laughed! She invited me into the house. Then she said I was a burglar, and she was going to shoot me."

Hart dropped his head.

"I know it's hard to believe," I said. "I couldn't believe it while I was running for my life."

"Oh, I can believe it," Hart said. "Mother was very coolheaded, and she had an extremely creative way of handling the truth. She wouldn't have wanted anybody to know about that car. Any more than she wanted anybody to know I'd been seeing a psychologist."

"She didn't want people to know you'd seen a psychologist?" I was mystified. "So what? So who hasn't? That's nothing to get excited about."

"It might have meant nothing to you, maybe, but to Mom it was the kiss of death to my political career."

"Surely people are not that ignorant. . . ."

But Hart was shaking his head. "It wasn't the mere fact that I was seeing a psychologist, Lee. It was what she was afraid I might tell him."

"Oh." Suddenly I didn't want to know any more.

But it seemed I was going to, because Hart went on talking. "You see, I killed my father."

I was silent, and Joe squeezed my hand.

Timothy spoke. "But this is stupid, my boy. Nobody killed your father. He fell! It was an accident. Nobody ever suggested it was anything else. And now both you and Olivia claim to have killed Vic."

Hart smiled at his uncle. "Mother didn't kill him, Uncle Tim. She was still trying to protect me. Me and my wonderful political career. But I can't stand to lie about it anymore. I killed my father. Oh, it wasn't murder — only manslaughter, I guess. Maybe even justifiable homicide.

"Fifteen years ago — when I was twenty — my father was drunk. He threatened my mother. I punched him, trying to protect her. He fell against the china cabinet, the one that held my grandmother's collection of chocolate molds. The cabinet fell over. It landed on him, and the back of his head was smashed in.

"I was willing to call the police. At least an ambulance. But my mother wouldn't hear of it. She got a wheelbarrow from the storage barn, and the two of us threw my father's body over the bank into the lake. His death was accepted as an accident.

"The china cabinet was smashed, and it had blood on it, and one of the molds — some kind of a bear — had a lot of blood on it. I broke the cabinet up with an ax, and we burned it in the fireplace. But we couldn't burn the doors, because of the metal and the glass. Mother washed the bear mold and tossed it and the other molds into a box in the basement of the bungalow. She put some other old kitchen utensils on top, made it look like a box of junk. The collection was too well known to simply get rid of, and I'm sure she figured it would end up going to a museum or something eventually."

He patted his uncle on the shoulder. "Uncle Tim didn't know anything about it. He found the kitchen utensils and molds in the basement and gave them to Gail to sell. The molds wound up being displayed at the TenHuis shop. At first Mother thought that was okay, but then she found out some expert on chocolate molds was going to come to look at them. Apparently Mother tried to break into TenHuis Chocolade and get hold of that bear mold before the expert could want to know why it had been treated badly. Gail must have figured out that the burglar used Uncle Tim's MGB, because of the broken taillight."

Tears were running down Timothy's cheeks. "Gail had seen the MGB," he said. "I showed it to her when she picked up the molds. She knew it had a broken taillight. She may have thought that I was the burglar."

I was having trouble taking all this in. "Did your mother use the snowmobile to chase me?"

"She did have the snowmobile out yesterday," Hart said.

"Why would she chase me?"

Hart rubbed a hand over his forehead. "I know that something you said upset her, when we talked outside the police station that morning. She must have decided you knew something. Maybe that Gail had told you about the MGB and its broken tail-light."

The chief came in then. The first thing he said was that Hart should get a lawyer. Then the chief instructed Jerry Cherry to let Jeff out of the holding cell, and he told me we could leave. He and Hart were still arguing about whether Hart should call a lawyer as Joe, Jeff, and I headed out into the winter dusk.

But as we stepped outside that dusk was shattered by strobe lights. I almost ran back inside. Two guys had been waiting, and I recognized them as part of the tabloid crew that had invaded Warner Pier the previous summer.

"Cool it!" Joe told them. "The story's inside the police station! Not out here."

The photographer laughed and flashed his strobe again. "That's not what George said."

"Shut up!" That came from his companion, a man with a notebook.

"You'd better get inside to talk to the chief," Joe said. "I think you're the first team on the scene, and this is going to be a big story."

"Wait a minute," I said. "Did somebody

from Warner Pier call you? George? George who?"

"Never mind!" The reporter grabbed the photographer and the two of them hotfooted it into City Hall.

Jeff, Joe, and I stood looking after them. "George?" I said. "Surely he didn't mean George Palmer?"

"Surely he did," Joe said. "George is on the park commission. I thought one of the commission members had to be the tabloid source. They were the only people who knew I'd approached Mike Herrera about selling the Warner Point property to the city."

"Why didn't you say something earlier?"

"I couldn't rule out someone from the lawyer's office blabbing. I tried to give George the benefit of the doubt."

"He's so obnoxious!"

Joe shrugged. "Well, I'll tell Mike Herrera what we've deduced, and Mike will call George's father-in-law, and maybe old George will have a new job pretty quick."

"Wouldn't that be great! Maybe Barbara can come back."

Jeff's jacket was still being held as evidence, so the three of us ran the two blocks to TenHuis Chocolade for a joyful reunion with Aunt Nettie and Tess. We were all in the workroom, jumping up and down and turning cartwheels, when someone came in the front door. One of the hairnet ladies went up to the counter.

I heard a deep voice with a Texas accent. "Ah'm lookin' for Lee McKinney," it said.

Jeff's eyes suddenly were the size of dinner plates. "It's Dad," he said in a whisper.

I sighed. I had to face Rich sometime. "Bring him back to the shop," I said.

Rich came in. Dina was with him. Dina's eyes locked on only one thing. "Jeff!" she said. "You're here!"

Suddenly they were in a three-way hug. "I'm all right!" Jeff kept saying. "I'm all right."

They finally loosened their grips and turned around toward the rest of us, all three of them with tear-streaked faces. And sometime in there Jeff's lip stud had disappeared.

Jeff started talking. "Lee kept working 'til she figured out who really killed that woman. She got me out of jail."

That led to more commotion, of course. Dina had to hug me — and after a minute, Rich did, too. They had to meet Tess. They had to confirm the news Jeff had told us earlier — they had gone to Mexico in an attempt at reconciliation.

Apparently it had worked. Dina held out her left hand and proudly showed off her new wedding ring. I was surprised at its appearance. It was a simple piece of Mexican silver. No clusters of diamonds. No ruby the size of an idol's eye. It was definitely a sincere wedding ring, not one to show off to your business associates. Maybe Rich actually had changed his ways.

I hugged her. Dina had always been pretty nice to me. "I want you two to be really happy," I said. I shook Rich's hand.

Then they had to hear the whole story of our burglary and the murder of Gail Hess. Through all of this, Joe leaned against a worktable, saying nothing. It was nearly an hour later when Rich looked at his watch and said, "Are we going to be able to find a place to stay?"

I called the Inn on the Pier and was assured they had rooms available. "Good!" Rich said. "Now, I already noticed a restaurant open down the street. I'd like to take everyone to dinner."

I looked at Aunt Nettie. She looked at Tess. Aunt Nettie used her mental telepathy powers and told both of us to say no.

"I think I'd better go home, take a hot shower and get into my flannel pj's," Aunt Nettie said.

"And I think I'd better go with you," Tess said. "I have to call my parents." Aunt Nettie patted her hand and smiled.

"Lee?" Rich looked at me.

Behind me Joe stirred. "Sorry," he said. "I'm taking Lee to the Dock Street Pizza tonight."

I went over to Joe. "You're sure?"

"I'm not taking another chance on losing you, Lee."

Then he put his arms around me, right in front of God and everybody. Which included Aunt Nettie, Rich, Dina, Jeff, Tess, and three of the hairnet ladies who hadn't left yet.

But Aunt Nettie had one more comment. "Before the party breaks up," she said, "would anybody like a sample chocolate?"

Rich had an Italian cherry bonbon and immediately began talking to Aunt Nettie about boxes to give as business gifts.

Dina told him to hush and picked out a raspberry cream bonbon ("Red raspberry puree in white chocolate cream interior"). "It smells heavenly in here," she said.

Tess went for a double fudge bonbon and Jeff asked for a Jamaican rum truffle.

"Could Lee and I take ours in a little box?" Joe asked. He took a coffee truffle ("All milk chocolate, flavored with Caribbean coffee") and I chose a Frangelico one. Aunt Nettie settled for solid chocolate with bits of hazelnut.

Ten minutes later — after we'd seen the others off and I'd locked up — Joe and I went out the front door. Joe took my hand again.

"Our friendship is about to meet a new challenge," Joe said. "The big question is, do you like anchovies on your pizza?"

"No!"

"Good! Come on."

We got in Joe's truck and headed for Dock Street Pizza. Right in front of God and everybody.

About the Author

JoAnna Carl is the pseudonym for a multipublished mystery writer. She spent twenty-five years in the newspaper business, working as a reporter, a feature writer, an editor, and a columnist. She holds a degree in journalism from the University of Oklahoma and also studied in the O.U. Professional Writing program. She lives in Oklahoma but summers in Michigan, where the Chocoholic Mysteries are set. She has one daughter who works for a chocolate maker and another who is a CPA.